"THE ACTION IS FRENZIED AND, AS THEY SAY, THIS DEBUT THRILLER COULD BE THE BEGINNING OF A BEAUTIFUL FRIENDSHIP."
New York Daily News

THE
SAPPHIRE
SEA

JOHN B.
ROBINSON

AVON BOOKS
An Imprint of HarperCollinsPublishers

This is a work of fiction. Names, characters, places, and incidents are products of the author's imagination or are used fictitiously and are not to be construed as real. Any resemblance to actual events, locales, organizations, or persons, living or dead, is entirely coincidental.

AVON BOOKS
An Imprint of HarperCollins*Publishers*
10 East 53rd Street
New York, New York 10022-5299

Copyright © 2003 by John B. Robinson
Map illustration by David Lindroth, Inc.
ISBN 0-06-052726-9
www.avonbooks.com

First Avon Books paperback printing: March 2005
First William Morrow hardcover printing: November 2003

Avon Trademark Reg. U.S. Pat. Off. and in Other Countries, Marca Registrada, Hecho en U.S.A.
HarperCollins® is a registered trademark of HarperCollins Publishers Inc.

Printed in the U.S.A.

10 9 8 7 6 5 4 3 2 1

This book is dedicated to:

Narcisse Randriamirado, for his courage,

and

Jean Phillippe Francois Truong Huu Khâ

(aka Mamy Kha),

for his warm heart, beautiful music

and wandering spirit

SAPPHIRES—The gem of the soul and autumn, the natal stone for September, was said to preserve the wearer from envy and attract divine favour. Fraud was banished from its presence and necromancers honoured it more than any other stone, for it enabled them to hear and understand the most obscure oracles. The ancients thought sapphire to be endowed with the power to influence spirits, to be a charm against carnality, to be capable of making peace between foes and to protect its owner against captivity. The Sinhalese respect the star sapphire as a protection against witchcraft.

—*Gems: Their Sources, Descriptions and Identification*, Fifth Edition, Robert Webster

Contents

1

HAPPY BULL

It was 6:45 A.M. when the sun's blazing rays of amber light finally blasted over the horizon. Lonny cruised down a stretch of open macadam flanked by lizard green hills and fetid rice paddies. He was past the mining camps and inside the King's Reserve. He had the throttle wrenched back, the clutch lever squeezed tight and was in the act of kicking the Japanese road pony into third. And it was just a flash. A hallucinogenic glint of phosphorescence in a crosshatched sea of chartreuse yellow, ocher red and black ash.

The motorcycle coasted at a high-pitched whine as Lonny's eye processed the color, and a magical sensation welled up inside his chest like a balloon. He told himself to push on but the curse and the salvation of Lonny's life was his eye. Lonny had a seeing eye. An eye that could weigh, cut and mount a gemstone by holding it to the sun. The eye of an artist. An eye that could see into things and take their measure.

As he whipped around in the saddle to locate the blue glimmer, the motorcycle veered into freshly tilled soil and his body catapulted forward like a human cannonball. He plowed into the sponge-like paddy helmet-first. Mud jammed up around the visor and left him with an intimate view of a tropical millipede. After two years in Madagascar there were still some mornings he found the place surreal.

It was the fourth time he had taken a digger, each time in a paddy, and each time it had required a team of zebu to pull the machine free of the sticky muck. But this time he was not overly concerned about himself, his predicament or the danger of getting caught inside the King's Reserve. He could feel his body temperature rise and his eye twitch as he thought about an improbable twinkle that promised a glimpse of the divine.

He pushed himself off the fallow ground and glanced around. In the near distance he spotted a middle-aged peasant sitting away from the deserted highway beneath a towering mango tree. A small figure who watched Lonny's ridiculous accident without understanding and without trying to understand. The peasant was lifting a blue stone up to the sun, as he had seen the traders do in the sapphire camps, trying to see what he could sense.

Lonny wiped the mud from his visor and surveyed the damage. The front tines of the motorcycle were twisted, the wheel rim bent, the engine covered with soil. With luck he might be able to ride it back to Diego-Suarez. He removed his mirrored helmet and walked woodenly toward the gigantic mango tree. His body was drenched in a heavy layer of sweat before he was halfway there.

"M'boulets tsara," greeted Lonny in the local dialect. Once a week he submitted to Antakarana lessons from Bishop McKenzie, an aged Scottish missionary who had not spoken English for months at a go before Lonny parachuted into town.

"M'boulets tsara," returned Jaoravo, the Happy Bull, a descendant of Jao, the Bull. Unlike the landless miners from the highlands and the south, Jaoravo's ancestors had cultivated this territory for a dozen generations. It was a part of his feet, his hands, his stomach. Everything he harvested he owed to the ancestors' good grace.

"J'achete des saphirs," said Lonny, switching to French. As a boy his French mother had impressed upon him that "the beautiful language" was the language of love. At New York University he had majored in French because it was supposed to be the language of literature and art. Yet in northern

Madagascar all his years of St. Exupéry, Sartre and Duras served a commercial end.

Jaoravo listened to Lonny and heard nothing malevolent.

"*Vous avez un saphir?*" continued Lonny, hoping he would not have to try the whole thing in dialect.

At the time of independence Jaoravo had finished his schooling and he was proud of his ability to speak French. The young men in the nearby village called him the Frenchman because they liked to tease him. He did not mind the teasing. He was proud of his ability to communicate with strangers. His own father spoke French and Jaoravo did not feel ashamed before the ancestors.

Lonny's legs were limber, as he had only been riding a short time, but he lost balance when Jaoravo rotated his palm and extended his arm to reveal a luminous sapphire the size of a swan's egg.

"*C'est un vrai saphir*," said Jaoravo. A real one. And he knew it was. For although he knew nothing about sapphires in particular, he sensed the force of the stone, and from what he had heard, all the good stones were sapphires. The stone had a presence not unlike the sacred tree where he offered white-faced male ducks to the departed. He had discovered the blue stone in his rice paddy as he turned the soil with a squared spade. He had been carrying it for months, but now he felt himself unaccountably sad and he wanted to make a tribute to the ancestors.

He wanted to sacrifice a zebu in their honor and he thought that if he took the disturbing blue stone to town surely one of the strangers would give him a zebu for it.

Lonny picked the wondrous sapphire from Jaoravo's work-beaten palm and held it against the washed turquoise sky. The stone was the color of a delphinium on the summer side of a mountain, as clear as a bell's chime. He closed his eyes briefly in delight and behind his eyelids he saw the magnificent sapphire float melodiously like a musical note. The gem did not filter the passage of light, rather it seemed to give value to the light itself. In one bright instant the contours of his soul shifted their shape. He knew, like a caged cockatoo who encounters her mate for the first time, that he was looking at the very conception of beauty.

"*Il est beau. Magnifique*," said Lonny, against all the tenets of his trade and his father's warnings about showing emotion in the presence of something valuable.

"*Merci*," said Jaoravo. He held out his hands to take it back, but Lonny had the gem up against the sky, plumbing its depths and calculating the type of cut that would bring out the stone's best nature. He had the impression he was gazing into God's iris.

It was Easter Sunday, a feast day, and Lonny had piles of local currency. Although his father insisted that he buy low-quality stones at cheap prices, he couldn't stop himself from gambling on larger crystals. He was tired of buying low-grade corundum destined for teenage mall rats and unsatisfied prom queens. The material was flawed and opaque. Ninety-five percent of it would have to be cooked to burn out the somber tone and transform it into the rich hues Americans preferred.

One carat commercial-grade sapphires were worth $40 at the final point of sale. Between the initial purchase price, export bribes, export costs, overhead, heating, cutting and sales expenses, he needed to buy several hundred rough stones every week to justify his father's investment. There were tons of sapphire within fifteen feet of the surface, but the miners worked with crowbars, metal sieves and five-gallon jugs of water. Production was limited. Even when Lonny found clean stones the size of a gram, his father complained that they rarely produced decent gems.

Lonny shifted the massive stone down so that it lay in his outstretched fingers and his shadow blocked any direct sunlight. Nine hundred and ninety-nine out of a thousand rough sapphires died instantly when shaded. They lost their fire, their resiliency, their ability to filter light evenly. They lacked a life of their own. Not this one. The stone's hue remained constant and its color value became deeper, more intense. The shaded hue resembled the color of paint used to highlight Mother Mary at

Lourdes; the same pigment chosen to bring her head into relief against the backdrop of angels. Not royal blue, that dark and radiant hue prized in Burmese sapphires, more like the lighter, piercing tone found in the gem-bearing wash of Ceylon. The color of a clear New England sky in the month of October.

How much? thought Lonny. He held the stone up to the sky a third time as if to check he had really seen what he thought he might have imagined. But he had not dreamed such beauty nor such value. Despite its massive size the sapphire had no deep pressure fractures that would diminish its worth on the grinding wheel; no color windows, no clear spots so often found in the average, everyday stone he was used to trading. The clarity and luminescence of this stone's character assured that only a come-again Caesar, an artist or a thief would ever appreciate it truly.

By force of will over emotion Lonny recovered his poise and placed the sapphire on the ground between himself and Jaoravo. The King's Reserve was a dozen miles beyond the mining camps and strictly off-limits. Over the past several months he had risked arrest to purchase spectacular eight-, fourteen-, and twenty-three-gram stones from peasants digging illegally inside the tribal boundaries. He knew they would be moving toward the camps this morning, attempting to trade sapphires for Three Horse Beer and sacks of rice.

Jaoravo wore a thin piece of linen wrapped around his waist and a rude vest of woven palm fibers. Against his calf lay the local version of a machete, which had a long wooden handle and short iron blade in the shape of a worn L. He was barefoot, and despite a diet of plain rice, an intestinal tract full of worms and recurrent bouts of malaria, was in pretty good health and harmony for a middle-aged man who lived in an isolated hut removed from a village and two days' walk from town.

The refracted heat of the humid earth baked Lonny's lean body as efficiently as a pottery kiln. The rainy season was just ending; tender shoots of new grass sprung everywhere from the once razed ground. He felt feverish rivers of sweat running down his cheeks, realizing at the same time that he was too drained to defend himself or even run in the case of danger. But standing there, like a lighthouse on an emerald plain, next to an armed peasant, in one of the poorest countries in the world, carrying enough local money to last twenty local lifetimes, Lonny knew he had to risk everything.

Lonny chose a raised root and sat beside Jaoravo. They sat beneath the landmark mango tree whose oviform yellow fruits were prized for their salty taste. On the periphery of the shade spot two zebu stood dumb and mute before a wooden cart with wooden wheels.

When he had first flown out of John F. Kennedy

Airport, Lonny wouldn't have known what to do with a zebu if one stepped on him. Now he traded in the native cattle frequently. Zebu were Malagasy cows with an enormous set of horns and a big hump on their backs. They were black, brown or brindled. Most of the time they were gaunt and smelled like walking dung heaps. Every Malagasy peasant aspired to own three zebu. One for the burial of his father, one for the feast of his mother, one to be sacrificed at his own death. Zebu were never butchered as everyday fare by the chronically undernourished peasants. Lonny quickly learned that the beasts represented spiritual wealth and wellbeing, not actual wealth.

Across the decaying paddies Lonny spotted Jaoravo's square hut. A few walls made of palm mats attached to seven vertical poles coifed with dead leaves and raised above the exhausted earth by a series of miniature stilts. Lonny guessed that if he stood in the middle of the hut and jumped up and down the whole contraption would implode.

Having grown up on the seventeenth floor of a skyscraper, Lonny found visits to the Malagasy countryside unnerving. In the bush there was no way to avoid self-exposure. In town there were hundreds of schemes, mountains of paperwork and thousands of people to occupy his attention. The last time he had stayed overnight in a village he was obliged to listen to his hosts engage in an extremely vocal sex act. The children, the in-laws and the woman's little sisters all commenting on the event, encouraging both husband and wife toward a loud and satisfactory conclusion. Lonny hadn't touched a woman since his legal separation from Cass. He hadn't held a child in his arms since he kissed his daughter, Annie, good-bye. Sexual liaisons were the reason he found himself in Madagascar to begin with and he hated to be reminded of his failures.

How much? thought Lonny ludicrously. As if the price of the magnificent sapphire could be decided in terms of money or barter. His father would have cringed at his lack of self-control. His father shepherded him into the stone business not because he liked Lonny, not because he thought much of his artistic worldview or his college degrees, but because he knew Lonny would be loyal. "It's better to be incompetent and loyal," said Cal, "than smart. Smarts can be taught." And as the only Protestant on the corner of West 47th and Fifth Avenue, Calvin Cushman knew a lot about smarts and more about loyalty. Which is why he had coaxed Lonny into the separation, legal and geographic, instead of a divorce. He felt Lonny and Cass should be loyal to each other in spite of her unexpected pregnancy, his adultery and both their lies. But Lonny hated himself for agreeing to let Cass retain primary custody in Manhattan while he tried to sort out his conflicted emotions on the other side of the world. He missed being a part of Annie's life.

Jaoravo was thinking not of his father but of all of his fathers. His father's father, and his father before, and his mother, and his mother's mother, and her mother. He would need to honor them properly to wipe away his melancholy. To materialize their spirits and offer them the blood of several zebu. If he did it right, on an auspicious day, with the agreement of his brothers and sisters, and in the presence of a good witch doctor, he was sure to be well received by the ancestors. There would have to be big plastic tubs of rum. And *salegy* music. And dance, and sex. Divinity, happiness, harvest and fertility. If it was done strictly according to custom, as it would be, the ancestors, the living and the unborn would all be satisfied. There would be a whole and he would be part of it.

"How much?" asked Jaoravo in solid, colloquial French. He moved next to Lonny on the mango root and he placed the gem in Lonny's hands. When the stone, its surface temperature warmed by the heat of Jaoravo's fingers, touched his soft pink palm, Lonny suspected the peasant was selling more than just a precious stone.

"You tell me how much you want," replied Lonny.

"How much is it worth?" asked Jaoravo.

"It is worth any price you wish," said Lonny. "But I cannot set the value for you. You must decide how much the sapphire is worth. You are the own-er." He forced the precious object back into Jao-ravo's grasp.

"But how much is it worth?" repeated Jaoravo.

"To whom?" asked Lonny.

"To you."

Lonny shook his head. "My friend, this sapphire is worth my father's esteem and my own self-respect. I am willing to pay you what you think it is worth to you. As a commodity it has no intrinsic value."

"A sapphire has no value?"

"No," said Lonny.

"Then you don't want to buy the sapphire?"

"That is not what I said. No single price can be fixed upon the value of a sapphire. What I am will-ing to pay and what you are willing to receive are two separate ideas. Perhaps I am prepared to pay nothing for this stone and you place a great value on it. Perhaps I place a great value on it and you do not care for it."

Jaoravo listened carefully. He tried to think of how his ancestors would have talked with this other, this tricky stranger with a silver tongue and eyes like piercing thorns.

"So what is it worth?" he asked.

"You tell me," said Lonny.

Jaoravo looked down to the exposed earth for support. He was the master of himself and his two wives and his six sons and his seven daughters and three fine zebu. He had been blessed all his life. The stranger was being very evasive and Jaoravo did not want to be tricked by a fine orator.

Jaoravo walked to the zebu cart and came back with a small container of cane rum. He offered it to Lonny, who put the scuffed plastic jug to his lips and let a mouthful enter. The homemade concoction was so bitter he choked, and to keep from spitting on the ground, and to keep from offending the ancestors, Lonny forced the nauseating fire down his throat. His head went light and a sweat broke out over his body. For an instant, when he saw Jaoravo spilling a tribute to the ancestors, he thought he had been duped into swallowing poison. But Jaoravo sluiced the divine spirit into his own belly. He shuddered. He coughed. He hawked a gob of bloodred sputum into the blackened dust. He tried to remember what he would need to satisfy the ancestors, himself and his wives.

"How much will they give me for the sapphire in Diego?" asked Jaoravo.

Lonny, eyes closed, head swimming, rum vapors swirling through his nasal passages like surgical anesthesia, "It does not matter what they give you in Diego. I will follow you wherever you go and buy it from the person you sell it to. I will buy this sapphire for any price."

Jaoravo wedged another shot of the divine spirit

into his soul and reflected upon Lonny's declaration. To ensure both his wives would give tributes to him when he departed and cover his bones in fine white cloth, they would need one good rice paddy each. He owned a small rice paddy of poor quality, but he knew that nearer the village there were many fine rice paddies of good quality, and if he had 6 more zebu he could buy enough land that each wife would have a rice paddy. 6 zebu is a good price for the sacred stone, thought Jaoravo.

While fighting through the layered meanings of the stranger's words the number 6 grew in his consciousness. The number 6 was a celestially whole number, the number of sons a man needed to carry his coffin to the family tomb. The sacrifice of 6 zebu as a tribute to the ancestors would be the most glorious thing ever done in the village. The 6 white-headed zebu. The number 6. He thought around the number 6 several times. Jaoravo allowed himself to believe that the meeting with the stranger was divine. A stranger guided to him by the ancestors. A stranger who would satisfy the hunger of the living and the warmth of the missing.

Lonny tapped his foot impatiently. He wasn't supposed to stop in the King's Reserve for any reason and he certainly wasn't supposed to be buying sapphires while stopped. If a military or gendarme patrol happened along they would confiscate the bulk of his cash. He hated waiting for anything but now he would wait, dodging armed men or perched on a mango root if need be. He would sleep in the squalid hut, eat badly hulled rice and give blood to malarial mosquitoes. He was willing to do anything to capture the most sublime rock he had ever held to the sky.

Lonny understood that his American conception of time, based on the rotation of the sun, measured by vibrations of a cesium atom and spread throughout the industrialized world like a religion of wall calendars and digital watches, was irrelevant in Madagascar. While most of the world celebrated the start of the new millenium, the year 2000, Malagasy peasants were just counting the moons since the last harvest. The Malagasy did not believe that minutes, hours or years were manufactured like metal spoons, that each one was the same as the next. In Lonny's experience, the peasants had no sense of the past, other than it was past; no conception of the future, other than it had not yet occurred. They lived in the eternal present as if it was all that had ever existed or would exist. The bargaining process could drag on for days.

As waves of clear light began to flood the land and Jaoravo struggled to put a price on his sacred stone, Lonny tried to inhabit the moment. But he could not. Besides weighing his chances of being arrested, his mind was busy thinking about the prospect of success. His reputation would be made for now and forever once he wrapped his hands around that ephemeral blue song. The foundation stone of his career. But would he find someone new? Would his soul bounce back with the same resiliency? His self-exile in Madagascar had strengthened his ability to make deals, to get the job done. Yet somewhere, in his belly, in the womb he would have had if he were born woman, he was less sure than ever that he was ready to love again. He wondered if luck and love were synonymous or separate, if Jaoravo's seasonal fires torched the medicinal plants with the weeds, leaving behind nothing but secondary growth, or if the fire purified the ground of the surface tangles and let the deep-rooted plants flourish in the cinders.

Lonny had always searched for the best stones. "A profit is a profit," was his father's maxim, but to Cal Cushman's bitter disappointment Lonny did not enter the precious gemstone trade just to make money. He found no satisfaction wholesaling kilos of dull, lifeless corundum, and maybe because of that, or maybe because he believed in possibility, or maybe because of his gifted eye, he was quietly obsessed with the search for a truly exceptional gem. And he had found it. Right under the noses of soldiers, gendarmes and a dozen gem dealers from Senegal, Thailand and Sri Lanka.

Just as Jaoravo sought constantly to appease the ancestors, to keep in contact with them and to consult with them, Lonny searched for beauty. He liked the fine things in life: books, films, jewelry, paintings, oriental rugs, wood boxes, carved statues. He supposed that was his original mistake. He had fallen in love with a woman five years his senior because she was beautiful. The visible pregnancy and their high-profile marriage increased the circulation of New York tabloids for months. The legal separation four years later and his flight to an impoverished agricultural country were equally dissected. But somehow, through it all, his faith that he would find a new kind of beauty in Madagascar had kept him alive. It had kept him vigilant to opportunity.

Lonny's mind imagined the sound of his father's voice when he called in the news. Although Cal had sent him to Madagascar to scope out the newly discovered sapphire deposits, he didn't expect much to come of the exercise.

Lonny's wholesale gem buying on the red-brick island was the extreme end of the business, far removed from the cutting rooms, spectrographs, dark-field loupes, calibrated scales, display cases, sales pitches, magazine models and auction houses of New York, Johannesburg, Geneva, Bangkok and Tel Aviv. Cal knew how dealers indulged themselves when they worked with relatively large sums of money in destitute countries. He frequently accused Lonny of whoring, taking drugs and avoiding responsibility. Lonny's insistence that something rare could be found in such an offbeat place only incensed his rigid father.

Jaoravo quietly held up his hand to ask for attention in the European manner, the way he had been taught by the French schoolmaster. As the ancestors had directed this stranger to him to satisfy their needs he must not forget a single thing. The cost of much rum, the special shrouds, sacks of rice from town, crates of beer, cigarettes, the musicians, the witch doctor, a tribute to the First Rooster. Jaoravo thought of the wonderful image of 6 zebu, and a patch of forest needed to feed them, and out of his mouth, unwillingly and far too quickly, as if it were not him at all, but really the ancestors who forced his tongue, he said to Lonny, "I want 66 whiteheaded zebu . . . 6 . . . 6."

"I accept your price," blurted Lonny without hesitation. He reached over and squeezed Jaoravo's knee and the peasant touched him kindly on the shoulder. Neither could speak for want of an adequate vocabulary. A vocabulary in which joy and exultation would be an approximation of their simultaneous state of grace. A moment that would change both their lives and the lives of their descendants.

Jaoravo placed the sacred stone in Lonny's cupped palms.

"Thank you," said Lonny. He was supremely happy to hold such a sublimely beautiful object, to have the desire of his dreams so close to his skin before anyone else knew of it, to touch the essence of something transcendent knowing he could never possess it.

Jaoravo offered him another slug of white rum. Lonny surveyed the empty road, spilled a tribute to the ancestors and drank with them.

"Now," said Lucky Lonny to the Happy Bull. "How much does a good zebu cost in paper money?"

2

DIEGO, MON AMOUR

There is no way for a stranger to win an argument about the relative merits of a zebu, its celestial lineage or its terrestrial price with a Malagasy peasant. After two hours of trying Lonny simply gave up. He was surprised that a military patrol hadn't hassled him already. He unzipped his knapsack and began throwing packets of Malagasy francs into a pile. The bills came in denominations of 25,000 *francs Malagasy* (fmg). Ten bills made a sheaf, four sheaves made a packet, each packet was worth a million francs. Lonny tossed sixty-six packets at Jaoravo's feet. Jaoravo refused to count the pile. Lonny added another ten packets. Jaoravo huffed contemptuously. In frustration Lonny dumped all the money in the knapsack onto the ground and showed the peasant the empty bag.

"*Ehh?*" pressed Lonny. The pile was worth $20,000 U.S. and was as high as Jaoravo's knee. Across the paddy three of Jaoravo's sons were dragging Lonny's motorcycle from the sticky earth using a team of zebu and hand-braided ropes. Lonny knew that Jaoravo had never seen that much paper money. The ancient Greek concept of "one million" was translated as "the number beyond which counting is possible" in Antakarana. Over a hundred million Malagasy francs lay on the ground before Jaoravo defying his ability to quantify it.

"*Yaa,*" said Jaoravo finally, nodding to Lonny, no longer thinking in French. He shoveled the pile of money into a wide raffia basket used for harvesting tangerines. He would travel all the way to Ambanja, where the zebu were fat, to purchase fine beasts.

Jaoravo had a huge smile on his face and talked fast in dialect about the motorcycle. Lonny nodded blithely as he scanned the road. Jaoravo clapped him on the back in a brotherly fashion and bid, "*Live well.*"

"*Live well,*" responded Lonny. With goose bumps covering his arm he caressed the stone and put it into the knapsack. His right eye fluttered uncontrollably with nervous tension. He jogged across the paddy and thanked Jaoravo's sons for their help with the bike. Clots of mud were impaled on the cylinder heads, the front fork was definitely bent.

It was thirty-five miles back to his house in the provincial capital of Diego-Suarez. Three hundred miles onward to the national capital of Antananarivo. The single road to Tana became a morass of deep ruts in less than one hundred miles. The riding was rough, with no guarantee the bike would make it. Not to mention the real threat of being arrested by unfamiliar gendarmes. Once he got there, if he got there alive, he wouldn't be able to export the sapphire through his usual channels.

Every few months Lonny flew to Antananarivo, bribed and cajoled a host of bureaucrats for the proper export documents, then personally carried his goods to Europe where they were transshipped to New York. Even when all the documents and export permits were letter perfect, he still had to bribe layers of policemen, customs officials and immigration agents to leave the country. He knew, beyond any shadow of a doubt, that the vultures in Antananarivo would summarily confiscate his incredible sapphire the instant they laid eyes on it—export permits or not.

It would be better, Lonny decided, to deal with the greedy bastards he knew than the devils he did not. He kicked his bike to life and headed back toward his house in Diego. He cruised carefully through the vibrant green countryside, dodging village goats and road chickens, leaning into curves, slowing across patchwork bridges, opening up where the tarred gravel snaked through smoking pastures. He carried the nylon knapsack slung forward, the stone snuggled against his belly.

Once he was out of the King's Reserve and across a long, waterless stretch of scrub, sinewy miners and their haggard women began flagging him down. Distant figures, like oversized ants combing a sugar pile, fanned out across the grasslands searching for a spot to dig stones. Here and there an isolated hut held precariously to the grass-covered hills. The closer Lonny came to the camps, the better constructed the huts.

Lonny finally spotted the platoon of soldiers that was supposed to monitor the road and strip-search traders who dared venture beyond the camps. Their Peugeot 404 pickup rested on three wheels and a mud brick next to the torched remnants of an old mama's hut that served cane rum. As he motored past, a sentry saluted with a sloppy, bloodshot grin. The man's rifle was muddy, his uniform rumpled and stained. Other members of the patrol lay motionless in the shade of a tree like victims of a failed coup attempt. The acrid smell of scorched fruit hung in the air.

Three hundred yards past the dissolute guardians, around a bend in the road, huts were jammed cheek to jowl and right to the pavement. It was a permanent riot as trucks, Jeeps, taxis, motorcycles and bicycles tried to negotiate a passage through a solid wall of peasants, miners and commerce. Vendors set out everything from dried fish to plastic combs in the middle of the traffic.

When Lonny first arrived in Diego there had only been a few dozen peasants out here probing the wilderness. Now there were close to thirty thousand people in the irrational grip of sapphire fever. There was no running water, no organized sewage treatment, no governmental authority, no police protection, no nothing. The California Gold Rush would have seemed like a well-organized brawl in comparison.

The miners recognized Lonny instantly as he tried to force his way through the squalor. Every grandma and squalling babe, every bucket-toting mama, every naked child and bare-chested miner thrust chips of blue at him. He revved the bike loudly and shouldered into the swirling mob, refusing to make eye contact. Normally he would have picked up a few kilos of stones. It was a feast day and there was desperation in the air.

A host of small girls waved to Lonny from an embankment. They were the same age as Annie and he usually bought them cakes, Cokes or candy when he stopped. They wore cotton dresses he had purchased in bulk and given away by the dozen. The image of his own seven-year-old daughter robed in a scratchy 40-kilo rice sack had pierced his general indifference to the poverty.

The road shimmered with heat when he broke free of the camps. Yam-colored licks of flame checkered the countryside where miners set fire to the ground vegetation. Here and there skirmish lines of black and white ibis faced the flames, hunting down insects and slow-moving lizards that were fleeing one type of death only to find another. The air carried the scent of burning grass above the pungent aroma of a night rain.

Lonny downshifted reluctantly forty-five minutes later when red-striped barricades and soldiers rose like mirages out of the mid-morning heat. Impassable roadblocks marked the limits of Diego-Suarez and regulated the traffic in and out of the town better than a tollbooth. Colonel Ratsimanga's soldiers manned the post, checking identity cards and keeping a close watch on the movement of people and goods. Lonny stared blankly at Lieutenant Rakoto while a conscript motioned for his identity card, motorcycle papers and driving license. Lieutenant Rakoto knew exactly where he lived, exactly what he did and exactly how far he could push the stranger without a reprimand from the colonel.

"Have you sapphires?" demanded Rakoto, a highlander with straight hair and light, Asian features. Ever since their seafaring ancestors migrated from Indonesia one thousand years before, the highland tribes had not married outside their caste. They remained racially and socially homogeneous, inbred, xenophobic, scornful and aloof from the theories of social and technological development that had transformed the rest of the globe. Their peasants starved, their women died for lack of decent pharmaceuticals, and still they looked down their brown aquiline noses at all the unfortunates not born to their lineage.

"None," said Lonny, dazed by the absence of motion.

Somebody was always keeping tabs on Lonny. Whether it was his house guard, Ali Mohamed, the disco girls at the Vo Vo, other expatriates, fellow gem traders, bureaucrats, miners or children swarming him for candy. His only true moments of physical and mental tranquillity came while riding the motorbike faster than a man could run.

Lieutenant Rakoto shifted his baseball cap and blinked. He had watched Lonny transport pickup trucks full of sapphires past his post. He knew Lonny played bridge with Colonel Ratsimanga on Sunday nights. He hated Lonny for his ghostly skin, his obvious wealth and disdain for protocol. Lieutenant Rakoto also knew enough to stand in the shade and blink quietly. He had asked a direct question, received a direct answer. He had done his job.

Lonny collected his documents and rode past the

entrance to the airport to the next barricade at the next shade tree. Two gendarmes, members of the National Police Force, stood there dressed in baby blue shirts with gold epaulets and fluorescent white pants. Scarlet kepis perched on their jet-black skulls and well-greased automatic pistols hung from open holsters. The older gendarme wore the chevrons of a sergeant. He saluted smartly as Lonny reached for his papers.

"Mr. American," said the gendarme, dismissing the documents with a wave. "It is the pleasure of the National Police Force to invite you to our Annual Ball. Entry passes are 10,000 francs."

"*Tsara be!* Super good!" said Lonny. "One pass for me." The police ranks were filled with *côtiers*, the coastal-dwelling Malgash whose blood had mixed with Africans. Their hair was woolly, their skin dark and pure. The *côtiers* detested the highlanders and had set up their own barricades to keep an eye on the "foreign" soldiers. Although Lonny felt more comfortable with the policemen than the military soldiers, he treated them with circumspection. He didn't know any of the superior officers personally, which left him open to petty harassment.

The gendarme laughed pleasantly. The American was courteous and spoke the local dialect. Perhaps, thought the sergeant, the American tribe was as different from the French tribe as the highlanders from the *côtiers*. He had been taught that Frenchmen were descendants of noble Gauls and the Americans descendants of untouchables and slaves. Perhaps this American was a prince in his country and the local Frenchmen mere bondsmen. Once a person travels from his birth village it is very difficult to place him in the proper celestial order. He wanted to ask the American for a small gift, but the ancestors would punish him severely if he demeaned himself to obtain a *petit cadeau* from the descendant of a slave.

The gendarme tore off a citation form, scrawled his initials in red ink, then presented the scrap of paper to Lonny as if it were an engraved invitation. Lonny stashed bills of different denominations in different pockets of his jumpsuit. The left front breast pocket carried ten 10,000-fmg notes, the left rear, a million's worth of 25,000-fmg notes. The right front, tiny bills for buying Cokes and peanuts, the right rear, his documents. He always kept money in reserve for unforeseen difficulties and he never showed all of it to anyone at one time. He unzipped the appropriate pocket and handed the sergeant a 10,000-franc note.

Both gendarmes snapped to attention and saluted precisely. It was their policy to treat a stranger as a stranger and avoid any interaction. Lonny carefully arranged his papers and zipped them back into his jumpsuit as the gendarmes retreated to the shade.

Now that he was back in Diego, Lonny could not

stop a bothersome new question from forming: How do I get the sapphire off Madagascar?

Diego-Suarez was an island within the island of Madagascar. There were no unsurveyed points of entry or exit. The military roadblocks were always manned. Secret policemen, immigration and customs men canvassed the rare flight to the exterior. Port officials and navy men searched ships leaving port. Diego existed apart. Days to the next large town, hundreds of air miles from mother Africa, thousands of nautical miles from Asia. A world within itself.

The buildings of Diego-Suarez spread across a small, easily controlled peninsula that jutted into a magnificent San Francisco–sized bay. The whitewashed walls and rust-colored roofs huddled futilely against the seasonal winds and the constant slap of the sun. The harbor welcomed an endless parade of tramp steamers delivering cheap manufactured goods from Asia and removing the island's natural resources.

Lonny pointed his road bike down the bare, overgrazed neck of land that connected the interior of Madagascar to the low-slung peninsula. A line of peasants in homemade clothes trudged the same direction. So did several zebu carts stacked high with tons of charcoal. A few desperate men, servicing those too poor to buy the charcoal, strained at rickshaws sagging with firewood. Lonny accelerated past them. They were all trying to make it into the provincial capital before the equatorial heat reached its mid-morning strength.

At the start of the peninsula Lonny passed the busy soccer stadium, the empty taxi brousse stand and the closed gas station. On a normal day the stadium would have been empty and the taxi brousse station would have resembled a fiesta. A taxi brousse was a small pickup truck fitted with a turtle-like shell. The top swayed with baskets of fruit, live hens and bulky merchandise. Passengers were wedged inside like livestock until every square inch was full to bursting. If it weren't for the taxi brousse, clunking down the rotten countryside roads, grinding through streambeds, throwing up billowing clouds of dust, the movement of society in Madagascar would cease altogether.

Lonny banked round the principal rotary and headed straight for the rue Colbert, the commercial heart of Diego. Smoldering garbage piles marked the intersection of minor streets in a town that had not seen organized refuse collection since Independence.

The principal rotary sat on the neck of the peninsula like an octopus, connecting and controlling the traffic in the town and around the bay. One arm of the octopus shot around the great bay of Diego-Suarez toward Ramena beach, the military camp and the Pass; another arm looped the opposite direction around the bay, toward the salt flats, the sterile pastures and the blunt tip of northern Madagascar itself, Cape Bobaomby; one arm snaked past the French consulate, the Christian churches and the slaughterhouse; another led to the bourgeois shops of the rue Colbert; another to the section of town inhabited by Comorians and abandoned by the local authorities since Independence; the most important road led out to the airport, the villages of the interior and would eventually lead a battered traveler past Antananarivo, through the highlands and across the desert, to Fort Dauphin, 900 miles to the south, the opposite end of Madagascar.

When the French first mapped the Bay of Diego-Suarez in the mid-nineteenth century there was not a single person living on the shores of the outsized bay. The surrounding land was poor and the Mozambique Channel offered better fishing. Although the harbor compared favorably to San Francisco, the narrow pass to the ocean (where Californians united their own headlands with a famous bridge) was next to impossible to navigate under sail. As a consequence it was the last great harbor on the planet to be colonized and permanently inhabited, at a time when great harbors were gradually losing their strategic and economic importance.

One hundred years after the French empire imported clerks and ditchdiggers of every race and religion, Diego was still a place where cultures clashed and mingled. Europeans who had been ostracized from their own societies by crimes or differences in perception regularly washed up in Diego like storm-tossed sailors. Living on small pensions dispensed by the French consulate, wire transfers from offshore bank accounts or bogus disability pensions, they made do. The free living and nonjudgmental *côtiers* welcomed them much as they had welcomed Captain Kidd and his libertarian pirates in bygone centuries. The collected miscreants of Diego reveled in their social, geographic and cultural isolation.

As Lonny crossed the empty marketplace he felt a much-needed boost. The market was his favorite part of town and on market day the throbbing concrete apron electrified his New York spirit. On market day there were young girls frying sweet bananas in hot oil. Peasants whacking the tops off green coconuts. Butchers hanging offal along a line of stalls that led to shrimp mongers and fishermen. Dark bars that sold palm wine known as cat piss. The auto mechanics were positioned next to the clothes re-sellers, sorting oily parts inches from freshly laundered secondhand clothes. Carpenters were to the north near the sandal makers, and all through the middle, in a great square crossed by shifting paths, pyramids of ripe vegetables and rotting fruit were tended by bickering women and stunned babies in the ferocious sun. The big market was ringed by the offices of medical doctors and European pharmacies, witch doctors and herb salesmen. On market days Lonny felt as charged and open to possibility as if he were sidling through the streets of Hong Kong with a fistful of diamonds.

This Sunday only masticated cane fibers and fly-licked litchi pits littered the slowly roasting square. A thick, filthy stench rose from the sugar-coated slab. Ships' captains, merchant seamen, dockworkers, day laborers, Coca-Cola salesmen, bus touts, Catholic priests, Lutheran ministers, choirmasters, Imams, truck drivers, deep-sea Comorian fishermen, penniless students, tropical shell bandits, grocery clerks, peanut girls, taxi *maîtres*, disco girls, best boys, bankers, lawyers, fortune-tellers, tour operators, cruising expatriates, stick-swinging policemen, machine-gun-toting soldiers and wide-eyed peasants were all sleeping off the bliss of the Saturday night fête.

Diego was a Casablanca without a Bogart. There were no hidden heroes in this far outpost. No single soul willing to risk his life or fortune for a cause. Destitute bureaucrats vied with pinched soldiers and squads of gendarmes to make a living off the isolated citizens. The tiny bit of real commerce that came through the port was heavily taxed by the central government, which led a culture of corruption and bred rival ministries competing against each other like criminal gangs. If God had asked just one of the residents to sacrifice himself for the sake of

humanity the town would have blazed in the glow
of His disappointment.

Along the rue Colbert, the self-styled Champs-
Élysées of the Indian Ocean, Diego boasted a disco
named *Le Moulin Rouge,* a restaurant known as *La
Tour d'Argent,* and a hotel *Georges V*—all badly
flawed negatives of the Parisian originals. Lonny
cruised half the length of the rue before stopping in
at the Glace Gourmand. The concrete café was
scrubbed and whitewashed for the expatriate families expected after the Sunday Mass. Out on the
usually bustling rue there was barely a soul to be
seen in the heat of the morning that followed in the
wake of a full tropical night. Lonny huffed a sigh of
relief and walked inside to plot his next move.

3

ANGEL FROM ANTANANARIVO

In the growing period, after the rain swept down and before the Eastern trade winds blew at a constant rhythm, the wet air blanketing the town was as cottony and humid as the inside of a dog's mouth. The cool ice-cream parlor served as Lonny's refuge and his second home. The owner, Alexis Grandmaison, was both a business partner and his best friend. Lonny removed a chilled Coca-Cola from the drink fridge and held the bottle to his forehead. Icy rivulets rode off the thick glass onto his face.

"Happy Easter," said a woman's voice in English.

Lonny turned around. It was about 10 A.M.

The sun raked the trunks of the palm trees and beads of sweat stood out on his forehead like fat raindrops. A heavy stench from the tuna fish factory enveloped the open terrace.

"You can call me Malika." She held out a freshly showered hand.

Lonny gripped the manicured fingers tightly in surprise. He had never laid eyes on her before, but he knew a pair of Calvin Klein sunglasses, a Prada handbag and Gucci mules when he saw them. The last time he had seen a woman wear apple-green Versace hot pants, or anything like them, was at Cartier's on 5th Avenue. She was an unsettling vision from his past life.

He directed her wordlessly to the table where he usually met with miners, merchants or bureaucrats. She had the prudence not to wear dangling earrings or a necklace that could be snatched off her body. He sat facing the rue and positioned her across from him.

"Who are you?" he asked. She had the smooth, light ebony skin of an African and a common East African name, but she spoke with a flat midwestern accent. The light framed her visage in shadow and her aura gave him a funny feeling, as if her best facet might be hiding a more insidious truth, like a ruby glued on top of a garnet.

"I work for the U.S. State Department," said Malika, as she examined her fellow American. He had a charming smile and a pleasant masculine neckline. His lean physique, sand-colored hair and deeply tanned skin were an unexpected bonus. She was disarmed by the mischievous lilt of his eyes.

"You're CIA," stated Lonny. She wasn't part of the regular embassy crowd. Regular Americans avoided him like a bowel ailment. They lived in Antananarivo on inflated salaries and diplomatic visas. He lived by his eye and his wits. The official Americans (diplomats, naturalists and aid workers) celebrated the Fourth of July, Thanksgiving, Christmas, Kwanza and Martin Luther King Day inside the courtyard of the barricaded embassy. For the past two years Lonny had celebrated the Fourteenth of July with the French at the consulate, the Twenty-eighth of June with the Malagasy in the dust, and spent the Christmas season buying rough sapphires for pennies on the dollar from undernourished peasants roaming the rue Colbert. There were no other Americans in Diego and the ones passing through didn't speak to him unless they needed to cash a traveler's check or receive emergency medical attention.

"I'm a diplomat," hedged Malika.

The Directorate of Operations had grudgingly accepted the resident ambassador's request that Malika fly in from Cape Town, Republic of South Africa, to speak forcefully with Leonard Cushman, G.G. (Graduate Gemologist), formerly of East 79th

Street, New York, New York, about his gem business. It was more dangerous than it appeared. In countries like Madagascar, disappointed American citizens with prominent families back home tended to complain loudly when the world didn't turn their direction. The directorate didn't think the cost of letting Lonny continue his various activities outweighed the risk he posed to their officer's cover, but she was sent to deliver a message anyway and she wasn't very happy about it. A congressional inquiry with her name on it would terminate her undercover career as effectively as a stiletto.

It was Malika's first mission outside of South Africa and already it was going badly. Part of her luggage had disappeared in Antananarivo. The hotel in Diego was filled with hissing cockroaches. There was a bare electrical wire hanging across the shower stall and no mosquito net to protect the nasty-smelling mattress.

Africa was supposed to be the place where Company officers padded their résumés and boosted their careers. African bureaucrats and military officials were poorly compensated and eager to get on someone's payroll. If an ambitious young CIA officer could recruit a couple hundred informants, add an arcane language to their quiver of arrows and pocket recommendations from the local ambassadors, the clean, well-lit capitals of Europe were the next stop. Just because the year-long tour of Africa was an obligatory rung on the career ladder didn't mean Malika had to enjoy it.

She had prepared for their conversation well in advance. She'd read the file at the embassy. Flipped through the tabloid clippings compiled for her in Virginia. It was obvious that Leonard Cushman could not be publicly embarrassed. His wife had already shared his sexual preferences and peccadilloes with 15 million New Yorkers. Daily readers of "Page Six," the *New York Post*, knew him as a toxic husband, an absent father and an incorrigible, gem-dealing playboy. His most intimate mistakes had been psychoanalyzed by gleeful columnists. Malika's plan was to play it straight. Instead of threatening him, she would offer to help. Explain the situation then propose an immediate, practical solution.

A lithe waitress came round the counter and took their order. A grand café au lait and croissant for Malika, a tall glass of ice for Lonny. The waitress called Lonny *cherie*, and approved of Malika's fashion sense with a wink. Behind the cash register Alexis caught Lonny's eye. The middle-aged Frenchman, still bleary from a long night at the disco, tapped his finger against the side of his nose. It was their signal for trouble.

"I'm here," announced Malika, "because the embassy is behind the proposal to classify the King's Reserve as a national park. The discovery of sapphire deposits has put the plan in jeopardy and may lead to the ecological destruction of the entire area."

Lonny nodded. Jaoravo's early-morning shots of hut rum made his body shiver in fits and starts. He was covered in agricultural grime and couldn't wait for a bath in the bay's salt water.

"Your status as an American citizen and your high-profile gem-dealing undermine the position of the United States Government."

Lonny examined the woman sitting across from him the way he would appraise a gem. She had round Caucasian eyes but a strong mahogany tone. Her hair was straight or straightened. Her taut nipples poked at the ribbed fabric of her competition orange tank top. Her arms were long and thin, unused to manual labor of any kind. If her beauty and clothing were meant to veil her true origins, like a fake diamond set in a platinum wedding band, the distractions were working well.

The waitress delivered the breakfast order to the table with another wink.

Malika stirred her coffee. She wasn't sure if Lonny was ignoring her words or weighing them. She decided to let the uncomfortable silence grow, the way she had been trained.

"I am American," stated Lonny, discovering a source of his irritation. "It is not my status."

"Yes," agreed Malika. A spoonful of coffee spilled onto her saucer. "That's why the embassy sent me here to speak with you."

"About what?"

"The Ministry of Foreign Affairs has evidence that you are falsifying the value of your exports and that you have undeclared sapphires in your possession."

Lonny locked his eyes onto Malika's, searching for his center of balance, hardly blinking. He became like the peasants who exuded nature's own innocence while pawning ground glass as imperial opal. Undeclared sapphires? Or one undeclared sapphire? There was no way she could know. He had only purchased the stone a few hours ago.

"I'm not sure what you're talking about," he recovered.

"Mr. Cushman, in a few days Madagascar will have a significant portion of its debt forgiven by the World Bank and the International Monetary Fund. When that happens the Prime Minister will declare the King's Reserve a national park. Neither the Minister of Foreign Affairs nor the American ambassador wants a diplomatic incident to endanger those proceedings."

"And so?"

"I'm here to pass on a warning that a regime known for its indifference to human rights is considering the arrest of an American citizen."

"Are you accusing me of lying to a dictatorship?"

"Yes."

"And my actions reflect badly on the 280 million Americans who can't find this place on a wall map?"

"Yes."

"The ambassador strongly encourages me to cease and desist before she permits the local authorities to press false charges and confiscate my goods?"

"Exactly."

"I'm a little confused," sighed Lonny, getting a feel for the conversation. "Does the ambassador want me to bribe somebody for her?"

"This isn't about a low-level shakedown," shot back Malika. "This is about a three-billion-dollar debt swap and pharmaceutical research. Once the King's Reserve is declared a national park, American teams will catalog the unique flora and fauna of the area for the first time in history. I'm sure you are aware that the only known cure for leukemia is derived from the rosy periwinkle, a plant first studied in eastern Madagascar. A park will protect the singular biodiversity of northern Madagascar. The next generation of aspirin or AIDS antiviral might be discovered in the King's Reserve."

Lonny let his eyes wander across the rue Colbert. On the empty lot facing the Glace Gourmand were the remains of ten dump trucks the European Health Commission had donated to the town. Because there was no money for gas in the municipal budget, the mayor had sold off different pieces of the trucks until they were absolutely useless hunks of iron. Someone had recently removed the windshields.

"The Prime Minister," continued Malika, "is chosen by the constitutional assembly and relies on support from specific tribal leaders. He called the ambassador because he will not risk stopping your arrest. He wanted to know if there were going to be repercussions. The ambassador expressed her concern over the situation but assured the Prime Minister that America respects the judicial process of independent nations."

"The judicial process of independent nations?" Lonny gave her a broad smile. "That's a good one."

"If you think," said Malika as Lonny refocused his attention on her, "the ambassador is going to let an irreplaceable piece of the earth's biosphere go up in smoke simply because a New York City playboy is being denied his basic human rights, you got another thing coming. The ambassador herself asked me to deliver this message."

"New York City playboy?" repeated Lonny. He watched as Malika forcefully bit into her croissant. He had met the ambassador one time and she had not been helpful. She spoke French poorly and seemed to think he was a nuisance. She devoted all her efforts to the Peace Corps volunteers, visiting them in remote villages where they hosted parasitic worms and walked miles for a pail of water. The creation of a high-profile park had to be her ticket out of the dreary ambassadorial ranks and into the upper echelon of Washington policy makers. If the deal fell through she would probably spend the rest of her career chaperoning church groups through the shanties of Kinshasa or Ouagadougou.

"How's the croissant?" asked Lonny.

"Tastes like a bicycle tire."

"How's the coffee?"

"Oily."

"Give me the bottom line," said Lonny. "What's the problem?"

"You are. You've paid off every civilian, police and military official from inspector to minister. According to Immigration you've been on rotating tourist visas since you arrived two years ago."

"So what?"

"So what! You're buying sapphires from the King's Reserve. You have been encouraging illegal mining in areas strictly off-limits to foreigners."

"You can't prove that."

"The First Rooster, the king of the Antakarana wants your head."

"I've never met him," countered Lonny. Unlike the French, the Malagasy had never deposed their own kings and queens. Hundreds of them ruled major and minor fiefs throughout the land. Under colonial rule they had been sidestepped but with the anarchy that followed Independence some had reasserted their hereditary rights and powers. The only thing Lonny knew about the First Rooster was that he drove a recent model Toyota Land Cruiser.

"You're contributing to the ecological destruction in the world's fastest disappearing forest," said Malika. "You're undermining the power of a legitimate tribal leader. You are threatening the future of a new park, the power of the constitutional assembly and the effectiveness of the Prime Minister."

"I'm providing starving people with money to buy food."

"You're taking advantage of people who are unable to defend themselves from economic predation."

"I'm exercising my profession and helping hardworking miners get a fair price for their labor."

"You're exploiting the situation."

"And how would you conduct business? Set up a miners' co-op?"

"Your conduct is outrageous and the ambassador wants it to stop yesterday."

"What do you want me to do?" demanded Lonny.

"Go home."

"What?"

"There is absolutely no logical reason for you to stay in this place."

"It's a living," said Lonny. Leaving Madagascar without the stone was not an option. A routine export permit was a straightforward lesson in institutional blackmail. He dutifully delivered televisions, packets of cash and ceramic tea sets to every bureaucrat with a rubber stamp and an ink pad. The stone would require a much higher level of bribery and he wasn't 100 percent sure if he could pull it off on short notice.

"Fly out with me this afternoon," she insisted.

"I can't."

"Why?"

"Well." He considered. "Today's flight stops over in Nosy Be. The delegate to the constitutional assembly over there promised to skin me alive the next time I set foot on his island."

"What did you do to him?"

"I refused to give him $25,000 dollars as a birthright."

"We'll take tomorrow's flight."

"That one stops in Mahajanga. Bubonic plague in Mahajanga. I'd hate to spend any time in their jails and there is a certain customs official who has his eye out for me."

"What did you do to him?"

"I went over his head and paid off his boss to import the motorcycle."

"How about the day after?"

"No good." Lonny shook his head. "If I get on a direct flight to Antananarivo my enemies will be waiting." He could picture the faces of a dozen low-level officials who would happily confiscate the stone. Commercial aircraft were out of the question.

"You're not making this easy," commented Malika.

"Why should I?"

"Because I'm offering to help you. And if you don't accept my help the ambassador is going to let you die in this shit hole."

"What makes you think I need your help?" asked Lonny.

She sipped her coffee and watched Lonny's vivid gaze follow the curve of her shoulder to the base of her neck. She had not expected him to bolt for the exit. Between his bitter split from the New York City publicist and the stinging separation agreement that took custody of his only daughter, he had no particular reason to go home. And Malika had no particular reason to force a confrontation. His family connections in New York were both real and powerful. The local ambassador just wanted something in the file cabinet to cover her back.

Sitting across from those lively brown eyes, the loose windswept hair, a completely unexpected thought crossed Malika's mind. She wore the clothes of a fashion model, but she had grown up in Minnesota, had a law degree from the University of Chicago and went to work in the sterile environment of an embassy every day. She'd seen magazine pictures of Lonny in a white tuxedo with starlets and models. He'd be good in bed. She reached into the $500 black-and-white leather "bowling bag" on the bench next to her and turned off the tape recorder.

"What do you do around here for fun?" she asked, tossing her hair.

"Swim at Ramena beach."

"Will you take me?"

"I thought you were reading me the riot act."

"I'm done."

"Seriously?"

"Yeah." She smiled seductively. "Pick me up here in an hour?"

"Sure," said Lonny. He was planning on a dip anyway. "Leave your stuff with the owner. He'll look after it while we're gone."

"See you soon," returned Malika as she stood up. She wanted to jot down her nonverbal impressions for the contact report. The Company governed the use of her time and manipulated her conscience at will, but she controlled the use of her body. Lonny's face bore the stamp of a ladies' man and she liked the idea of using her natural talents to tactical advantage. He had full lips, grizzled cheeks and a jaded twinkle in his eye that promised an intimate knowledge of female pleasures. In comparison to the overweight, world-weary diplomats of South Africa he positively vibrated with testosterone.

Malika snatched up her little bag and was out the

door with a shiver. She felt his silent regard when she turned her back. It was difficult to remind herself that he was a privileged white boy in jeopardy of ruining a multibillion-dollar debt swap.

4

FRIENDS

Lonny sipped his cold Coke thoughtfully as a *pousse-pousse*, the wide Malagasy version of a rickshaw, clattered down the incline of the rue Colbert out of control. The man in charge of the cart was sprinting in bare feet while a towering load of charcoal threatened to overtake him from behind. He held on to the front bar of the *pousse-pousse* for life itself. When his load tipped backward he was left dangling in the air, legs churning uselessly. When the load shifted forward he ran as fast as possible to avoid being crushed.

The *pousse-pousse* men came from the Antesaka tribe in the southeastern part of Madagascar, near a place called Vaindranogrado ("where one buys water"). They were internal exiles, wandering the large towns of Madagascar, selling their back muscles to pay off elaborate funeral tributes to their ancestors. They were the only tribe of hurried men Lonny had ever met in the tropics. They worked dawn to dusk pulling heavy loads, then hired themselves out as night guards. They honored their ancestors with toil and were impatient to return home as redeemed men. The Antesaka considered the trials of this life only a brief moment of pain before the eternal bliss of tending zebu.

"Poor bastard," said Alexis in French. He left the ice cream counter and sat down with Lonny. His face was drawn and his eyes dull from a lack of sleep. Most Sundays he was in bed after running his disco all night, but it was Easter and he expected a large crowd for ice cream as soon as the churches let out.

"He'll outrun it," said Lonny.

"I was talking about you," said Alexis. "That's the first time I've seen you speak English. I didn't know you could smile."

"Lay off."

"As soon as you go home to your family."

"What family?"

"That famous wife you're always talking about. Your daughter, your fabulously wealthy father. That family."

"You don't know the first thing about my family."

"Very good. Very good." Alexis raised both his palms off the table in a gesture of surrender. "Do it your own way. Be like me. A fifty-seven-year-old expatriate."

"You could go home if you wanted to."

"Who wants to live in France on a pension? Do you know how much it costs to live in a socialist country?"

Alexis had retired as a flag officer from the French navy after the Persian Gulf War. He had begun his career in Diego-Suarez, when it was the most important French naval base in the Indian Ocean and had kept fond memories of those days for thirty years. He moved to Diego as soon as he retired and started businesses providing the two things that sailors dream about monotonously: ice cream and women. He was by far the most successful French resident in town. Whenever a merchant ship, fishing vessel or naval frigate came into port, the officers crowded into the Glace Gourmand by day and the sailors mobbed the Vo Vo Club by night. After a few pints of free ice cream, an open bar tab and escorts of solicitous young females, seasoned captains offered him liberal contracts to provision their ships.

"Tell me about the lady," said Alexis. A visitor from the capital meant news and the political situation all over the island was extremely tense. There were wild rumors circulating through the newspapers and the streets.

"She was from the embassy."

"Don't hold out on me," said Alexis. He kept a stash of cash and a loaded gun behind the counters of both his establishments. He was ready to cut and run on a moment's notice. "Tell me what she said."

"She wants me to leave the country."

"Are you going?"

"I'm not ready."

"A ship without a compass will never arrive at port," said Alexis.

"Don't start that again."

"People like you don't live in places like Diego-Suarez, Madagascar. People like you live in cities. People like you call the plumber when the toilet clogs."

"I go wherever there are stones."

"You don't belong here."

"I already told you that when I first got here I wanted to kill myself," said Lonny. He preferred to talk about money. Alexis brought in huge quantities of local currency from his businesses. Lonny took the Malagasy francs off his hands and compensated him with dollars transferred from his own New York reserves to Alexis's account in Paris. It was done word of mouth, without written contracts of any kind, and they had developed a close relationship based on mutual trust.

"Then what happened?" prompted Alexis.

"Don't you ever get tired of the same conversation?" asked Lonny. "We go back and forth on this five times a week."

"Tell me again," encouraged Alexis. "I'm waiting for the day your story is going to change." Alexis took a gambler's interest in Lonny. He figured the odds at 3 against 2 that Lonny would leave Diego happy, 5 to 4 that he would get his ass handed to him in some major way, and 6 to 5 generally. But he also had a hunch, a 1500 to 1 long shot that Lonny just might find or do something in Diego-Suarez that had never been done before. An educated American who could speak both French and Antakarana? Lonny was a unique genre of *Homo sapiens* on an island renowned for its odd species.

"I'm a competitive person." Lonny suddenly picked up their shopworn conversation with a sly new grin. "When I saw the Thais and Senegalese making money, I thought, I can beat them. I can outtrade them any day of the week. It became a game."

"I set up the disco for the same reason. Just to see if I could do it."

"Except I was playing the lottery."

"Keep on."

"If I had stuck with small stones and paid average prices, I would have made 20,000 dollars a kilo. It's not much by the standards of West 47th Street but it would have been 200,000 dollars a year net."

"Real money."

"That's what my father said. But you know I did something different. I specialized in big stones. Ones that cost a few thousand dollars each. Crystals . . . 10 grams, 20 grams, 35 grams. The stuff nobody else would touch. Cracks and inclusions are impossible to identify until the stone is cut."

"And you made money."

"I made some, lost some."

"So why are you still here?"

"I'm waiting for one truly exceptional stone."

"But you can't find it and you never will. It doesn't exist except in your head." This was the part of their endless conversation that Alexis enjoyed the most. It allowed him to delve into the general weakness of the American character and the insidious effects of Hollywood movies. Their banter up to the present moment was simply a setup for his attack on the American way of life and a defense of French intellectual standards.

"It does exist," said Lonny. "I found it this morning."

"Of course you did."

"Take a look." Lonny unzipped the knapsack and placed the huge sapphire on the table like a poker player laying down a straight flush.

"*Sacré Madonna!*" Alexis grabbed the stone. It was as smooth and heavy as a ball bearing. He rolled the heptagonal object around on his fingertips. Warmth radiated from its surface and it was so crystalline that it actually sparkled. He hefted the stone into the air, letting it rise a few inches above his outstretched palms then scooping inward on its downward fall.

Lonny plucked the stone out of the Frenchman's grasp and put it back in the knapsack.

"Bravo." Alexis tipped an imaginary hat his friend's direction. "I never doubted you."

Lonny burst into laughter at the lie.

"Now tell me how can I get off Madagascar without being searched."

"Well," said Alexis. "That depends on where you are headed."

"It doesn't matter."

"A med-evac plane could take you to Africa, the Seychelles or La Réunion."

"What if the airport were blocked?"

"Then a dhow to the Comoros."

"My watchman is from there. They're midway between here and Africa."

"It's just three days' sail. Mayotte's the closest to Madagascar, then Anjouan, then Mohéli, then Grand Comore."

"What's it like at the moment?"

"Three of the islands change governments about every six months. Forget about them. Mayotte is the place to go. It's still considered French territory."

"How would I get out of Mayotte?"

"If everything is going great you hop a direct flight to Paris. If things fell apart you could always charter a yacht to South Africa. The police are there to prevent undocumented Mahorias from flying to France, not survey European yachtsmen."

"The islands of the moon," said Lonny, remembering a folk tale he had read about an exiled Zanzibari prince. "The stepping-stones to Africa."

"I know some people there."

"I don't need your help."

Alexis tilted his head back, pursed his lips then knocked his knuckles against the table. "Where did you get that thing?" he asked.

"Does it matter?"

"If you got that one from the same place you've been getting the other ones, it matters."

"Who cares?"

"The First Rooster will care," said Alexis, keeping an eye on the rue Colbert. There was a clink-clink of prisoners coming down the sidewalk. Eight men were shackled in a line by their right ankles. Several had bone-deep sores and walked listlessly, others scavenged edible garbage. A guard trolled behind them, threatening them when he felt like it, herding them this way or that with a knotted whip, as if they were goats.

"I don't get it," said Lonny, tearing his eyes away from the condemned men.

"The First Rooster is a gendarme."

"What the hell does that mean?"

"You've just given the First Rooster an excuse to challenge the military."

"How did I do that?"

"The gendarmes are the only organized force in Madagascar capable of standing up to the military. The First Rooster is leading a coalition of tribal leaders against the Admiral. They are backing a strong Prime Minister who will take power away from the presidency and give it to the constitutional assembly."

"Meaning?" Lonny didn't follow Malagasy politics. He found it difficult to decipher the daily accusations, protests, grenade attacks, jailings, death threats, disappearances and defamation in the local scandal sheets.

"You took a valuable mineral from the King's Reserve," explained Alexis. "Since it's the military's responsibility to prevent unauthorized mining in tribal areas, they can be held accountable."

"How long do you think before they find out?"

"A week."

"I don't believe you," said Lonny, getting up from the table. "Nobody knows what's going on out there. It's the Wild West."

"I can help," offered Alexis.

"I'll get back to you," said Lonny. Alexis loved conspiracy and doom. He found third world politics more entertaining than the World Cup and created rumors to pass the time. Although he trusted Alexis more than all the other expats combined, Lonny wondered if he could count on the Frenchman when his future was at stake.

Lonny hopped the iron rail dividing the café from the street and climbed aboard his motorcycle. He rolled it down the rue Colbert, silently wending his way through the perspiring streets. Forty years after independence from France the architecture of Diego-Suarez was distinctly colonial, whitewashed arcades and yellow balconies, false second stories and rubble-filled lots. The rue itself was paved but the side streets were simply gouges that drained to ramshackle alleys. Colonial-era mansions sat above the waves of corrugated iron huts like tall ships stranded at low tide. Outside the Vo Vo Club torn condoms and vomit stains marked the passing of another Saturday night.

But Lonny saw something more sinister in the fresh light of morning. Wind-beaten BUVEZ COCA-COLA! signs hung outside every shack, the lone video store advertised Disney movies in Arabic, beer bars served Heinz ketchup remaindered from Argentina, the telecommunications up-link hooked into American technology put there by NASA. Caterpillar bulldozers smoothed the roads. Airplanes in and out of Diego were serviced by Boeing. American industry subtly dominated every aspect of the Malagasy economy. Suddenly there seemed to be a remote possibility that Malika and Alexis were both telling the truth: A multibillion-dollar deal did hinge on getting rid of him, and the *côtiers* really were prepared to take on the highlanders. Perhaps the American ambassador had a right to be concerned for his health.

At the base of the rue, Lonny popped the motorcycle clutch and roared up a side street toward his residence. His elegant villa faced east, on the eastern edge of the peninsula, catching the breezes that blew in off the Indian Ocean. The walls of the house were made of brown limestone blocks quarried from the outlying hills. He had a well-knit lawn of garnet green grass and a spectacular view of the topaz bay from the rear veranda. Rows of citronella drove away mosquitoes, pots of geraniums fended off flies. The palm-lined street in front of his compound led directly from the shops of the rue Colbert to the rear gates of the *Lycée Français*.

Ali Mohamed opened the gate at the sound of Lonny's motorcycle. He was a giant, leather-skinned Comorian fisherman no good for the sea and nothing else mattered. He guarded Lonny's house for wages because he did not feel like dying just yet and his children did not want to feed an old man who did not work. He wore a hand-stitched prayer cap and read the Koran in Arabic to pass the interminable days.

"*Shikamo*," greeted Lonny in Swahili.

"*Marahaba,*" responded Ali politely but somewhat vexed. He had explained to Lonny several times that it was the watchman's duty to initiate the greeting ceremony.

Lonny tromped into the house to shed his jumpsuit and boots. His Swahili was a remnant of a semester's worth of night classes at the 92nd Street Y and tanzanite purchases on the steppes below Kilimanjaro. He enjoyed expressing himself in foreign tongues for the way it enhanced the routine of daily living. "I wash your feet" and "I let you wash them" created a bond that transcended the monotony of a *bwana* and his guard trading pleasantries.

And he spoke Swahili for the drama of it. The old man liked to tell the other watchmen that Lonny had visited the Comoros and other such lies. It gave both of them an up, joint membership into a club whose admission fees could not be paid for in money or blood. There were no other Americans in Diego and no Comorians from Ali's island of Anjouan. In the absence of true peers their stranded vocabulary made them friends despite their differences in color, culture and age.

Lonny turned on the kitchen tap. The pipes spat and eventually a thin brown stream of dubious liquid emerged from the faucet. He opened the doors to the veranda and scooped some cool water out of his emergency barrel. The barrel was half full and the stagnant water smelled of rust. He stripped to boxers and poured a measure over his neck without relief. The boat bottom red bluffs hovering over Ramena beach reminded him of Malika's invitation and the clean water that lay across the bay.

Lonny entered his small gem lab in his underwear and closed the doors behind him. He removed the stone from the knapsack and held it in the palm of his hand. Corundum were the second hardest stones on earth. They were brought to the earth's surface by volcanic magma under intense pressure and heat. Even though he believed the stone was corundum from the way it held his body heat and its extreme density, he needed an objective test. He took out a series of ten hardness pens and scratched them against the stone. He breathed a sigh of relief when only the diamond pencil made a small mark.

In eight years as a gem trader Lonny had bought thousands, tens of thousands of pieces of corundum all over the world. Opaque corundum is just a dull, heavy stone without any particular value. Transparent corundum changes its name and becomes a specific gemstone, like a woman who marries into a royal family. Transparent red corundum is known as ruby. All other transparent varieties of corundum—blue, pink, yellow, orange, purple, green, white—are called sapphires.

To determine the sapphire's true quality, Lonny needed to check the four C's: clarity, color, cut and carat weight. He would also need to examine it in different lights: incandescent, fluorescent, halogen and xenon. The wavelength of each light brings out different qualities in a sapphire the same way a person reveals different characteristics under different circumstances.

One of the tricks to buying gems on the equator, when they are going to be sold in the gray light of the Northern Hemisphere, is to light them with a 60-watt household bulb. If they sparkle, or at least remain colorful, the gem is exceptionally clear and will sell in any country, at any jewelry store, any day of the week. Lonny turned on a bare bulb hanging from the ceiling. The incandescent light hardly penetrated the stone's surface yet the sapphire held the color of the evening sky.

Lonny flipped off the unshaded lamp and turned on a fluorescent office fixture also mounted on the ceiling. Two fluorescent tubes, their overlapping oscillations simulating natural daylight, created the same fire inside the stone as he had seen in the field. The gem was truly crystalline, a quality that allowed it to refract even the weakest amount of natural light.

Using a piercing halogen flashlight, Lonny turned and twisted the stone in every conceivable way, trying to catch the merest hint of an interior crack. The stabbing light would catch the most imperceptible flaw and reveal it as plainly as a sword driven through the stone's heart. Stare as he might, he found nothing. All the more remarkable because sapphires from the region were known for their value-killing cracks and fissures.

For the color test Lonny used a broadly focused xenon flashlight to illuminate the gem so that it glowed like a neon space rock. In northern Madagascar the best gems were pale ocean blue hinting toward green. The cleanest, sharpest stones had a certain resemblance to robin's egg blue. But this stone was different. It fell on the red-purple side of the blue color continuum. With xenon lighting it took on an azure cast. A very light, very even blue with a touch of violet.

It was so perfect he feared it was a fake. African dealers flew into Madagascar with trunks full of cheap synthetic sapphire. They traded fake crystals for real crystals using a simple ploy. Whenever a miner arrived with a particularly good sapphire, the dealer would offer to swap stones instead of buying it for cash. The unsuspecting miner would examine the lab-grown crystal, find it superior to his own in clarity and size, then agree to the trade. There were so many synthetic sapphires in circulation that even Lonny had bought a few.

The shape of the stone argued for its authenticity. Lonny had visited high-temperature, high-pressure furnaces in Russia and China. The material they produced was either long and cylindrical or blob-like. Both ends of the stone he held in his hands exhibited perfect hexagonal form with basal planing. The stone actually looked like two hexagonal pyramids bonded together at the base. It would have been next to impossible to produce such an object in a man-made oven.

In the end, it came down to the color blue and Lonny's ability to interpret its many hues. Lonny had an eye for blue. Some dealers stuck with green, spending their whole careers in emeralds. Perhaps a dozen colored-stone dealers in the New York were capable of dealing only in red, a life surrounded by rubies their reward. But Lonny knew blue. He made his living off the color and he felt he was as good as any other dealer in the world when it came to blue sapphires. There was another sapphire that he had personally examined with the same sublime quality: Ruspoli, Louis XIV's milled rectangular cube. During the years of the French monarchy, aristocrats, aesthetes and priests traveled the Continent to stare at the "divine light" of the stone. Lonny's eye, and his mind's eye, compared the two stones and found their purity identical.

Large, clear sapphires were so rare that each one had a name. Lonny ripped through his bookcase for a gemology dictionary and quickly came across a list: St. Edward's Sapphire; Charles II's Sapphire; Catherine the Great's Sapphire; the Logan Sapphire, 483 carats; the Bismarck Sapphire, 98.57 carats; Ruspoli, 135.80 carats; the Star of India, 536 carats; the Midnight Star, 116 carats; the head of Abraham Lincoln, a carved stone of 2302 carats. Lonny used his oversized mining scale and a calculator to work out the weight of his own massive specimen—16.4190 ounces @ 28.35 grams an ounce equaled 465.47865 grams; @ 5 carats a gram it came to 2,327.39 carats in the rough.

"I've done it!" he whispered to himself. "I can't believe it, but it's true!"

In his hand Lonny held the largest, most perfect sapphire ever discovered.

Lonny unlocked his small lab and nervously paced the bare house for a place to cache his future. Tupperware containers of lemon-yellow sapphires and a chrome 9-mm pistol were jammed under the kitchen sink. Two buckets of flat pleochroic titanite crystals were stashed in the shower stall. Heavy bundles of local currency were in a locked metal trunk bolted to the bedroom floor. Even if Alexis was right about the highlanders and the *côtiers*, Lonny still had a week to come up with a plan.

The best place to hide the stone was out in the open. Paint it white and lay it on the garden path or flick the guts out of a big papaya and mire its blue wonder in the orange flesh. But neither solution would do: Whitewash doesn't stick to a sapphire and he didn't have time to go searching for market mama with an extra papaya. Outside the walls of his compound he could hear the slow passing of the chain gang.

Where can a person hide something in a tropical house? There are no real closets, no attics or basements, the walls are made of stone or concrete. He looked around and in looking he found himself in the same position as the victims of Rwanda. Rafter mamas. The women who stuffed themselves into the ceiling tiles while *genocidaires* decapitated their husbands. Lonny popped a cardboard tile and jammed the knapsack into the crawl space between the ceiling and the roof. He hoped the imaginations of the Malagasy were like those of the Africans, rooted to earth not the sky.

5

RAMENA BEACH

Dressed in sandals, a tank top and knee-length swim trunks, Lonny rode back to the rue Colbert for his 11 o'clock rendezvous with Malika. Businesses along the rue were shuttered and the streets dead, but Lonny knew that other parts of town must be hopping. The soccer stadium, the movie theater and the bars in particular.

When he awoke to predawn yells of, *"charbon, ehh!"* and the slow crunch of *pousse-pousse* wheels, he had not expected much out of the day. But now he suspected that this day, an Easter Sunday of no particular importance, foreshadowed by nothing, foretold by nobody, was to change his destiny.

Malika reappeared at the Glace Gourmand

wearing a single-piece swimsuit and a sleeveless blouse knotted at the navel. The stretchable cotton suit gripped her palm-sized breasts like hands and the V-cut crotch rode over her pubic mound like a tongue.

Lonny was stunned by Malika's femininity. Not her clearly revealed anatomy, not her soft vulnerability, not her carefully chosen enticement. What floored him was the way his physical self, long sheltered and purposely avoided, reacted so strongly to her attitude. Her willingness for self-exposure, her calculated disregard for daytime decency and all standards of reserve. Urges that he had not dared himself to experience since the separation from Cass were suddenly thrust upward from his dormant loins.

"Wow," remarked Lonny.

"My last post was Rio," she said not too innocently.

"Well, let's mount up." He winced at his own words. Malika swung into the saddle and wrapped her arms around his waist.

Alexis's straining eardrums nearly popped when Lonny added a gratuitous twist of throttle to his kick start. He ran out to witness the scene as Lonny stamped into first and screeched down the rue.

"*Excellent!*" he said, sucking in his breath with Gallic pride.

Lonny could not concentrate on the obligatory

tour. He was thinking about the last time an American woman wrapped her hands around his waist and pressed her inner thighs to his back. He was thinking about Cass. The way she would lie back and say, "Tell me what you want." He had been a twenty-two-year-old graduate student when she dazzled him into her sleek twenty-seven-year-old bed. She knew tricks he hadn't dreamed of, how to oblige his fantasies and make him feel powerful. She had used her potent sexuality and worldly charm to manipulate him into the worst mistake of his life: fatherhood. He had been blinded by her social contacts, her ease in obtaining invitations to the charity balls and media events his own father shunned. How could he have done it? How could he have fathered a child when he was little more than an adolescent himself? Malika reminded Lonny of Cass. Her sexuality was just as alluring and just as dangerous.

"This is the rue," explained Lonny. When he turned his head the wind slipped by his sunglasses and forced a teardrop. He turned anyway because he liked the blurred intimacy. By now he hoped Cass had stopped involving Annie in her personal dramas. Hoped she had found a man her own age. Hoped she had stopped calling newspaper columnists every time she wanted to inflict pain on him.

He banked at the end of the rue and circled around the bust of a French general who watched over the working port and the clover-leaf bay like an ancient deity. He rounded the pedestal twice, forcing Malika to snuggle her tummy close against his vertebrae, before righting the bike and surging away.

"You want to visit the waterfront?"

"Don't slow down," yelled Malika.

They passed the back of the Alliance Française, the regional governor's house, the military barracks, the post office, the city hall, the gendarmes' barracks, the central rotary, the Allied war cemetery, a shrimp factory, and were on their way around the bay.

Her eyes were closed and her head tucked into his neck.

Out in the bay there was a tiny island called the Sugar Loaf. The rocks along its top edge created the eerie image of a man bending backward to the sky and screaming in agony. Malagasy witch doctors held annual ceremonies to appease the spirit, but every time Lonny passed the island he could feel the man's pain. The last protest of a soul denied justice.

For centuries dreamers and vagabonds had been drawn to the bay's undeveloped shores. It was a place of inexplicable passions, unforeseen circumstances. It was a place where the sun-enforced siestas bred children with blue eyes and black skin, black eyes and blond afros, green eyes and Persian curls.

It took them forty minutes to bump and grind

around the bay before they came even with the pale cranberry cliffs that hovered over the white sand beach. Lonny had utterly forgotten that Easter Sunday was the one day that Diego's most refined transported themselves to Ramena for *morenge* fights, cockfights, picnics and *salegy* dancing. Zebu carts were piled high with singing, swaying families. In a few hours bush taxis, town taxis, military buses and even a 1936 Dodge deuce-and-a-half with a U.S. Army star would be slouching toward the beach. The afternoon festivities marked the change of seasons, the comeback of the incessant winds and a slight lowering of the temperature.

Ramena beach was already packed with resplendent Indian merchants who lorded their town-earned wealth over the villagers. Naked village boys splashed in the water defiantly. Little village girls walked between beach bungalows selling sweet treats made of coconut shavings and molasses. Here and there were nascent groups of French expatriates or a Swiss tourist. The tourists carried cameras; the expatriates drank or smoked together in the shade.

The Indian merchants created an economy of penury, monopolizing the importation of essential items and keeping prices for manufactured goods artificially high. The secret to their financial success, in stark contrast to the failure of the European development banks and local custom, was that they never gave credit, for any reason, to anybody.

The Malagasy hated the Indians with a passion. They knew the immigrants had purchased most of Diego from departing colonists for the price of a stale baguette. Dada Idi Amin, the illiterate Ugandan dictator who expelled Indian merchants from Central Africa, was the secret hero of every bribe-taking bureaucrat, politician and police chief. The Malagasy found nothing more galling than to watch colonial clerks prospering in the land of their ancestors.

A trickle of sweat ran down Lonny's chest from the rising heat of the bike and the descending knock of the sun. An intimate slick of warm perspiration bonded Malika to his back.

"Tide's out," said Lonny, surveying the garbage-strewn mud flats and the uneasy crowd. "Let's ride to the old legionnaire's camp at the Pass and swim off the pier."

"Anybody there?"

"No, everyone will be at the village preparing for the fights."

"Let's do it."

A mile down the beach, past the village and around a gentle outcropping of rock, the abandoned camp blossomed as if it were a mirage rising from the sands. The camp consisted of four large barracks, a wash house and a few detached officers' quarters built of hand-hewn stone. The half-moon cove beckoned like a postcard from the Caribbean. Where the eternal tides had breached the bay's limestone hills and cut a narrow pass to the sea, a stone pier topped by a lighthouse ran into the tepid ocean. Four enormous naval guns guarded the Pass against phantoms that had never come. In her head Malika pictured the recruiting posters: LIVE IN MADAGASCAR! WARM SUN, FRIENDLY NATIVES! LIBERTY CALLS! DON'T MISS YOUR OPPORTUNITY! The Central Intelligence Agency sold her a similar bill of goods before they sent her up the Amazon.

Malika loosened her grip on Lonny as he negotiated with the military guard. The soldier insisted on a week's salary for passage then refused to give any sort of receipt. He had no gun, no uniform, no boots. Lonny paid. He wove the heavy road bike over the split tennis courts and gunned it across the shell beach onto the pier.

They dismounted and stood side by side taking in the view.

"This is so romantic," breathed Malika. "A man, a motorcycle, a deserted fortress."

"I didn't realize diplomats were dreamers," said Lonny.

"Not dreamers, fantasizers. Fantasy is a severely underrated coping mechanism." She turned toward him, placed her hands on his hips and kissed his neck.

"You taste like road grit," she said, licking her lips. "Tell me what I taste like."

"I don't trust myself."

"What's not to trust?" Malika untied her blouse so Lonny could take in the full effect of her Brazilian-cut bathing suit.

She placed Lonny's hands on her hips.

"Go ahead," she dared him.

He drew her in and kissed her exposed neck.

"You taste like cocoa butter."

"Nicely done," she complimented him. "I told you I wouldn't bite."

Lonny resisted the urge to get down on his knees and bury his nose in her belly. Although disco girls proposed him nightly, he hadn't been spoken to in such a calm, sincere way since his arrival in Diego-Suarez. He hadn't realized how much he missed it.

Swells from the open ocean rolled through the Pass, creating an eddy behind the stone jetty. Lonny pulled a mask and snorkel from his saddlebags and moved out over the bright neon reefs and little multicolored fish. From time to time he glanced in Malika's direction as she swam languidly a few feet from the barnacle-encrusted steps. She reminded him of forgotten lovers. Of nights in Tucson and mirrored bathrooms washed in flickering lights. She was running around in his brain where she had no right to trespass. What was she up to? A weekend tryst far from prying eyes? Of course she must have read his file back at the embassy, knew about his well-documented infidelities and marital neglect. What was her game? Conquest?

Cass had been an easy conquest. Slaps and tickles when they began their love affair, verbal jabs and marriage counseling soon after the wedding. She was worried that he no longer found her attractive, became jealous when he came home late, began breaking plates if his plane was delayed in Lagos, Windhoek or Phnom Penh. If he was home, she complained he wasn't earning enough money. When he was abroad she accused him of neglect. Society photographers thought she was an ice queen, but Lonny found her just the opposite, insecure and emotionally unstable.

The judge hadn't bought any of his excuses. He gave primary care to Cass and three weekends a month to Lonny until reconciliation or divorce. Annie, the seven-year-old wonder girl, slowly moved beyond his reach. She no longer shared her morning routines and nightly school reports. If something happened to her she confessed to her mother or her nanny. He was pushed out of the picture.

Why did he do it? Lonny's goggled eyes followed a clown fish flitting in and out of a carnivorous sea anemone, immune to its poison. Why did he start combining his wife's pleasures with those of outside women? Why did he confirm her worst fears? He did it because he was immature. Because he thought women his own age would validate his masculinity and make him feel good. Because he was mad at his mother for abandoning him. Because he was young, and he traveled, and he hated staying in empty hotel rooms. He did it because he could and he was pissed-off at Cass for becoming so irreversibly pregnant.

In Diego, a sexually open port in a sexually open society, he didn't do anything with his sexuality. He could have had a different girl every night for a few francs. A permanent mistress for the cost of a dress, a pair of shoes and a monthly payment to her parents. But he didn't. He protected his newfound chastity by cultural belittlement. He told himself he would not sleep with a Malagasy girl, ever, and denied that their Asian features and African sensuality aroused his lust. He became so far removed from his own nature that he wondered if he was homosexual. The slender curves, the uninhibited dress code, the lack of pretense. All the things he would have fallen for in Chelsea were a turnoff here. He told himself he would get AIDS. Madagascar would kill him. The culture gap became his only shield against the complete disintegration of his self-worth. He felt that if he went native the last thread of his self-esteem would fray irreparably.

Malika was American, challenging and magnetic. A midwestern girl with fashion sense and lo-lo's that made his fingers curl with anticipation. She aroused him like a theater-darkened squeeze. What to do? pondered Lonny. Fight the current of desire or ride the new moon's tide to the open sea?

Colonel Ratsimanga yelled at Lonny as he

snorkeled serenely in the whip-o-whirls of the bay. Soft swells surged, the ebb tide tugged and Lonny was loath to leave the waters. His mask enabled him to float inside the blissful world of fishes. The colonel's insistent yelling canceled the pleasure of that short-lived escape.

As Lonny hauled himself onto the disused wharf he noticed Malika was fully covered. She had one beach towel wrapped around her waist, another draped over her shoulders like a shawl. Six soldiers stood inches away regarding her every nook and cranny without the slightest hint of shame. They might have been village headmen silently debating the bearing capacity of an untried cow.

"*In vo vo?*" What's happening? said Lonny.

"*Tsy tsy vo vo,*" said the colonel.

"*Kabare?*" Any business?

"*Tsy kabare,*" said the colonel. Then switching to French he said, "Now let's drop the jokes. I don't speak this coastal dialect any better than you do."

"*Oui, mon Colonel,*" acquiesced Lonny, directing the colonel's attention to Malika. "May I introduce an American from Antananarivo? She calls herself Malika."

"Peace Corps?" asked the colonel.

"No. I am a registered diplomat in the service of the United States of America," replied Malika with surprising panache.

"Ehh," grunted the colonel.

"Colonel Ratsimanga and I play bridge together most Sunday nights."

"It seemed like a good day to inspect the base, with everyone in town visiting Ramena," said the colonel. "The guard does not have your entrance marked in the visitors log."

"There must be some mistake, Colonel. I paid him 5,000 francs."

"Show me the receipt," demanded the colonel.

"I don't have a receipt."

"It is not correct."

"*Mon Colonel.* I paid the soldier at the gate 5,000 francs but he did not give me a receipt."

"The situation is irregular," said the colonel.

"The man at the gate is responsible," replied Lonny.

The colonel turned to the soldiers, who were still watching Malika as if she were the last drop of fresh water on earth, and said, "Arrest the guardian."

Their eyes remained anchored.

The colonel stamped and the fully armed men were in a foot race for their victim.

"They are like children," remarked the colonel.

"Big children," said Malika.

"Yes," replied the colonel, giving her his full attention. "They are the descendants of slaves and will always need direction. Even so, I would like each of them to have a pair of boots. This morning I turned out 400 men for review. Only 20 have boots."

"If the politicians didn't eat your money every soldier would have a pair of boots."

"Everybody must eat," said the colonel. "If I did not take rice from the soldiers' mess my family would be skinny like them."

"Is there anything else I can do for you?" asked Lonny, trying to move Colonel Ratsimanga along.

"There is," stated the colonel, bracing himself on the crumbling jetty, the lighthouse hovering over his shoulder. "There is a story that a stranger bought a sapphire the size of a watermelon from the King's Reserve. In fact, they say the stranger was not French. In fact, some peasants have mentioned an American. On a motorcycle. The story says this stranger paid 66 zebu for a sapphire. What do you know about this?"

Lonny was dumbstruck. The bloated bureaucracy was incapable of delivering the mail, building a road or maintaining electricity, but lines of communication were fantastic. It hadn't been more than six hours since he had paid for the luminous rock and already Colonel Ratsimanga was on to him.

"I don't know what you are talking about."

"It must be quite valuable, of course," continued the colonel, unfazed by Lonny's bald-faced lie. "A sapphire as big as a watermelon might sell for a 100,000 dollars in America. The person who has it must be very careful."

"Why should that person be careful?"

"Because we are such a poor people. Even if the sapphire were only the size of an orange I imagine it would be very valuable."

"As big as an orange?" Lonny squeezed disbelief into his voice.

"If you happen to discover the owner of this sapphire before I do," said the colonel, staring straight into the back of Lonny's eyes as if he were interrogating a bound captive, "please tell him to seek my protection immediately. Otherwise he is likely to be murdered."

"Murdered, Colonel?"

"We are such a poor country. Why would a Malagasy let a stranger steal the wealth of his people? This person," the colonel turned toward Malika, "is in very great danger and he doesn't realize it."

"Unless he has hidden this stone somewhere," said Lonny. "Or sold it."

"Yes, of course." The colonel still addressed his comments to Malika. "In that case he would be tortured, then killed."

"Torturing an American would have consequences," said Malika.

"For whom? The American who has his scrotum crushed with a brick? Or the colonel who is promoted to general? I think the President would be quite pleased with the officer who presented him with a national treasure."

The colonel turned to Lonny. "A good bridge

player counts the points in his hand then listens for his partner to bid. Neither knows what the other is holding but good partners come up with the right contract every time. Once the contract is made the cards simply need to be played. The conclusion is foregone. Make a bad contract and you will always lose, even if you start with a good hand. Think about it."

The colonel walked on the uneven stones past Lonny, past Malika and on down the pier until he reached the beach. Everything around them was under his command and most of it had been sold for personal gain. Roof tiles from Marseilles went to a restaurant, copper wiring to the mayor; the solar panel installed on the unblinking lighthouse had simply vanished. Upon reaching the sand Colonel Ratsimanga pivoted abruptly and walked back to the mute pair.

"What does he want now?" asked Malika.

"I can't even imagine," said Lonny.

"I have considered it," announced the colonel peremptorily. "A simple flogging may not be adequate for a soldier who has let two foreigners into a highly restricted military base. I will court-martial the soldier and you will testify at the proceeding. You must not leave Diego-Suarez. In fact, I request your travel documents."

"Be reasonable, Colonel."

"You are a witness in a court-martial proceeding. I request your means of identification. In specific, your passport."

"Excuse me, Colonel," interrupted Malika. "Mr. Cushman is an American citizen. I am a representative of the American embassy. If you are going to detain Mr. Cushman I will have to file a formal protest with the Department of Foreign Affairs, the Military Command and the Prime Minister."

"Madame. If you insist on interfering in this matter I will ask my soldiers to physically examine you and properly establish your identity."

"You wouldn't dare," said Malika.

"Don't tell me how to conduct my business," the colonel bristled. "You are a woman, a stranger and probably the descendant of a slave. I'll do with you as I please."

"I'm a registered American diplomat and when I get back to Tana I'm going to crucify you," Malika responded with hollow anger. She had neither the time, the clout nor the clearance to seek revenge.

"Yes. But you are in Diego. The capital is a long way from here," said the colonel with impeccable logic.

"I will give you my passport and we can discuss the case later," Lonny broke in.

"That would be to your advantage."

Lonny fetched his navy blue passport with dispatch. Although the threats were routine, the idea of Malika pinned to the ground by a mass of hands turned his stomach. He did not mind a confrontation with the colonel, he had had several in the past, but he did not want a third party scarred for his actions the way Annie had paid with her childhood because of his inability to strike a deal with Cass.

"No disrespect, Colonel," said Lonny, handing over his only outward proof of nationality.

"Don't go anywhere," said the colonel. He slipped the passport into his crisply pressed shirt pocket and headed back toward the beach and his posse of thugs. The sapphire was his ticket out of this hellish command. He would be promoted and posted back among his people in the highlands. It was unfortunate that the American had discovered the stone instead of a Frenchman, an Italian or an African, but he would work around the handicap. One way or another he was going to leave Diego with another gold stripe on his uniform.

"I need a new passport," said Lonny.

"Come to Antananarivo and I'll type you a new one myself," Malika responded.

"I can't," said Lonny.

"Stop making excuses. Just get on the plane with me and your worries will be over."

"There's too much at stake."

"Like what?"

"I can't tell you."

"Then what am I going to do about you?" she asked peevishly.

They both watched as the colonel's men kicked the lethargic gate guard into the backseat of a tiny Renault 4L before sitting on top of him and slowly driving out of sight. They weren't coming back anytime soon.

"Evacuate me," said Lonny. In Madagascar he had learned to negotiate against the entrenched bureaucracy from a position of permanent weakness. It meant risking everything each time, dancing the razor's edge of failure.

"How?" asked Malika.

"Charter me a med-evac from Antananarivo. When it lands here the doctor can diagnose me with a critical condition and the plane will take me to Johannesburg."

"Won't Colonel Ratsimanga be watching you?"

"The colonel is known for holding fanatical reviews of his troops from 6 to 7 A.M. every morning. Have the pilot land at 6:15 and file a flight plan for Tana. At 6:30 A.M. we can be airborne and he can change direction. The embassy in South Africa can issue me a new passport."

"You've got it all worked out, don't you?" Instead of this man abiding her request to leave Diego on the afternoon plane, he was asking her to work for him. Their fleeting intimacy had been replaced with adrenaline from the confrontation. He felt full of masculine self-assurance because he had pro-tected her. She needed to seize that energy, reshape its form and thrust.

Lonny walked to the end of the pier then dove off into the thin blue sea. A pier built by the dragooned dregs of the French empire. A useless tyrannical pier whose only purpose had been to labor soldiers scarcely better than slaves. In a few days he would be homeward bound. He had already missed the im-portant gem shows in Arizona but if he needed to drum up publicity a tour at the Natural History Museum of New York and a loan to the Smithson-ian would do the trick. He turned his face back to-ward the pier in time to see Malika shed her swimsuit on the hot stones. She arced gracefully into the bay like a siren and swam toward him push-ing out concentric rings of sea water.

Tiny droplets coursed down her face, her eyelids were wide-open, her face flushed. Beneath the sur-face Lonny could see her uniformly brown breasts and shaved pubis. The refracted light seemed to penetrate Malika's smooth recesses in a new way, the way afternoon sunshine will pierce a stone's in-terior and accent its strongest hue.

"Is it true that you bought a big sapphire from the King's Reserve this morning?" asked Malika, tread-ing water.

"Of course that's not true," he lied. "Sapphires the size of a watermelon just don't exist."

"Did you buy it from the King's Reserve?"

"I don't know what you're talking about."

"You handle yourself like a professional," complimented Malika.

"Were you scared?" Lonny smiled right back.

"I like men who protect their interests."

"Are you one of my interests?"

"I'd like to be," she returned.

"Wouldn't that complicate matters?" asked Lonny.

"It might clarify them."

She backpedaled with an easy smile then sank into the bellflower blue ripples. Her pointed feet, defined ankles and hard calves shot from the bay like an upended ballerina. Her legs scissored open then submerged beneath the aquamarine curtain. She surfaced two body lengths away and began swimming butterfly strokes toward the pier. Her naked torso rising and falling through the gentle swells like the slick back of a porpoise.

He followed her slowly, letting the salt water carry his weight. They stood close to each other on the small beach next to the pier until he wrapped his arms around her splendid shoulders and pulled her against his chest. She grabbed his ears and kissed with an open mouth. They spread warm towels on the hot sand and let their lips explore each other's thighs, nipples and necks. For a tropical instant they lost themselves in a place without memory beneath the shadow of the rusting guns.

6

PARADISE NORTH

Malika felt a surge of triumph mixed with a flood of relief as she regarded Lonny on the towel beside her. His eyes were closed, his mouth slack and slightly ajar. In less than four hours she had overcome his initial hostility to create a bond of tenderness and familiarity. It validated her new approach. Instead of flying in from Antananarivo and laying down the law like an Assistant District Attorney, she had gently ensnared him in a web of conflicting emotions. He had tasted the honey, now she could play the role of the righteous queen bee.

She beamed at the thought of Lonny in Antananarivo that evening. There would be no more American citizens exporting sapphires from northern Madagascar. The ambassador would be placated. The debt swap and the national park on track. The new Prime Minister as good as installed. Malika could head back to Cape Town on the first available flight.

Lonny stirred himself awake. He could feel the renewed press of tropical heat and the itch of salt drying on his skin. Any other Sunday he would have headed back to Ramena. Sat under the wide shade of a badamenia tree. Searched for a few beers, some rum and a couple of Malagasy musicians playing guitar, vahila or bongos.

"Your plane leaves at 3 P.M.," remarked Lonny, with his eyes still closed. "We'll both have fewer problems with Colonel Ratsimanga if you get on it."

"Are you anxious to get rid of me?"

"I need you in Tana to arrange that med-evac."

"You need me for more than that."

"Of course I do," said Lonny, sitting up.

"Then why don't you come with me on the 3 o'clock flight. You can stay at my hotel. I'll get you a new passport. You'll be safe."

"It's not a good time for me to leave Diego."

"Why not?"

"I have unfinished business."

"You've been losing money since you arrived," snapped Malika.

"How do you know?"

"Try and remember who I work for. If you get on

that plane with me this whole thing will be a pleasant memory."

"It's not that simple," said Lonny.

"Yes it is," said Malika. "It's that simple." She
turned her back on him and pulled a cotton sun-
dress out of her shoulder bag. She stood up, let him
survey the full stretch of her naked body, then let the
cloth drop like a curtain. In a blink she transformed
herself from vixen to angry African-American.

Lonny experienced a pang of regret as she
marched over to the motorcycle in exasperation
while he picked himself off the beach. Their moment
together had been so real, so connected. He didn't
understand why she was suddenly so miffed. He
couldn't imagine what he had done to piss her off.

They rode across the pier, the vacant camp and
the village in strained friendship. Hundreds of spec-
tators were packed into a zebu pen to watch
morenge fights. The ritual fights were normally
arranged by village elders to settle differences between rival men, but on Easter they were strictly a
spectacle. Townspeople and villagers matched up
against each other; the first person to get in a good
head punch won the round and advanced toward
the finals. An Indian merchant had put up 50,000
fmg, $10, as a grand prize.

During the times of the legionnaires the village
hosted *morenge* fights every weekend. Back then
Ramena was a destination not a village, with water-

skiing, scuba diving, paddle-boats and nightclubs. Back then the road was so good that Alexis claimed it only took fifteen minutes to get to Diego.

Now the road was littered with crashed taxis, broken *pousse-pousses* and wandering zebu carts. The pavement was bad enough to prevent high-speed accidents, but not good enough to keep the various modes of transport from falling to pieces. A broken cart formed an impromptu roadblock where drunken men were trying to extort money. Lonny shot off through the bush, circled and found the road a few hundred yards later.

By the time Lonny and Malika straggled back around the bay, picked up her bag at the Glace Gourmand and zoomed to the airport, Lonny realized there was going to be a problem securing a boarding pass.

The barefoot soldiers manning the airport's candy-striped gate delayed them further. The soldiers eyed Malika and bantered with Lonny in dialect. They enjoyed posing banal questions and watching him struggle to respond in their language. His occasional use of the active tense caused them to giggle. Did he think he was an ancestor, all knowing and all wise? "Words should be round like cups not sharp like arrows," proverbed one soldier.

The airport made Lonny nervous. There were too many officials gathered in one place. In Dar es Salaam businessmen and bureaucrats might choose to rub elbows at the yacht club, in Nairobi the golf course. In Diego they all collided at the airport like opposing electrons in a badly planned fusion experiment.

A lone mango tree stood in the center of the airport parking lot, its roots bucking against the sealed earth, its lower leaves actually singed from the reflected force of the sun, its bark clawed and doodled upon by stranded airline passengers. Dry heat distorted other features of the area, radiating off the blacktop as if it were the belly of a cast-iron stove. Painted in Nantucket red on the side of the whitewashed terminal were the words *"Bienvenue à Diégo-Suarez—Le Paradis du Nord!"*

Inside the oven-like terminal, where dispirited travelers had passed days of their lives hoping for a ride to somewhere else, a tense and nervous crowd surrounded the checkout counter. A ticket in hand meant little until the boarding pass was issued. Even then passengers had to rush from the gate to the plane to make sure they actually had a seat.

"This could be a challenge," commented Malika.

"It never gets any better," replied Lonny. "Give me your ticket."

"Get one for yourself too," she said.

He shoved his way into the sweaty crowd. No one gave him the slightest leeway. A disco girl from the Vo Vo blocked with her slender hip, a businessman kept his elbow sharp. In a panic Lonny pinched a plump Indian woman's midriff roll. As she jerked round he thrust his arm past her shoulder and winged the folded ticket to the counter. An annoyed clerk glanced up and Lonny rubbed his thumb and forefinger together in the universal sign for bribery. The clerk nodded, Lonny retreated. A few minutes later, when Malika's name was called out, and she stepped over trussed baskets and homemade suitcases to receive her boarding pass, fellow travelers tisk-tisked their disapproval. The clerk winked at him and Lonny knew the man would pass by the Glace Gourmand later in the week for his reward.

"I need air," said Malika, emerging from the pack like a wilted daffodil. Her torso was drenched with perspiration, her face covered with trickles of sweat. Her aureoles made wet brown splashes against the inside of her yellow dress.

"Why don't you stand outside? I want to see who's here."

"You're wasting your time," said Malika. The cool pleasure of the seashore had melted away like a single lick of strawberry sorbet. Lonny obviously didn't have a ticket for the plane and she was tired of playing nice. Her house in Cape Town had air-conditioning and a pool.

On the back side of the wall separating the ticket counter from the bar, Lonny found a significant portion of the town's French residents. They were expatriates on teaching contracts at the lycée, pensioned legionnaires, tax cheats, deadbeats, criminals on the lam, con artists. They came from the troubled departments of their native hexagon, Haute-Savoie, Moselle, Finistère. They had made immoral decisions, married badly or thought they were going to outsmart the system. Those that came with a little money left with less. Those that came with nothing traded the tarnished prestige of their French nationality for shelter. Most could manage a legally registered marriage, which conferred French citizenship on the new spouse and guaranteed a spot at the lycée for the kids. There were more French citizens in Madagascar than in all other African countries combined, 25,000 souls, the sedimented refuse of the post-colonial order.

Mixed in with the expatriate cabal were two African gem traders from Senegal, a clique of Indian merchants, the French consul and the Right Honorable Bishop McKenzie. The group's dress ranged from the elegant one-piece robes of the West Africans to plastic slippers, stained T-shirts, spandex shorts, open-collared shirts and various shades of sunglass. It was as ugly and as unpromising a lot as ever there was. Lonny raised his hand in a sweeping gesture and his nighttime companions cheered him like a brother.

He went down the line greeting each person in

turn, touching him on the shoulder, nodding vigorously, shaking hands.

"*Salut*, Monsieur le Consul."

"Why, it's the baker from Lyon paying cash!"

"Allo Dede, are the tourists treating you right?"

"How is the restaurant, Lucia?"

"Dabo, you bought that four-gram stone I had first dibs on."

"Umbertto, the immigration man hasn't caught up with you!"

"And I feel good, Philippe, thanks for the compliment."

"New merchandise from the capital, Ibrahim?"

"Xavier, you're too thin. No work for your truck?"

"Salutations, Doctor."

"Monsieur Mordant, no girlfriends? The wife back already!"

"How is that English Land Rover of yours, Jean-François?"

Covered in a hot lather Lonny worked himself over to the bishop, who appeared sour and not in the mood to be caught among such blasphemers.

"Why, Bishop," said Lonny, finally switching to American. "I thought you would be celebrating Easter among the faithful."

"Who needs God if not the blackest sinners?" asked the bishop loudly enough to be heard over a diesel truck engine. The thin, haggard old bishop was attired in a purple shirt embroidered front and back with a large gold cross that made him look like a uniformed Christian soldier living the fresh hells of a modern crusade.

"We need to talk about your dialect lessons," said the bishop, vising Lonny's underarm as tightly as a rugby player in a scrum.

"Shall we?" He used his chin to point to the far end of the terminal. The plane was late and no dumb fools stood around looking expectantly for its imminent arrival. Soon the apron would be crowded by the local greeting committee: panicked outgoing passengers, the airport director, a trio of policemen, the ground crew and pushy taxi drivers vying to get the few unmet passengers into decrepit taxis. All the folks who make flying into a forgotten paradise like Diego-Suarez like landing in Times Square on New Year's Eve.

The Admiral's informant stood to one side carefully surveying the scene. He wore a suit, tie and miniature, aggressive eyeglasses that served no practical purpose. From what Lonny understood of Malagasy politics, the Admiral had been a brutal dictator who sought refuge in Paris when he was overthrown by a popular revolt. To prove to the world that Madagascar was capable of democracy, the head of the opposition party called for free and open elections as soon as possible. The Admiral flew back into the country with a symbolic payload of rice, only a few short years after fleeing with the palace toilets, and won the election.

The province of Diego, where the popular revolt began, not only voted against the Admiral, they tried to secede from Madagascar when he was inaugurated as president. To quell dissent the Admiral installed his nephew as the regional governor, sent Colonel Ratsimanga with a brigade of troops and kept a tribe of informers on his payroll. In response, the *côtiers* let the road between Antananarivo and Diego fall into total disrepair, voted against the national government at every chance and ignored the contrary directives of the Admiral's 35 different cabinet ministers. The *côtiers* and the highlanders were stuck with each other more by the accident of geography than any type of cultural affinity.

Lonny caught the informer staring at him.

"Let's go," said the bishop, steering Lonny out of the crowd and over to the vacant baggage claim area like an unruly boy.

"Your family has a lot of money back in the States, isn't it true, Lonny?"

"My father has money," responded Lonny.

"You've gone to some of the best schools your country has to offer. New York University, Columbia."

"What's on your mind?"

"You had a marriage and a girl child but brought

them both to ruin through wantonness and neglect."

"I'm not sure how much of a marriage I had."

"You have a fine villa near the French lycée."

"Get to your point, Bishop."

"You're in a lot of trouble, laddie."

"Why's that?" said Lonny, surprised but not caught off-guard. An Anglican bishop might call a lot of things trouble.

"An inebriated peasant named Joaravo spent the morning telling the world about his good fortune. A sapphire this big"—the bishop cupped his two hands as if he were holding a cricket ball—"that he sold to the American for 66 zebu."

"It's true," said Lonny. He had lied to lovers and lawyers but never a clergyman. The man was wasted from years of trekking into the countryside. Pock-marked from burrowing worms, pale from feverish attacks, righteous from witnessing cruelty. He was living proof that a preacher could survive the absence of an audience.

"Did you buy it inside the King's Reserve?"

"Yes."

"Then you must present it to the King of Antakarana. The land and its riches are his ancestral possessions."

"And if I don't?"

"The gendarmes will burn out your eye sockets with a tire iron," said the bishop. "They will hook up your testicles to electric wires, use flesh-cutting devices and rub chili peppers into your open sores."

"I have no intention of giving the son-of-a-bitching king my sapphire," replied Lonny. He did not blame Jaoravo but the news worried him. The bishop was not the type who spread false rumors.

"Not a person in this town will take the side of a stranger against the First Rooster."

"You're a Scot, Bishop McKenzie. Are you telling me to give up the stone without a fight?"

"Let go this obsession of yours."

"How do you know about the king?"

"He telephoned the French consul and Monsieur le Consul said it was not his job to protect or defend American citizens."

"What do you mean telephoned? Where is this famous king?"

"The king is in Antananarivo on tribal business."

"Are you positive?"

"The consul's cook is an Anglican parishioner. He answered the call and then overheard the consul speaking to the king while he served lunch."

Lonny scratched the back of his hand nervously. It was so wet that his fingernails tore off a layer of skin and left behind red welts.

"Why are you telling me all this, Bishop?"

"Because the unrepentant are damned to eternity's hellfire. You are not. I can see God's mark upon you. A chosen son. A prodigal."

"Come off it, Bishop. I don't even know what a prodigal is."

"A wasteful soul. One who denies his Christian upbringing for the pleasures of flesh and the thrill of travel."

"I didn't realize travel was supposed to be thrilling."

"Why did you find a sapphire on Easter Sunday?"

"I was the first person down the road."

"What do you know about sapphires?"

"How much they cost."

"Do you know sapphires are a Christian stone?"

"I suppose."

"That the prophets describe God as seated on a throne of sapphire?"

"So?"

"Do you think it's all a great accident? The ten commandments were written on sapphire tablets. Jerusalem is built on a sapphire. Jewish rabbis used to wear sapphire studs over their hearts. Even the Pope, when he is coronated by the cardinals, is given a sapphire ring to wear on his wedding finger. The sapphire is God's attempt to reconcile mankind to Himself."

"And you want me to get rid of it?"

"Aye. It serves no earthly purpose."

"Then why did God show it to me?"

"He offered you a sacred sign on the day of His

son's resurrection. A symbol of His faith in you."

"I'm a gem dealer," said Lonny. "I buy and sell gems. That's what I do. I can't just give away the finest stone I've ever seen."

"The devil has got hold of you!" The bishop seized Lonny's arm. "Drive him out before vanity becomes your misfortune. How many people have missed their signs? How many people never got one? Think about the scoundrels at that bar. How did they get here? How will they leave? And the Malagasy? Why do they live in such wretchedness? Why has God sent them to this island? You cannot deny His will as Jonah tried to do. You must hear His word. He speaks in every language, in blue stones and baby girls. You must leave this place at once to carry out His plan for you."

"When will the king come back to Diego?" asked Lonny. His eyes still shined but a deep sense of chagrin defeated his inner bravado.

"He arrives on the plane."

"And what if God meant for me to keep the sapphire?" Lonny asked feebly. "What if this is my fate and it is His way of helping me?"

"Fool!" exclaimed the exasperated bishop.

"I must know the nature of my sin before I can repent it."

"Vanity will be the end of you."

"I don't understand your words or your God," fought back Lonny.

"You are worse than ignorant. You think but refuse to know. You listen but refuse to hear."

"Fuck off."

"And you too," nodded the bishop. He wiped his
thumb across his brow so that it dripped with
sweat. Using his own perspiration as Holy Water he
jabbed at Lonny and made the sign of the cross
upon his forehead.

"By this cross let the word of God enter this
man's heart."

The bishop then turned away wistfully, as if he
saw the intransigence of his own youth reflected in
Lonny's eyes. He left the young American with a
sad nod and walked silently across the terminal for
a glass of Scotch. The broken slope of his shoulders
made the large gold cross on his back sag like the
fronds of a battered palm tree.

Lonny looked toward the crowded bar for support but no one had noticed the exchange. The
French expatriates of Diego-Suarez were like the
residents of Pompeii thriving in the shadow of Vesu-
vius. He could not turn to them for understanding;
they were oblivious to the disaster that was upon
them and not one cared for redemption. He stumbled out of the stifling airport terminal and stag-
gered to the mango tree where Malika stood in the
shade with the taxi drivers.

"See anybody you know?" she said.

"Everybody."

"An ugly lot."

"I spend every night with that lot."

"Do they buy sapphires from the King's Reserve too?"

"They might, but I don't."

"You're lying."

"I appreciate your feminine intuition," said Lonny. "Just do your job."

"My competence and loyalty have never been in question."

"Neither have mine, sweetheart."

"Then here's a plane ticket," returned Malika testily, holding up a valid boarding pass she had just bought off a businessman for three hundred dollars. "I want you to get on that plane."

"For your sake or mine?"

"For yours, sweetheart. I've got a diplomatic passport and the embassy looking out for me. Who's looking out for you?"

"I can take care of myself."

Malika pursed her lips thoughtfully.

"Come on," said Lonny. "I'll get you into the VIP building on the other side of the terminal."

"Why should we go there?"

"Because you'll get on the plane before everyone else."

Lonny picked up Malika's handbag and walked her over. He gave the soldier outside the building a ball of little notes. Inside the small, square room there was a simple wooden bench. A large sliding glass door looked out onto the runway.

"Do you think the ambassador will accept my plan?" asked Lonny.

"She's got nothing against bona fide medical emergencies."

"What does that mean?"

"She doesn't like you."

"Does that mean she won't help?"

"That means you've got to cover your own back. You understand?"

"No."

"She's not going to stretch herself for you."

"Will you arrange the med-evac or not?"

"I have an extra boarding pass for this flight," said Malika with finality. "It's the best I can offer you."

"I can't do it," said Lonny. "I still have unfinished business."

"I suggest you wrap up any loose affairs as fast as possible," Malika said angrily. She would have to fudge the contact report and cover her tracks. His sexual talents might have exceeded his reputation, but it wouldn't exactly benefit her career if the Company found out. "I'll see what I can do about getting you another passport."

Lonny had confidence that Malika could swing a new passport and a med-evac plane if she put her

mind to it. Their noontime tryst counted for something. He decided to make sure she got on the plane
but hang back where no one would bother him. He
ended up squatting with the taxi drivers under the
mango tree. The chauffeurs looked like one-lunged
trumpet players, their left cheeks bulging with khat.
They took turns sucking warm Coke through a nail
hole punched into a capped bottle.

The circle of men was ringed by a circle of white
Renault 4L taxis. The little cars were one-quarter
the size of an average American Chevrolet. Their
engines were no bigger than lawn mowers but they
transported tons of matériel. The mayor issued a de-
cree limiting the number of passengers to eight for a
car most Americans could not have squeezed five
into with a hydraulic jack. Their ground clearance
was such that they ruled the unmaintained tracks of
the countryside. When they became bogged down in
sand or mud their passengers simply disembarked
and pushed the miniature vehicle beyond the trouble
spot. Each driver was proud of his conveyance and
they all sent pictures of themselves posing in front
of the cars to impressed relatives in the far bush.

To entertain the gathered men, a taxi *maître* told
jokes and related tales of his misadventures. Lonny
laughed easily with the drivers. The stories were full
of good intentions and high hopes and ended with
maître defeated by the hands of fate or the superior
intelligence of women. Lonny understood the taxi

drivers just as well as he understood the French expatriates, and neither group, with their anecdotes and particular intoxicants, appealed to him anymore. With the sapphire in his possession it seemed that he was something entirely new in these parts—a man with options.

The French consul came out to the middle of the inferno and Lonny stood up to meet him. The drivers bowed their heads deferentially in his presence as if he were a cabinet minister or gendarme commandant. Without letting go of Lonny's hand, the consul walked him back across the scorching asphalt to the door of the terminal.

"I can help you," said the consul. He was a small, white-haired man with a well-trimmed beard. He had a self-inflated air of wisdom and sobriety despite service in dozens of diplomatically unimportant countries and ill-considered affairs with unattractive women that had ruined his chances to do better. He had invited Lonny to play bridge Sunday nights mainly because he was not French. The French community in Diego despised the consul, and now Lonny knew why; the man lacked loyalty to his own kind in a country ruled by tribal passions.

"How's that?" said Lonny.

"I know you paid a large sum of money for a sapphire of great importance. I know that the king wants this sapphire and the king will have the sapphire. What I can do is arrange a fair price."

"If I were French? What would be a fair price?"

"I am not the law in Diego. Even if you were French you would have to respect the rights of indigenous peoples."

"Indigenous rights are important when the Quai d'Orsay is no longer in charge? When de Gaulle massacred 100,000 Malagasy *côtiers* in 1947, who was the law then? Who stood up for indigenous rights in Diego then?"

The consul let go of Lonny's hand. "Monsieur, you have no idea what you are saying. In 1947 there was a Communist-inspired insurrection against the legal authority of the land. Times have changed. We must all recognize the new climate and adjust to it."

"You have no jurisdiction over me and neither does the king."

"You like to stir up shit storms," said the enraged consul.

"And you like to play with little girls on scholarship at the lycée," retorted Lonny.

"My private life does not concern you."

"And the sapphire does not concern you."

"Political unrest concerns me. You are making a mess that the French will pay for in their pocketbooks and with their blood."

"What are you talking about?"

"The Malagasy look at you and see a white man who speaks French. If there are problems they will take it out on the French. It is the tribal mentality.

Very basic. Your bumbling may cause French citizens to lose respect in the eyes of the natives. Once respect is lost, French property and French lives will be next.

"The most important thing in these third world countries," the consul stuck his finger in the air like a professor, "is to maintain order. The Malagasy prospered under French rule because we were even-handed and very firm. You have never seen political unrest in Africa. It is like wild fire. One event can set off something entirely unrelated. I appeal to your sense of decency!"

"My sense of decency is different than yours," Lonny responded. If the French had implemented their original vision each former colony would still be learning about *"nos ancêtres les gaulois."* Reading their way up the Western canon from Socrates to Françoise Sagan until they were intellectually prepared for the burdens of liberty, fraternity and égalité.

"Will you at least discuss it with the king?" insisted the consul.

Lonny considered. He hoped to be out of the country as soon as possible, but if the med-evac fell through he needed a secondary plan. "If you will host a bridge game next week for Colonel Ratsimanga and the king, I will attend," he proposed.

"Not next week," replied the consul. "Tonight as usual. If it is agreeable to the king, the colonel is not otherwise occupied and you hold to your word."

"Next week would be better for me."

"If you don't come to my house tonight I'm not sure you'll be able to come next week."

"What does that mean?"

"I strongly suggest you play cards with me to-night."

"I'll see what I can do," returned Lonny.

The consul nodded his clenched jaw then walked to his four-wheel drive.

The airport's siren blasted a warning to napping goatherds and Lonny heard the jet plane as it circled the field. Within minutes the king would touch down and Malika would take off: One wanted Lonny dead, the other wanted him out of the way. The bishop condemned him, the consul washed his hands clean and the colonel had confiscated his passport. His popularity among the decision makers in Madagascar had unquestionably reached its nadir.

The king of Antakarana was the first out of the Boeing 737. A hoard of wives and concubines, whom Lonny had not seen nor suspected, rushed to the foot of the stairs and sang out in wails of happiness. When the First Rooster reached the bottom step they spread their shawls on the runway. The First Rooster walked across their colorful cotton wrappers to his Toyota without ever coming into contact with the ground. The Land Cruiser sped away followed by a pickup truck full of heavily

armed gendarmes and a lorry filled with singing
women. The whole scene unfolded so quickly
Lonny was not sure he had seen anything at all.

Sleepy baggage handlers suddenly rushed the
plane like frantic circus clowns and disembarking
travelers fought for palm-fiber suitcases under the
belly of the jet. Ticketed passengers jammed the terminal's exit, impaling the trio of policemen. Taxi
drivers and porters lunged into the fray, bellowing
for clients. The kicks and cudgels of the beleaguered
authorities did little to calm the situation. Lonny
circled the terminal from the outside and watched as
Malika made an undignified dash for the plane's
rear stairway.

Two small boys pulled at Lonny's shirt as he retreated to the knife blade of shade hugging the terminal wall. They were completely naked except for
the sticks they held in their hands. On the edge of
the runway Lonny could see their goats beginning
to stray. He dug into his pockets for some bonbons.
He gave each child a few candies and smiled as they
tittered away, happy as could be.

Annie was about the same age. She had beautiful
locks of chestnut brown hair in a rumpled mass. She
was learning to read, learning to write, and she
wanted a scooter. Every time Lonny permitted himself to think of her he was stunned and amazed by
how fast she grew, how smart she was and how
much he missed her. Last Christmas she had sent

him a fax asking for an EZ Bake Oven, a Get Real Girl and world peace.

"I miss you, Annie," Lonny said out loud as he watched the departing passengers fight with each other. He wanted to fly to her. To read her chapter books. Talk to her about the Emerald City and Harry Potter's latest Quidditch match. He wanted to start over but he didn't see how he could do that without the sapphire. It was late in the game and he was far from home.

7

LAST CONVERSATIONS

Sometime around 4 P.M. the Air Mad Boeing 737 to Antananarivo finally rumbled down the airstrip and groaned into the stale air. The jet wash tugged at Lonny's sweat-soaked garments as he watched the plane struggle over the looming volcano. His shirt was drenched and his pants legs stuck to the vinyl saddle of his bike when he climbed aboard. Working the motorcycle gears like musical scales, he left the airport and overtook the caravan of fat taxis fleeing the terminal. The front wheel wobbled worse than before.

The road back into town was obscured by hundreds of people lounging on the roadbed across from the soccer stadium. They sat on the level pavement, blocking traffic and turning the area into a fairground. Lonny approached the scene at forty miles an hour, shifted to neutral, flooded the engine, then forced it to backfire with a ripping *bamh!* Men, women and children dove for the ditches as he swerved through the middle of the panicked crowd like a jinni.

The motorcycle ran out of road at the bottom of the rue Colbert and Lonny nearly overshot Akbarely's *Maison de Joaillerie*. Although a solid metal curtain sealed the display windows tightly, a few sharp knocks brought Akbarely to the side door of his gritty establishment. The pallid Indian paused at the spy hole then cracked the door and motioned Lonny inside.

On top of buying rough stones and exporting them to his father, Lonny ran a side operation to add spice to the daily routine. He hired a Sri Lankan cutter to polish a small quantity of commercial-grade sapphires. He lent them on credit to jewelers who set the stones in coppery gold and sold them to sailors, expats and disco girls. When a piece cleared Lonny was supposed to receive his share of the profit. The retailers appreciated the scheme as a way to swell their inventory and Lonny traded his experienced eye for hard cash. It should have been easy money, but the retailers were slow to pay out and lied about their sales.

"Good day, sir," greeted Lonny.

"Good day to you, sir," replied Akbarely in perfect English. In earlier days he had managed a duty-free jewelry mart at the Dubai International Airport, United Arab Emirates. The UAE was a thriving, open-minded country on the Persian Gulf, sandwiched between Oman and Saudi Arabia. The province of Dubai was a bustling hub of world trade. As a result Akbarely was one of the few people in Diego connected to an international phone line. For most residents the greater world was unimaginable. A place as unreachable as heaven or hell, Paris or Moscow.

"I would like to telephone my father in New York."

"I'm afraid it is not possible."

"Why?"

"You are in big trouble with the authorities. Even if they saw you here I would have problems."

"Just a ten-minute phone call."

"Quite impossible." The placid Indian grinned as if he had just given Lonny a gift.

"How much of a premium do you want?" countered Lonny.

"The colonel told me you are not to use the phone. Quite impossible for any price."

"I'll forget the five thousand dollars you owe me to make one phone call."

"It is not a matter of dollars."

"You're quite right," said Lonny. "Nothing I can offer you in Diego has any worth. You are a simple man and do not need vast quantities of money."

"Correct."

"What if I sold your debt to Colonel Ratsimanga and had him collect?"

"You cannot sell my debt. It is a personal matter between you and me."

"Incorrect," Lonny pronounced succinctly. "I'm going to sign it over it to Colonel Ratsimanga. I'm sure you'll pay him."

"You cannot come into my shop and threaten me. It is against the custom of civilized people. It is barbarous."

"I want to conduct a little business over the telephone, OK? You let me call, I forgive your debts. It's a good deal."

"I will not be threatened," nodded the Indian. "But for the future of my business I will permit you one phone call." He placed a rotary-dial telephone on the sales counter.

"Give me the other phone. I don't want you to listen in."

Still smiling, Akbarely placed an ultra-modern, portable, push-button phone on the countertop.

"Wait outside," said Lonny.

Akbarely bit his cheek and went to post lookout on the stoop of his shop.

Lonny held on to the phone, just staring at it, figuring out what time it would be on East 79th Street. He pushed the little button on the portable black handset and listened for the dial tone. He pushed it off again when he realized he had forgotten the number. He remembered writing it down. In indigo. In his traveling address book. On the right side of the page. On the bottom. *My Father at Home*. He closed his eyes tightly and concentrated intensely. He remembered things visually, like exact images of rough stones, particular hues that called out for a match, and he tried to envision the page until it formed as a picture in the recesses of memory and he could make out round numbers. Twos, of course—212. Then a pair of 8's, and a 6 and a 4, 3, 8, 6. He opened his eyes. He punched the lighted dial pad and telephoned directly to his father's New York City penthouse from a fifth-rate jewelry store one third of the way around the terrestrial globe. It was eight hours earlier back home, 8:30 A.M.

He sucked in his breath and gathered his courage as the phone rang. Sunday mornings his father cut synthetic rubies in his mahogany-paneled gemological library. Rubies were difficult stones to shape because the human eye doesn't process red color variations well. It is easy to misalign a facet or cut the apron too thick. Beyond technical skill the cutter has to be able to envision the finished gem and judge its future ability to capture light. Lonny practiced cutting with real, commercial-grade stones, but Cal was much more prudent. They were like an unhappy family of musicians where the father had broken into the business by sticking to the basics and his son was born with perfect pitch. Lonny's father exercised his eye incessantly. Lonny knew what he was looking at the instant he beheld it.

"Hello, Father."

"Lonny! Can you call me back? I'm cutting the table of a three-carat ruby."

"No, I need help."

"Why?"

"I found a 465-gram sapphire."

"You mean corundum?"

"I said sapphire."

"Gem-grade corundum?"

"Otherwise known as sapphire."

"Don't talk back to me."

"I'm not trying to."

"What color is it in natural light?"

"Prize Ribbon blue."

"What color in incandescent?"

"Starry night."

"Clarity?"

"Right back at you. No cracks or inclusions visible to the naked eye."

"Shape of the rough?"

"A perfect crystal. Twinned hexagonal pyramids with blunt tips, classic basal planing."

"Are you on something?" said Calvin Cushman, a gemologist with over forty years in the stone trade, turning the idea over in his mind.

"There's a visible star dead center."

"Are you drunk?" Cal started over, pondering.

"No, sir. I found a star sapphire as big as Abe Lincoln's head."

"There are plenty of big corundum formations."

"This is a gem-grade sapphire," swore Lonny. "As clear as Raspuli."

"Did you buy it?"

"Yes."

"How much?"

"20,000 dollars."

"Are you out of your mind? It costs 20,000 dollars for a rough stone?"

"It's worth it."

"You'd better hope so."

"Listen. I've made arrangements to get to South Africa later in the week but I need a friendly reception once I get there. You know what I mean?"

"Why are you trying to skip town?" Calvin Cushman asked suspiciously, letting the stratospheric static hum. "What kind of trouble are you in?"

"I bought a perfect sapphire. Other people want it."

"I don't believe you."

"You've never trusted me."

"You've never proven trustworthy," replied his father.

"Listen," said Lonny. "I know you and I still have some issues to work out. But I need your help right now."

"You're an embarrassment," said Calvin Cushman and he hung up dismissively. He detested lies and he knew there was no such thing as a 465-gram gem-grade sapphire. It would be worth millions, tens of millions of dollars. He didn't believe his disreputable son for an instant.

"You jerk!" Lonny screamed into the dead handset. And in a moment of clarity, the type that comes when rage strips every other little thing bare, he realized his father would never accept him as he was and there was nothing he could do about it.

Cal Cushman still blamed him for his mother's love affairs. Annabelle, *la belle de la France.* She took Lonny to plush hotel suites where he watched cartoons and listened to her shrieks coming from the other room. After one particularly long afternoon Cal dragged the truth out of his eight-year-old son. It was only later, when Lonny destroyed his own marriage by conducting his own affairs, that he realized his mother had used him as a messenger. And his father had chosen to shoot the messenger. It wasn't his fault that his mother committed suicide, his father blamed him and he had been sent to boarding school in the wilds of Connecticut when he was nine years old.

Lonny remembered how glorious it had been to hold Annabelle's hand when they said the Lord's Prayer together at the Église Française du Saint Esprit on East 60th Street. He was surprised by the old feeling of loss. He realized that she would have helped him now, that she would have believed in him and trusted him, that both he and his father were missing something in their lives that had never been replaced. They were both wounded by her suicide, both angry with her and each other, both alone with their pain.

"You are finished? Yes?" Akbarely came back into the shop. "Your continuing presence is making me very nervous. You must leave my place of business."

"Yeah, yeah, yeah," said Lonny, staring vacantly at the merchant, regrounding himself to the premises.

"A deal is a deal. One phone call for five thousand dollars."

"What was the deal exactly?" asked Lonny. "That you get my gem stock when the colonel arrests me?"

"You are quite mistaken," the agitated man replied. His hands began moving quickly in small circles, like a boxer fending off blows. "Please leave my store right away."

"Don't tell him I made a phone call," threatened Lonny.

"Quite mistaken," repeated Akbarely, nodding, smiling, hands aflurry.

"You are a lying thief."

"Attention," the merchant corrected him sharply. "I am not a thief. You traders come and go. It is us merchants who take all the risks. When Colonel Ratsimanga is mad at me, where can I run? What country will accept a small businessman from a poor country? No, no, I am not a thief. I am a businessman. If you stay in our community I will do business with you and support you. But if you run away I must do business with the colonel. You must see matters from my own point of view."

"I do not."

"It is such a shame." Akbarely shook his head horizontally in that strange Indian manner. "We are such good friends."

"We are not friends," said Lonny.

"Such an extravagant person! A man in a country such as this cannot afford to lose friends," declared Akbarely. "I should try my level best to accommodate the colonel if I wore your sandals."

"I hope we never see each other again."

"If you truly feel that way then I must do you a favor to regain your confidence."

"Tell me what the colonel said to you."

"That is not possible."

"Then what are you going to do for me? Bring me soup while I rot in prison?"

"If you so wish, I will do it!" smiled the merchant. His wife could make an extra plate of food out of her market allowance. The American would be a lucky man indeed if he could swallow when the colonel finished with him.

Lonny threw the handset at Akbarely and kicked the door open. He laid a slick of rubber on the boiling asphalt and hot-rodded his bike toward the top of the rue Colbert. Preoccupied with the feeling of his father's betrayal, Lonny rode into a deep pothole. The handlebars of the bike twisted out of his grip. The wobbly front wheel failed to recover, the bike lay down and Lonny held on in terror. The wide cylinder heads kept the heavy motorcycle off the ground and protected his left leg during the short slide, but it was a near thing. A moped rider howled at him as he lay on the pavement. The rich American fallen in the center of town. Taxi chauffeurs jeered. Showers of self-loathing dripped off his eyebrows like tears and the midday heat swelled. If I could have reached my arms through the phone lines I would have strangled that bastard, thought Lonny.

He lay underneath the bike for an emotionally explosive moment then drained to a defeated low. Getting the sapphire off Madagascar was up to him alone. He couldn't count on help from his rich, well-positioned father comfortably ensconced in New York. The thought left a bitter taste in his mouth, but a true taste. Everything depended on his own actions. His father had never helped him when he needed it most.

If he could mislead the colonel and forestall the king he would be airborne in a day or two. When he landed in Johannesburg his fictitious medical condition might distract the customs officers from frisking him. For all the thousands of dollars' worth of gem stock stashed in his house, and the tens of millions of Malagasy francs locked into the trunk at the foot of his bed, he did not have enough hard currency on hand to buy his way out of the slightest misunderstanding. He'd have to risk it anyway. He had the suspicious feeling that events were beginning to accelerate.

Once he had dusted himself off and found that he was miraculously unhurt, the right thing to do, the thing any Malagasy would have done, was sit to in the shade and wait for a friend to drive by. But Lonny was not one of those people who is good at waiting. Which is how he thought of it. He thought that time was something that could be measured, a quantity that could be saved or wasted. He fervently believed that each person was allotted a certain amount of time and that life itself was a race against an invisible clock. He did not comprehend the Malagasy notion of existence, which accepted life as an endlessly flowing river. The Malagasy did not believe that days were minted like coins to be added

up, divided or lost. As a result Lonny began march-
ing through the backside of Diego because he could
not sit still like a normal person.

Walking Diego was an experience for Lonny. He
was so accustomed to zooming past everything that
familiar buildings took on different shapes. Inside
dark doorways he nodded to the folks who lived in
the colonial debris. They took shelter from the blazing sun under tin roofs that baked them half to
death. He did not pity them. He had visited the
highlands and seen the naked hills and the starving
peasantry, and he knew the *côtiers* were more fortunate than their cooler, more elevated brethren. They
had something to eat.

He had walked every section of the town at one
time or another, from the filth of *Tanambo Cinq* to
the airy heights of *Hôpital Be*, trying to get a measure of the place. Traversing the car-shattering
streets and meniscus-shaped alleys was an odd pleasure. Women tended charcoal braziers underneath
shade trees and small boys played with plastic bags
bound into soccer balls. Even though Lonny had
not strolled these back alleys for months he was
known in *Le Quartier d'Avenir*. Girls plaiting each
other's hair giggled after he passed and married
women beckoned brazenly to the delight of their
neighbors. A man with cash was hard to come by in
broad daylight.

Several men lay in a sliver of shade outside the

Mena Lounge, stupefied by the mixture of heat and alcohol. Temperature bands of distended air radiated off the bar's red roof and Lonny felt the punch of a blast furnace as he passed the open doorway. A prostrate figure called up to him.

"Hey, stranger."

"Hey hey," said Lonny. It was his mechanic, Jaojoby.

"Where's my son?"

"I had an accident."

"Where?"

"Over by the post office."

"It's too hot to walk in the sun."

"What choice do I have?"

"Now you are a real Malagasy!" Jaojoby worked very hard on Lonny's motorcycle, fixing the punctured tires, changing the oil, replacing broken headlamps. He didn't have many tools but he knew how to use them. Nobody in town was allowed to touch Jaojoby's son without permission.

Lonny romanced his mechanic with crates of beer and issues of *Sports Illustrated*. It wasn't like New York, where you drove your machine to a dealer and the thing fixed itself. In Diego a good mechanic protected your machine while he stole parts from you didn't ask who. A bad mechanic sold your motor's inner workings to your neighbor and you realized it fifty miles into the bush when the pistons seized.

"Will you go help our boy?"

"I'll go right now and put him in my own shack for the night."

"*Tsara be*," said Lonny.

"Give me money for repairs," begged Jaojoby.

"You're not going to repair it. You're drunk."

"I'll fix it when I'm sober."

Lonny took some notes out of his back pocket and gave them to the mechanic. "Keep the bike well concealed at your house and I will come for it later."

"Live well," said Jaojoby.

"Live well," replied Lonny.

As soon as Lonny was out of sight Jaojoby bought a round of Three Horse Beer for his friends littered across the ground. Contrary to his neighbors, who generally cursed short-term expatriates, Jaojoby found working for strangers paid off.

8

THE GREAT GATSBY

Lonny continued angling his way across Diego's grid of alleys as if he were descending a broken staircase. A goat named Lolita spotted him from her garbage perch and trotted up. She was a favorite in the *quartier*. The heroine of many tales.

"Hi, you sexy thing," greeted Lonny. He drew a greasy paper note from his pocket and offered it to her.

"Baah," returned the welcoming goat. She nibbled the bill gracefully, money or a banana being equal to the old pro.

Lonny continued through the linking streets and alleys, wincing at the smells. The open sewer, the internally combusting garbage, the crushed

rats and rotting fruit peels added their own elements
of unchecked decay. The wafting odor of the seaside
slaughterhouse carried the stink of lingering death.

Following his senses without concentrating he
wound up beneath the bluff where his house sat and
the *Lycée Français* perched. His body was covered
in a sweat so profound his pants legs were soaked
through and the inside of his slick thighs were
chaffed raw. He did not want to retrace his steps
around the bluff to the front of his house. He picked
out the footpaths that the neighborhood boys used
to ascend the steep incline and resigned himself to a
stiff climb. One foot after the other. He would have
traded a matched pair of garnets for an ice cold
glass of water.

Before he reached the top of the bluff, the edge of
his lawn, he heard unfamiliar voices. He snuck up
the last bit and peered into his own compound like a
burglar. Thirty feet away a swarm of soldiers were
in the process of dismantling the house. They
looked like a well-organized moving crew, carrying
furniture and appliances out the door as adroitly as
a squad of Brooklyn repo men. Colonel Ratsimanga
surveyed the liquidation from a lawn chair. He had
erected a large parasol for shade and looked as well
ensconced as Gatsby.

Colonel Ratsimanga was following his own
timetable. He had Lonny's passport and now he
was looting the house. Lonny was sure that if he

stuck his head above the grass the colonel would chop it off.

Lonny slithered a few feet back down the eroding slope on his stomach, hiding under the canopy of broad-leafed banana trees. The ground was dank and fetid, filled with crawling insects and tiny itchy things that made his skin suck in around his bones.

Patrolling soldiers rustled the leaves near the edge of the escarpment. Lonny jammed his face into the hot earth. He could smell the soldiers sweat-worn bodies. He was too scared to twitch. He could hear their breathing. Clods of dirt rolled into his hair. He clenched tight his body—eyelids, hands, toes and intestines—while an uncontrollable shiver of panic welled inside his chest with the force of a sneeze.

"You're dead," said a soldier, and fired a string of three machine-gun bullets.

"The colonel's going to whip you until you bleed," said another soldier.

"I heard something."

"Little boys."

"Something else."

The colonel barked and the soldiers ran back to the house. Their bare feet pounding the wiry grass like drumbeats. Warm trickles of urine snaked down Lonny's legs, mixing with red dust, pooling on the tops of his sandals. A spray of diarrhea coated the inside of his pants and a crease of pungent bile seeped down onto his balls.

He lay motionless in his filth, listening for footsteps, and after some minutes rolled onto his back. An engine started and the drift of voices moved away. He closed his eyes to the heavens. The relentless sun, the shame of filth, the drain of sex and the despair of his father's rejection overwhelmed him. His body collapsed inward and carried him away. It came as ecstasy, the release from physical cares, the slip of worry.

The throng grows until it is a crowd, the crowd until it encompasses the entire unorganized settlement. They press Lonny twenty deep, making him the hub of a circle that takes in even the half-wits trying to shade themselves with their own palms. They reach out to him as if he's their salvation. As if his word could save them from their surroundings. Their desperation smells like opportunity.

The 60-million-year-old blocks of limestone coral eroded into acres of razor-sharp needles. Overgrazed grass slopes covering short volcanic cones, gem-bearing pipes. The Sacred Lake filled with crocodiles, the Green Lake full of eels, the Emerald Forest a hallucination of hanging thorns and roots clutching to rock. Men and women comb through the wreckage of charred shacks to find cached treasures. Some of the stones are still hot when they press them into his hand. The village in cinders.

Even in the last hour of their need the miners remember to rub their stones in honey to better hide the flaws. His hands are sticky, palms dripping with perspiration and caramelized sugar. He glances at thousands of stones as hundreds of eyes interpret his every expression. He manipulates the little pea-sized rocks with his right, shades with his left, letting the sun illuminate telling inclusions.

It's easy to buy. Black corundum. Bi-colors. Greens in great quantity. Olive oils for burning. Dog tooths with windows down their center axis. A sky blue Ceylon, to flip. Lemon yellows, pale pinks, blood oranges. Padparadscha. Stars.

He wants to stop buying. "Tsy, tsy," he hisses and hisses. Every time he walks the mass moves like a wheel and rolls with him. New stones are pressed into his hands as fast as he can call out their names. Apatite. Opal. Amber. Sphene. Iolite. Orthoclase. Amethyst. Aqua. Onyx. Garnet. Zircon. Peridot. Tsavorite. Emerald. Tourmaline. Citrine. Agate. Alexandrite. Rubellite. The sun is colored by the stones and the rays pierce his eyes.

At last the crowd parts and a little girl wearing a rice sack walks to him. She slips a light object into his honey-covered hands. He smiles at her while he holds it to the light.

A beautiful piece of glass, he says. Harvey's Bristol Cream.

The girl holds out her hand for money. He

reaches into his shirt pocket and gives her the entire packet. And her smile grows larger and larger, and the stone in his hand becomes heavier, and when he looks at it again it is a fine azure sapphire. And she is gone. He yells at the miners with their stupid crowbars and metal sieve hats but they do not hear him. He wanders like a white apparition through a teeming camp of somber Malagasy peasants.

The chill of the approaching sunset woke Lonny with his feces dried into a thin crust around his loins. He scrambled up the slope onto his lawn and walked across the springy grass to the open house. The cabinet underneath the sink gaped open and neither his bucket of gems nor the pistol nor the cash were there. The faucets were missing, as was the flush toilet and all the light fixtures. Gemological books were dumped on the floor and the bookcase carried off, the rind more useful than the fruit. A truck must have transported the fridge, the cooker, the bed. Various ceiling tiles were broken and scattered across the ground.

"Damn," he cursed. He ran to the kitchen and popped the tile where his knapsack was supposed to be hidden.

It was gone.

"Damn! Damn! Damn!" swore Lonny as the impact of the empty space hit him. He was a marked man. No question about it. The colonel wouldn't have stolen the sapphire and his belongings if he thought Lonny would be alive to lodge a complaint. Without money or the gem the colonel had cut off his means of influence.

He had lost the most precious sapphire in the world. No one would ever believe him and it hardly mattered. And yet it seemed like any damned fool in Diego-Suarez would have know better than to underestimate Colonel Ratsimanga. He doubted that even Alexis would help him at this point.

For lack of anything better to do, Lonny stripped off his filthy clothes and squatted next to the rain barrel. He lathered up with Ali's thin bar of soap as he forced his brain to overcome its numb panic. All his relationships in Madagascar were based on money. How much he needed to pay for a certain object or service and what the other person owed him in return. He couldn't think of anyone who would help him for unselfish reasons. But there was one person who might. Malika.

He jumped up and ran naked into the open house. The old rotary phone was still operational because it was hard-wired into the wall. A phone without a phone line was useless in Diego. He picked up the receiver and carefully dialed the number marked in pencil on the wall.

"American embassy," a gruff American voice answered.

"This is Lonny Cushman in Diego-Suarez. I need

to speak with Malika, the commercial attaché. It's an emergency."

"Please hold." Lonny had no idea where he was calling. The few seconds he waited felt like hours, his hopes hanging precipitously to the static.

Malika's voice came on the line, "Why are you calling me?"

"I should have gone with you," acknowledged Lonny. "I made a mistake."

"I'm not in Madagascar to serve at your beck and call."

"Colonel Ratsimanga is about to arrest me."

"On what charge?"

"Does it matter?"

"What do you want me to do?"

"Stop them. Call somebody."

"I can't do that," said Malika.

"Why not?" said Lonny, trying to keep his voice even. Soapy water was puddling on the concrete floor of the ransacked house.

"Like I tried to tell you this morning, sweetheart. I'm here for pharmaceuticals, not human rights."

"Can you do anything?"

"I'll inform the ambassador. Are you in custody now?"

"They're after me with guns."

"Try running," said Malika. "They might not chase you."

"What?"

"Run," urged Malika.

"What about the med-evac? Can you arrange it for tomorrow morning?"

"That's impossible. The American embassy can't be involved in aiding or abetting a fugitive."

"I need your help."

"I'll see you get a consular visit."

"I'll be dead by the time you get here."

"It's a little too late for regrets," said Malika.

Lonny kept the phone to his ear as she hung up. There would be no magic airplane lifting him to freedom, no saving miracle to unlock the handcuffs as he dangled from an O-ring.

I did it again, thought Lonny, gazing at his exposed penis. I had an affair with someone who cared less for me than for what I could do for her. It needn't be Tucson, Las Vegas or St. Louis. It didn't have to do with Cass. It was a flawed decision-making process that combined physical attraction with opportunity and loneliness. Each time it had ended in misery. He had traveled 8,000 miles from home, lived a celibate lifestyle for two years, then committed the same mistake at the first opportunity. He couldn't escape from himself.

He had failed. He was a failure. If he survived the Malagasy jails he might hobble around the Museum of Natural History as a docent. He could lead tours through the collection of famous colored stones and cursed diamonds. He would explain the four C's and the importance of color variation. Or he could work from a wheelchair as an in-house gemologist at a jewelry mart, screening out synthetic imitations, squeezing traders down to their lowest possible margin. He had squandered his gifts.

He possessed degrees in liberal arts, fine arts and gemology. He was a sharp trader, a loyal friend and a regular marathon runner. He was so many things. He had made himself into so many things. He had been convinced that education, friendship and physical endurance were the base elements of the laser beam that would allow him to penetrate life's obscure mysteries.

He had overlooked love. They didn't teach it in schools. His father didn't know how to share what little of it he contained. The memory of his mother's reckless emotions spun him in a vortex. Like the preoccupied gem cutter who overpolishes each facet of a diamond until it is perfectly cut but so small as to be worthless, Lonny finally recognized his separation from Cass was the last gleam of a marriage that had been hopelessly flawed from the outset. Only the intertwined strands of their daughter's DNA bound them to each other and Annie was so distant she might as well have been born to a different father.

Cass had insisted on retaining custody. And Lonny, with shop hours and last-minute plane rides, knew he would lose the argument. A mother's biological claim to her children's early years appeared invincible. Play groups and daytime trips to visit the polar bears in Central Park were organized by women for women. Cal wouldn't help him financially if he stopped working and it seemed beneath contempt to sue Cass for support. By the nature of her ovaries she had been granted the benefit of doubt. Men without their children were as common as a bushel of lacquered emeralds in the diamond district.

In the hour of his defeat the flaws that shattered his marriage became startlingly obvious. It had been a mistake from day one. He should have accepted legal and financial responsibility for Annie's conception but refused marriage. Marriage was supposed to be a choice. An institution entered into freely and with devotion. He had never loved Cass. Perhaps she had never loved him. They had shared good times, movies in Paris, dancing on New Year's Eve, Mardi Gras in New Orleans. She was a beautiful person and a disastrous mate. The part of him that admired her was lost amid the recriminations, the therapists, the shotgun wedding in front of a city clerk and news photographers.

He had fathered a child with a woman he did not love. He had committed adultery while pretending to be faithful. He had even tried to use the discovery of the sapphire to blackmail his father for trust he knew the old man couldn't give. It was his fault for being so damned self-centered, every bit of it, and he didn't know how he would ever be able to forgive himself for being such an egotistical bastard. By following the same path as his mother he had alienated himself from his peers, his only daughter and his aging father. He felt more alone than he had ever been in his entire life.

If he killed himself he wondered if Annie would ever understand. Is it possible to love someone you have only known in another context, in a different place, as another person? Would a thread of understanding and compassion still connect their souls? Annie would be wearing her spring outfit today. A cotton party dress, patent leather shoes, an egg basket. She would look so bright and cheery that nobody would ask the little girl, Whatever happened to your daddy?

Annie was the only person he had ever loved as an adult, who loved him, unconditionally. Whether she was happy or sad. She loved him. When Cass was angry, he could see the light go right out of her eyes. When his father felt threatened he pushed Lonny away instead of bringing him closer. His mother had abandoned him in a laisez-faire manner, the same way she would stride down the sidewalk without worrying if he got lost in the crowd.

He walked back outside to the rain barrel. The dusky bay was spectacular in its undeveloped grandeur. The red-brick hills, the dappled aquamarine water, waning shafts of sunlight illuminating the alabaster sands of Ramena beach like a sound-stage. Yet melancholy feelings cruised through his mind like black submarines. He had never lived anywhere so scenic, anywhere so utterly sad and depressing.

Annie had a smile that could light up the skyline. She skipped out of school, down the stairs, up the sidewalk, jumped into his arms. He loved building imaginary castles with her on the couch. Making turrets out of pillows and dungeons underneath. In her world Princess Annie had a dog named Tu Tu, a cat named Miaou, a rat called Rainbow and a friend known as Lucy. Annie was the best thing that had ever happened to him. She was the only reason not to follow his mother into oblivion.

Lonny realized that he had allowed himself to be outfoxed by the colonel because he hadn't been serious enough about keeping the sapphire and going home.

The affair with Malika was exactly the type of thing his father faulted him for over and over again. It didn't have to do with sex—it had to do with remaining emotionally centered and alert. If he ever wanted to hold his daughter again he needed to wipe away his suicidal thoughts and get the job done. Annie was waiting. Recovering the sapphire and returning to New York were the first steps he needed to take toward making the world right.

* * *

Lonny circled the house searching for anything the soldiers might have left behind. Out front he discovered Ali guarding the curb from no one in particular.

"I wash your feet," said Lonny, in Swahili.

"I let you wash them," responded Ali. He grinned at Lonny's nakedness. "I thought you were dead."

"As God wishes."

"Indeed."

"They took everything."

"Not everything." Ali levered himself off the curb with his walking stick and withdrew a set of Lonny's clothes from the bushes.

"Where did these come from?"

"I saved them for your funeral."

"How thoughtful," replied Lonny. As he put on the blue cloth pants and collared shirt he imagined resting in them for eternity. They seemed rather inadequate. Ali had also saved his good European sandals, odd footwear for a voyage of no return.

"What is the problem?" asked Ali.

"The colonel took an important sapphire from me."

"Does it have value?"

"As much as you can dream, Ali Mohamed. A fishing boat with an engine. A bungalow in concrete. Four wives. A plane ticket to the Comoros."

"Is it enough to return you to America?"

"More than enough."

"Does your father know you found this stone?"

"He discharged me from his service."

"Completely bad," said Ali. *Mbaya kabisa*.

Ali communicated very well in French, and to his children and wives he spoke Malagasy. But to speak Swahili was a privilege and a pleasure. It reminded him of his youth, his brothers and his first wife. It brought back memories of what he had left behind in the Comoros to eke out an existence in Madagascar. And after all the years, the absurd politics, the unfaithfulness of his women, the forgetfulness of his children, he and the American often talked together about going home. The American reminded him of what it was like to be young and in the imagined debt of older men.

Ali had passed sixty years in Diego. He remembered the way the kilted Scots and Kenyan askaris landed on the unprotected side of the bay, beyond the salt flats, bypassing the huge guns and the lethal barracks of the Vichy legionnaires guarding the Pass. He could recall the panic after the Japanese mini-subs torpedoed a British destroyer. During the Cold War he saw the departing French sailors burn their houses before the North Koreans and Soviets moved in, only to watch the French come back again later when the North Koreans and Soviets moved out.

With his own eyes he had seen the president's

men kill his second wife. He had seen his own son in a soldier's uniform holding a rifle. He had fished for lobster and the great hammerhead shark. He had hooked a tuna so large he towed it to shore. There was a time he could afford a Coca-Cola every day; the neighbors' cooking fires swirled around him and his word was righteous.

But Madagascar was a country of blood. A place where the ancestors walked and genealogy determined caste. The descendant of a slave remained an untouchable slave. The descendant of a freeman, only that. The offspring of the nobles, forever powerful. He wanted to embrace Lonny, for in spite of a lifetime in this land, and two Malagasy wives, and so many children, they were both strangers in Madagascar.

"I know something you do not," said Ali.

"What?"

"The French consul was here."

"What?" A bolt of paranoia and a wave of hope shot through Lonny simultaneously.

"He took something from the house."

"You let him in?"

"Completely."

"When?" asked Lonny.

"Ten and a half."

Lonny sat down on the curb, completely befuddled. He knew Ali was trying to give him an important piece of information, but what was it? He hadn't even returned from the Glace Gourmand at 10:30 A.M.

"Ten and a half in the morning?" Lonny asked Ali. *Saa kumi na nusu asubuhi?*

"Ten and a half in the afternoon," said Ali, amazed that Lonny could be so dense. *Saa kumi na nusu mchana.*

Ten-thirty in the afternoon? Lonny tried to fit it together. They were speaking Swahili, therefore they must be talking about Swahili time. The Swahili day begins at 7 A.M. (one o'clock) and ends at 6 P.M. (12 o'clock), following the rise and fall of the sun. There are twelve daytime hours and twelve nighttime hours. In Swahili time six o'clock, high noon, was twelve o'clock in the European system, since the midpoint of the Swahili day corresponded to the zenith of the sun.

"Do you mean," Lonny said, switching to French, "at 4:30 in the afternoon?"

"Yes," replied Ali. "*Quatre heure et demi l'après-midi. Saa kumi na nusu mchana.*"

"I see," said Lonny. Ali was staring at him as if he were mentally defective, as if translating equatorial time to American time in Madagascar while speaking Swahili and French and thinking in English was as simple as opening a bottle of Three Horse Beer.

"Where did the consul go?"

"To the consulate," replied Ali.

All the pieces of Ali's puzzle suddenly fell into

place. At 4:30 P.M. Lonny had been on the phone with his father. It would have been just like the cunning, politically savvy consul to steal the stone a step ahead of the soldiers. The consulate was considered French territory and legally beyond the reach of Colonel Ratsimanga.

"I need to visit the consul."

"Yes, yes." Ali lifted his head vigorously.

"Will you do me a last favor?" asked Lonny, who knew he did not have the right to ask the old fisherman the least demand.

"Yes?" responded Ali.

"Tell the owner of the Vo Vo I will need his help."

Ali's eyes opened wide. "The Vo Vo? I might kill those girls if they try to ride me!"

"Will you go there?"

"Completely."

When Lonny rose, Ali rose as well. They kissed each other's cheeks in the French fashion then Lonny marched down the deserted street to make the deal of his life. He felt soap clean and cotton loose. The evening carried the slightest sting of the coming breeze.

"Don't worry," Lonny promised Annie. "I'm going to find a way back home even if I have to call on the winged monkeys."

9

THE KING, THE COLONEL, THE CONSUL AND THE KNAVE

The sun blinked down over the horizon and cast a black shadow across the town at 7 P.M., just as Lonny approached the French consulate. There was a platoon of soldiers lounging by the gate, harassing girls who strayed near and shining their flashlights at passing cars. Lonny greeted them going in and they sang return greetings like a church choir. It was the quality of their boots that unnerved Lonny. They were the colonel's best men.

Intertwined laces of rose, ivory, tangerine and Morganite bougainvillea formed a canopy over the stairs ascending to the consul's veranda. The consul had set out a card table, a miserly bar and an array of rancid camembert from his last trip to Brest. The First Rooster sat on a bamboo-framed couch with a minder by his side. He was a hereditary king with the blessing of his tribe, not a flaccid bureaucrat or a uniformed lackey. His impressive girth and fierce visage were a marked contrast to the knobby bones and humble demeanor of his subjects.

The colonel, standing, eyes bloodshot and weary, drank Johnnie Walker Black Label neat. He swayed back and forth on the balls of his feet, occasionally losing his balance and reaching out to the edge of the bar. Lieutenant Rakoto was stationed at the foot of the stairs.

The king drank nothing. Although he had been educated at the National Police Academy and visited Paris on a junket, he was raised in the bush. In the bush, where sorcerers and demons roamed in broad daylight, and poison was the preferred method of revenge, a person never accepted a drink from anyone living outside his own household.

The consul talked to both of them about the difficulties of getting his middle-aged daughter into the diplomatic service. He went on quite naturally even though he knew neither man was listening, and indeed, he barely knew what he was saying himself. His insides were twisted into knots. If the American did not show, the colonel would round up the Europeans in the district on charges of conspiracy, collusion or just criminally deficient melanin. Should the colonel choose to deport the most unsavory French citizens his esteem would rise in the capital while *la patrimoine française* suffered indignity. If that happened the ambassador would retire him immediately. The cold drizzle of Finistère would make a poor swap for the vivacious schoolgirls of Diego.

Lieutenant Rakoto smiled broadly at Lonny when he put his foot on the first step leading up to the veranda.

"Who would have guessed we would see each other twice in one day?" said the lieutenant.

"You'll never touch me."

"I'll cut your eyelids off so you never forget me, dirty Frenchman."

"I'm a dirty American, you cannibal."

"*Tsy, tsy*," whispered the officer. "A dead Frenchman."

Lonny felt the force of the lieutenant's malice pass over him like a gust of wind. He remembered the first time he had been mugged on Seventh Avenue. He was so surprised. The gangbangers just wanted his money but they would have killed him for it. Killed him for money. He was ten years old, home on vacation, and he had taken money for granted his whole life until that day. And now Lieutenant Rakoto wanted to kill him not for money but for who he was. A stranger. A condition he could not alter for all the money in the world.

"What a pleasure," greeted the consul effusively

upon Lonny's appearance at the top of the stairs. "May I present you to the First Rooster, His Most Royal Highness the King of the Antakarana?"

"This is the young man we have heard so much about. *Salut*," said the king, not rising. Lonny bowed slightly.

"Come for a hand of bridge?" asked the colonel unpleasantly.

"Good evening, Colonel Ratsimanga. We seemed to have missed each other earlier in the day."

"Diego is such a small town. I suspected we'd catch up to each other."

"Not Diego. Antsiranana," interjected the king, speaking to the colonel for the first time and in French. "The name comes from the ancestors." Like many of the smaller tribes living on the coast, the Antakarana had been forced to acknowledge the de facto power of the highlanders. But *côtiers* refused to acknowledge any sort of highland cultural supremacy. Rather than accepting highland Merina as the national language, the elite preferred that their children learn French as a second language and they spoke French to the highlanders to drive the point home. As the leader of the *côtier* opposition to the president, the First Rooster never let an opportunity to criticize his highland enemies pass him by.

"With all due respect to your ancestors," replied the colonel. He and the king were used to sharp arguments and unresolved conflicts. As the president's military representative in Diego, and a sworn enemy from a competing tribe, he would not stand to be corrected. "I believe the French were the first to establish a village on this bay. Although I am quite against strangers renaming parts of our country, this place had no name before the Europeans built a naval base."

"Perhaps that is true," argued the king. "The Antakarana are peasants, not fishermen. And our histories do not include the names of all the places around this bay. But surely the highland colonel must recognize that replacing colonial names with Malagasy ones is good for the nation."

"It's good for your tribe because it gives you ancestral claim to a place you have none," retorted the colonel. He despised the ignorant *côtiers* and their petty kings. His ancestors had crushed the king's ancestors with their wits and their muscle. He was not about to allow the First Rooster to create myths and lay claim to things that did not belong to him. Better to call the town Diego-Suarez than Antsiranana if it denied the king the slightest advantage.

"Please," said the nervous consul. "Let us play cards before we discuss politics. Lonny, may I serve you a drink?"

"Betsilo gray wine," said Lonny

"Excellent choice," commented the colonel. The grapes were grown in the highlands by a Swiss expatriate.

"The colonel and I will play against you and His Highness."

"There's no need to go through with the charade," said Lonny. He had momentarily forgotten about the invitation to play bridge.

"I insist," snorted the consul.

"Then shouldn't we have at least two tables? Where are your wives?"

"This is no place for ladies," remarked the First Rooster.

The protocol involved in seating a politically active *côtier* king and a militarily powerful highland colonel taxed the limit of the consul's diplomatic arts. He managed it, however, and got all of them facing each other across the flimsy table, knees practically touching. Each player received a ready hand. Given the delicacy of the situation, the consul had prearranged the distribution so there would be no surprises.

"Pass," said the king without organizing his cards.

"One heart," bid the colonel.

"One spade," overbid Lonny.

"Two spades," declared the consul, shooting Lonny a homicidal glance.

"Double," replied the king.

"Four spades," said the colonel, and they all let the contract lie.

The king led with the ace of diamonds. When the colonel's dummy was laid out there were only two diamonds showing, the queen and a six. The consul threw in the six. Lonny had a void in diamonds. He took a deep breath then committed the crime that would ever be confused and misunderstood by those who later tried to sort out these peculiar events in forgotten bars and on crumbling verandas. He trumped the king's ace.

"Incredible," burst the king, slamming his palm on the table and forcing the cards to jump involuntarily.

"Don't take him seriously." The consul attempted to placate the First Rooster as he played a low diamond from his own hand.

Lonny collected the trick and led with the eight of clubs. He knew that if he played the game for any length of time the other players would capitalize on his mental fatigue and use it to their advantage. He needed to stay focused and cards were the last thing on his mind. Where had the consul stashed the sapphire? Did the other players know he had it?

The consul ducked the finesse and the king picked up the trick with a jack, nothing higher showing in the dummy. His minder gathered the cards and the First Rooster sent the king of diamonds into the melee.

The consul released the queen from the dummy.

The king glared at Lonny. Lonny grinned back.

Lonny ran his index finger over the tops of the rigid cards. He tapped the edge of a throwaway card, danced over to another, then trumped the whole thing again out of a sense of mischief and desperation.

"Impertinence!" The king folded the playing cards into his massive fist.

"I bet no one ever did that to you before," exhaled Lonny. He'd come to bargain for his life not play cards. After being invited to play regularly with the consul last year, Lonny had taught himself how to count points, bid and finesse by reading a book expedited from Bordeaux. Without local access to the World Wide Web he was forced to puzzle out the arcane bridge terminology by himself, alone and in French. The other players at the table had been sparring for years. At the National Military Academy in the highlands, bridge was a graded class, as important to an officer's career as the knowledge of rifles or roadblocks.

"Myself," said the colonel, "I wouldn't have trumped the king right after he took the queen."

"Play," demanded the consul, grinding his molars.

Lonny nodded to the king and played spades. The consul easily collected the remaining tricks and made the contract without much effort. During the consul's deft run the king threw his creased cards toward Lonny in a desultory and menacing manner.

During the next round of bidding the king opened with a weak one club bid. Lonny upped it to four clubs immediately and left the king with an impossible four hearts contract when he converted to a major suit.

"Provocation!" said the king when he saw Lonny's dummy. The consul chopped his incisors together forty or fifty times and the colonel ate his lips.

"I am trying to make a point," said Lonny.

"That you can ruin a card game?" said the disgusted king.

"Yes. This is a four-handed game and any one of us can spoil it."

"You are in possession of something that belongs to my tribe."

"Are you interested in purchasing it?"

"You will give it to me," replied the king, throwing down his cards and pushing the table away from his chair into Lonny's stomach.

"I wish it were that simple," said Lonny, pushing the table back, glancing at the nervous consul. "The colonel wants me to give it to him as well."

The king frowned at the colonel. "The *vatomanga* is no concern of his. It is an ancestral treasure."

"Incredible," returned the colonel. "The sapphire has a tribal name!"

"I have never seen it," said the king. "Our storytellers say the *vatomanga* has many flat faces but no sharp edges. It is the size of a mango and the weight of red mercury. It has a six-pointed star in the center."

"Well, that's a closer guess than the colonel's," said Lonny, unnerved by the king's perfect description. "He said it was the size of a watermelon."

"You," interjected the colonel, "have removed a mineral belonging to the Malagasy Republic from the soil without proper documentation. I am responsible for enforcing the law. The sapphire must be forfeited to me immediately."

"You are a mere army colonel," scoffed the king. "An officer of the Malagasy Armed Forces is charged with maintaining political order and chasing bandits. The issue at hand is property theft.

"The *Gendarmarie*," continued the king, straightening himself up, "is responsible for recovering my possession. You do not enforce the law, you maintain order. You are nothing more than a guest in this section of the Grand Island. Understood?"

Colonel Ratsimanga glared at the king.

"*Comprend?*" the king repeated in French. He did not deign to speak his own language to a highland foreigner.

The king spoke precisely without using any two-headed verbs or subjunctive conditionals. Lonny had never heard the naturally ambiguous French language used so directly in Madagascar. There was nothing Colonel Ratsimanga could do but withdraw to the bar like a wounded clerk with his ego rammed down his throat.

"Huummph," snorted the colonel. He poured himself a full water glass of whiskey.

The king's gaze drifted from the colonel's sweat-stained back to Lonny's poker face.

"Our history," said the king in his regal bass, "tells of a great king who possessed this sapphire before the invasion of the highlanders. It was a gift from the most powerful man in the world, the sultan of Zanzibar, Seyyid Seyyid, and a token of his brotherhood. The stone bestowed second sight on the king, allowing him to outwit his enemies. It was lost when his bearers were attacked by a crocodile crossing a flooded rice paddy. The *filanzana* overturned. The king drowned. The stone disappeared. It is said a great mango tree sprang from the earth and protected the stone with its roots."

"Very touching," muttered the colonel.

"Very," said Lonny. He suddenly realized why the sapphire looked different from the thousands of others he had purchased in the region. The *vatomanga* had been imported! His eye had been right. The king was telling the truth.

"Armed with French gunpowder," continued the king, "the highlanders invaded during his son's reign and massacred nearly all our people. The king's hiding place was betrayed by his brother Jao. Now Jao's descendant has betrayed the tribe for the second time.

"You," the king leaned forward and pointed his massive index finger at Lonny's heart, "have taken our tribe's ancestral treasure from the hands of a traitor. He had no right to sell it and you will give it back to me!"

Lonny sat immobile, sweat dripping off the tip of his nose like a faucet. The colonel was dangerous but he had been temporarily neutralized. The consul lay as flat as an envelope. Lonny concentrated on the king. He needed to convince the king that their interests were the same.

"I would like to make you a proposal," bluffed Lonny, boldly staring back into the eyes of the First Rooster. The consul was the only one who knew he didn't have the sapphire.

"There is nothing to talk about," stated the king, glaring at the American.

"On the contrary," replied Lonny. "In spite of the stone's history, I believe I have a strong and legitimate claim to ownership due to the method of discovery and the nature of the purchase transaction.

"My good fortune can be ours to share," he went on, addressing the entire veranda. "I did buy the stone on the king's ancestral lands and will concede his interest. The state also has an interest and I accept the colonel as the government's representative. The consul can act as a guarantor, a neutral fourth party.

"I propose that we work together to bring the

sapphire to market in a way that will benefit each of us. The king will receive money to protect his lands, the colonel's family will be taken care of for the next thirty years, and the consul is entitled to a large honorarium for his efforts. If you permit me to arrange the sale we will all be significantly better off in a few weeks."

"You are in no position to make demands," said the colonel, as pretentious as ever.

"You are a criminal," blustered the righteous consul. He couldn't figure out where Lonny was headed.

"This is a good proposal." Lonny raised his voice. "I talked with a representative of the American ambassador today and the embassy will support my actions. I can be in South Africa in a few days and each of you can be millionaires by the end of the month. The four of us are in this thing together. Either we all win or we all lose."

"A million U.S. dollars?" The consul was bug-eyed. He had no idea that it was that valuable.

"A million dollars each," said Lonny.

"It is my stone," declared the king. "It is not for sale."

"*Tsy, tsy!*" the colonel negated the king.

"I have talked with the American ambassador about you," the king said to Lonny. "She does not approve of your actions. She has promised me many millions and the support of the American government to turn my lands into a World Heritage Site."

"Let me tell you a secret, King," said Lonny. "Nobody in Washington, D.C., gives a ding-dong about your highlanders, your *côtiers*, your 18 tribes, your hereditary castes, or your damn reserve. If the current ambassador is trying to turn a few acres of tribal land into an ecological preserve it's an extracurricular project. Over the next forty years that area is going to become the largest sapphire mine in the world. There are 60 meters of gem-bearing gravel laid over bedrock and 90 square kilometers of sedimentation from the volcano. I saw it the second I laid eyes on it. The sapphires are going to give you more money than you and your tribe will ever be able to spend, but your ancestors will curse you for it. The only way you are going to save your ancestors' soul ground is by preventing more miners from trespassing. The creation of a National Park will only transfer administrative control of your lands to the bureaucrats in Antananarivo. You need cash right now to arm your warriors."

"Nobody is going to arm anybody," interjected the colonel.

"What's your point?" asked the king condescendingly, ignoring the colonel. He knew that the American had spoken the truth the way a child unwittingly spills a family secret to a visitor.

"Your fat ass is perched on the richest sapphire deposit in the world. You can afford to pay me a fair price for my discovery. If you don't, you and your tribe are going to lose everything."

The king stared at Lonny.

Lonny wanted to backtrack, to reformulate and expostulate his crude threat in a more elegant way. But it was too late. He could speak French with childhood slang, in the stiff academic manner or as plainly as an African truck driver. He lacked the subtle verb forms and mature vocabulary to convince with graceful oratory. His comments were all too direct and presupposing. He did not own the proper rhythm, the correct cadence or accentuation. Instead of projecting himself as a well-educated man with a sound proposal, the king, the colonel and the consul were put off by his Anglo-Saxon directness.

In Lonny's deathly pale skin and satanic brown irises the king saw Jao laughing. Jao the original traitor, the one who had sold his tribe to the highlanders. The wicked and cunning Jao whose descendants were banished from royal ceremonies and funeral dances. He saw Jaoravo, the Happy Bull, calling up his ancestors, and those ancestors jumping in delight and in ecstasy. He saw low buildings and his own corpse. He saw the death totem over his tomb split and decay, the treasure buried with him looted, his sons and daughters scattered. In his outstretched hand he saw the *vatomanga*, the rock, clean and blue, the color of shallow water when viewed from a height, and he saw it fall from his hand into the void. The eternal night from which there is no sunrise.

Inside the king's piercing stare Lonny glimpsed charred devastation. Black ash, red earth and the night. He saw drums and bodies, and his own body moving without him, and the circles of oblivion. All around him were hellfires and damnation, and just beyond, through the white heat and the yellow tongues of flame, a speck of some other color, the slightest flicker. He stared into the king, aware of the colonel, somehow knowing what would happen next.

Colonel Ratsimanga watched Lonny's oration and the contest of wills from the bar. The king did not impress him. He knew the story of the king's rise, how he had outmaneuvered his older brother by reciting more proverbs and speaking through the night to the tribe's elders. Parlor tricks and wind hardly made a man. He teetered unsteadily next to the bar, his anger and impatience as finely stretched as the bubble that keeps a full glass of water from spilling past the edge. He fumbled inside his field jacket for Lonny's chrome-plated pistol.

The consul gazed at the disintegration of his career much the way a seaman watches a tanker break in two, its oily cargo slowly spreading out over the waves. Any hope for political calm had been dashed by the American's unpredictable appeal to individual greed. The colonel was as dangerous as a boa constrictor hovering over a water hole. The king simmered like a pot. In a previous era the consul would have had them all arrested just so he could think straight.

"*Ah zallah!*" exclaimed the king. He tossed the flimsy card table across the terrace. He would kill the stranger who dared look into his soul and threaten the well-being of his tribe. He would rip him limb from limb and use his head as a throne ornament. He lunged toward Lonny, his large fists expanding, sucking Lonny into his embrace.

Lonny scrambled backward. Colonel Ratsimanga blinked. Just as a jazz musician can feel the rhythm of a jam session and make space for a new riff, the colonel was a man so well versed in physical violence that what seemed like a desperate situation to a civilian appeared to him as the opportunity of a lifetime. He drew Lonny's 9-mm pistol from his waistband and shot the king through the forehead. The bullet repainted the consul's veranda with a tapestry of blood.

The First Rooster, king of the Antakarana, died instantly. His body collapsed facedown into a lumpy heap. His head whacked the floor and his eyes rolled in their sockets. Quivering bits of bone, hair and brain matter sprayed up against the wall.

Lonny crouched behind the overturned card table expecting the shiny pistol to swing his way. He recognized it as his own and he thought, I'm going to be killed with my own handgun. But the colonel only leered at Lonny in a perverse manner.

"The king is dead," shouted the consul in disbelief, his career irreplaceably shattered like a bottle of Château Lafite-Rothschild dropped onto cobblestones.

The colonel yelled to Lieutenant Rakoto and the junior officer came running up the stairs brandishing a cocked AK-47. The king's minder bolted for the stairs where Lonny heard him run past the lieutenant's men to the sound of gunfire.

"Arrest this man," said the colonel, pointing to Lonny. "He has killed the First Rooster."

"You murdered him!" protested Lonny.

The colonel ignored his plea and waved the 9-mm pistol at his chest. "This is your pistol. The king was killed with it, therefore you are the murderer."

The Malagasy logic behind the declaration hit Lonny like a punch. The king's bright blood oozed out over the dull crimson tile. He died in a polo shirt, khakis and flip-flops. A modern king.

"I'll tell you where the sapphire is."

"I don't need it."

"Why not?"

"Your arrest will serve my purpose."

"You can't arrest me here," protested Lonny. "The consulate is French soil. I have immunity."

"I waive it," said the listless consul.

"I haven't told anyone where the sapphire is," said Lonny. "Call your ambassador. I am a guest in your house and here by your invitation. You'll face charges if you hand me over."

The consul reconsidered. "Colonel, would you be so kind as to delay your arrest until I call the ambassador in Tananarive?"

"Make it fast," snapped the colonel. He poured himself another finger of whiskey. Lieutenant Rakoto bared his teeth at Lonny. He would shove fire peppers up the American's nasal passages and rub the juice in his eyes.

The consul entered the house through an open doorway. The living room was separated from the veranda by a screen of opaque glass slats and a decorative security grill fashioned out of cast iron.

The men on the porch watched the consul's shadow as he opened an enormous freestanding vault that dominated one wall of the living room. He removed a suitcase-sized, battery-operated satellite phone and dialed directly to his embassy on the encoded line. Through the haze of frosted panes Lonny spotted a spectral blue halo from deep inside the safe.

They could hear the consul arguing forcefully over the phone, then less forcefully concurring with statements made by the party on the other end. Lonny stepped over the inert body of the dead king and strode to the entrance of the house. As he did so the lieutenant pointed the automatic rifle at his head.

"Where are you going?" demanded the colonel.

"To the bathroom. I don't want to shit in my pants."

The officers giggled with the acknowledgment of their own power, as they had seen plenty of prisoners foul themselves, and Lonny walked off the veranda unmolested. The living room was decorated with original artwork and sculpture by Madame le Consul. There were phallic pieces of coral, erotic collages fashioned out of glossy magazine pages and all sorts of sado-masochistic imagery created with agricultural debris: broken balls, rusted chains, antideluvian keys, ox-driving whips. The consul turned to Lonny as he entered then turned back to the safe, saying, "Do you understand my position? Do you see?" all the while.

Lonny paused inside the room. He hadn't visited corundum deposits in northern Thailand the day the Khmer Rouge massacred everyone at that site. He flew out of Angola minutes before rebels mortared the airstrip and recaptured the diamond mines. A Greek emerald merchant was killed at a police checkpoint in Nigeria the afternoon Lonny was supposed to accompany him. In those places he had avoided death by his absence. Now, with the lieutenant's stare on his back, he had never been so aware of the Grim Reaper actually stalking him.

"*Dègage!*" the consul shouted at Lonny in annoyance.

Disengage? thought Lonny. No. This certainly wasn't the time to disengage. The door to the veranda had a self-locking mechanism that could only be opened with a key. Guests were always locking themselves inside or out by accident. He drew in his breath, plucked a rawhide whip off the wall and kicked the door shut with his heel.

"*Tsy-eh!*" shouted the lieutenant.

The consul's eyes flashed with fury and Lonny slashed him across the arm, telephone, cheek, nose and forehead with the stiff zebu-hide quirt. The man's face blossomed red with a stripe of shock. It was sickening. The first time in his life that Lonny had aggressively attacked another human being.

The colonel opened fire at Lonny's shadow from the veranda.

Lonny dove for the protection of the steel safe as 9-mm pistol bullets ricocheted around the concrete room like hornets. He crouched against the massive steel door and snatched the sapphire off a pile of documents. The consul was howling in agony and confusion. Lonny quickly crawled over him toward a hallway that led toward the front of the house.

The lieutenant blindly unloaded 20 copper-jacketed AK-47 rounds into the milky glass slats.

Lonny scampered sideways into the kitchen, killed
the lights, unlocked the side door and peeked out.
Soldiers were running up the driveway toward the veranda at the back of the house. He could hear the
lieutenant hammering on the wrought-iron grill.
Lonny ran down into the night, sprinted across the
compound and leapt the security wall on nothing but
adrenaline.

10

AT THE VO VO

The oily light of an open-wicked flame cast flickering shadows over the disintegrating pages of Ali Mohamed's Koran. He sat on the cracked concrete curb in front of the American's empty house. He did not read so much as soak in the presence of the book, the promise of peace written between its far covers. He had never made the voyage to Mecca, nor could he recite large tracts of the holy text, for he was a fisherman. He accepted his limited knowledge of the Almighty with resignation. Not all men were destined to enter the realm of paradise. Not all men were given the ability to understand the will of Allah.

There was a knot, a shiny bulb of skin and pus growing out of his armpit. Some days it rapped his heart so sharply he wanted to lance it with a fish-hook. Other days it sat as complacently as a rubber ball. Herbal teas and hot poultices had no effect. He needed the kind of medicine that came from a plastic bottle. He went to see his daughter so that she could take him to the *Hôpital Be*. She refused. It is not like before, she said. You need money to go to the hospital these days. I have no money to spare on an old man.

He did not argue. He could see the children and the mouths. He was not angry with her. She did not make the rules. He was angry with the others. The president, the colonels, the nobles. The big bellies who controlled the red stamps, the guns, the medicines.

The only person who respected him was the American. He knew that *mchele* meant hulled rice and *wali* meant cooked rice. He knew that *kula* meant to eat, and *kusaidia* meant to help. The American called him *mzee* which was proper, and even *mlimu* (teacher) which was an honor. They shared proverbs and argued over the interpretations. His favorite, "*Haraka haraka haina baraka*," meant "Hurry has no blessing," but the boy translated it as "Haste makes waste," which was not quite correct. He tried to teach the boy that Allah determined life's tempo; the boy believed his own tempo need only be regulated to make it more efficient. How Ali laughed at the boy's notions.

And now the American was missing. Panting soldiers came for him. They spoke short, angry words. They said the boy killed the First Rooster. But he did not. Ali knew this. The American was leaving Diego. He would not kill the king of the Antakarana over an ace. He was clever, the American. He spoke Swahili correctly. His nouns corresponded to the right verb class, his vocabulary was book-learned. In his country he must have been a favored son before he clashed with his father.

Ali left the Comoros because of his own Baba. A man too proud to fish with his son. Angry if the younger man caught more tuna, or rays, or sharks. But he could not throw the fish back into the sea. He had sailed from Anjouan a lifetime ago and the voyage haunted him now that he was old. The pain of the decision surfaced from time to time like a coelacanth hand-lined from the depths of the Mozambique Channel, an accidental reminder of a vanished world. Why should a man be forced to exile himself from his birth village because he was more successful than his father? He would like to meet his own sons again and forgive them for abandoning him.

Ali folded the Koran into a cloth sack and hung it on the gate of the American's compound. He knew that today was a holy day for the Christians. The day the prophet Jesus was resurrected from the dead. And the soldiers fired their guns. The First

Rooster had been murdered. Disco girls would be dancing and drinking alcohol. None will be saved, thought Ali. Allah pardons not the weak.

He locked the gate and went to find the owner of the Vo Vo Club.

The Vo Vo occupied the best piece of real estate on the rue Colbert, about halfway down, on a popular corner within sight of the Glace Gourmand. The imposing facade was two and a half stories tall, complete with arches, balconies, a red-tiled mansard roof, a street-level arcade and a walled courtyard. Alexis had leased it from a widow in La Rochelle who possessed the original title. Various politicians had tried to appropriate the building for their own use, but the widow's husband had been an administrative officer in the Colonial Office and the paperwork was airtight. Alexis liked to stand in front of the Glace Gourmand and gaze over at the impressive edifice. It reminded him of better days.

The inside of the Vo Vo resembled a cheap, off-Broadway theater. The windows had been boarded over. The concrete walls were painted flat black. Exposed pipes and bare wires hung from the ceiling. Interestingly, a tremendous 80-foot-long, horseshoe-shaped bar occupied the center of the cavernous space. A polished dance floor the size of a stage lined one side of the room. Bare metal stools welded in place around chest-high tables covered the remainder of the floor space. Seven days a week multicolored lights, whirling disco balls and high-intensity strobes pulsed to the ever-present beat of thump-thump mix music.

On a slow night thirty girls might dance with each other in sports bras and spandex micro-minis so tight they looked like skin grafts. A sparse audience of aroused expatriates, businessmen and bureaucrats would drink whiskey and buy beers for the women who lifted their spirits. Intercourse cost about 15,000 fmg ($3.00). Mothers came to sell their daughters, husbands their wives, brothers their sisters. The money went to pay school fees, settle charges with the state-owned electricity company, buy cooking oil and sugar for the kitchen. Sex meant survival in every sense of the word. The highlanders condemned the *côtiers* with a word imported by Welsh missionaries; the *côtiers* chided the highlanders for a severe lack of imagination. Women traded their warm bodies for cash and men paid the market rate to relieve a share of loneliness. In Diego a night bathed in the rotating colored lights was a way to stave off the madness of living.

The interior of the Vo Vo could accommodate boatloads of contentious Basque tuna fisherman or a French minesweeper's entire complement. It was a throwback to the era before airplanes and E-mail, when a seaman needn't worry that his significant other would surprise him in a port thousands of miles from home. Alexis usually supervised his bartenders from a position inside the horseshoe, halfway down the vast bar on the side away from the dance floor. He used a reading lamp to illuminate a long ledger of names and how much they owed him. The only customers who pestered him were the ones he had already denied further credit.

Lonny paused outside the entrance to the Vo Vo. There was music pounding through the thick walls but it seemed strangely silent. The regular policemen posted near the door were nowhere to be seen. The women grilling little sticks of meat on the side street were gone.

Lonny ducked under the courtyard arch and peeked into the bar. The strobes flickered across the empty dance floor and the music echoed against itself. Ali was sitting at the far end of the bar top. Lonny moved toward him cautiously.

"You're late," said Alexis, popping up from a hiding place behind the bar. His shirt was torn, his lip busted, one side of his face swollen. The cash register was smashed open.

"I see the soldiers got here before I did," remarked Lonny. It had taken him nearly thirty minutes to make his way from the consulate to the Vo Vo without being spotted by Colonel Ratsimanga's men.

"*Shikamoo*," said Ali Mohamed with evident glee. He was holding a Coke. It had been years since he had crossed the threshold of the Vo Vo.

"*Marahaba*," responded Lonny.

"You are not dead!" grinned Ali.

"What the fuck is going on?" demanded Alexis.

"Colonel Ratsimanga shot the First Rooster at the consul's house," declared Lonny.

"*Oh, la Madonna!*"

"They're trying to pin it on me."

"Abandon ship," said Alexis, one nervous eye on the door. "Gendarmes versus the army. *Côtiers* versus highlanders. Every man for himself."

"We're in this together," Lonny shouted at him. "You can't just leave me here!"

"Says who?"

"If they get me, they get you." Lonny raised one eyebrow in a wry, comic manner as if to say, You know what I mean? and Alexis slapped him so hard that he jerked backward like he had been clotheslined. The sapphire spun lazily on the hardwood.

Ali picked the sapphire off the dark floor, put his hand under Lonny's arm and raised him to his feet.

"That wasn't necessary," mumbled Lonny, holding the side of his face with two hands. The pulsing lights made him dizzy. The skin on his face tingled sharply like it was reviving from a case of frostbite. He could pick out the nearby pop of isolated gunshots over the music.

Alexis grabbed Lonny by the arm and dragged him to the farthest, darkest corner of the bar top. Ali tagged along behind the pair.

"That's the key," Alexis motioned to the stone in Ali's hand, "isn't it?"

"Back to 'we' again?" returned Lonny.

"It'll start as a vendetta between the highlanders and the *côtiers*," explained Alexis, "and end up as race riots. I saw it happen in '94 over in Mahajanga. They'll burn out the Indians then move on to the strangers. If the gendarmes catch us we're going to be paraded down the rue Colbert with placards around our necks. If Colonel Ratsimanga's men get us we'll have to ransom ourselves out of the barracks. Either way, I'll lose everything. They already stole my car."

"That stone is worth a thousand discos," said Lonny. "Help me get out of this place alive and I'll give you ten percent."

"Fifty percent," said Alexis. He had no idea what the stone was worth.

"Twenty percent," Lonny bargained instinctively.

"Forty percent," threatened Alexis. "Or you're on your own."

"Deal," said Lonny. If Colonel Ratsimanga caught them it was a moot point.

"Where do they expect you to go?" asked Alexis.

"The airport."

"Where else?"

"Antananarivo."

"Why?"

"I might get help from the embassy."

"Is that it?"

"Yeah, that's it. The colonel will be searching for me on the road and in every town between here and Antananarivo. The gendarmes will be looking everywhere else. Any questions?"

"We have to avoid roads, towns and airports."

"Where does that leave?"

"Cape Bobaomby," said Ali Mohamed. He had been shadowing the conversation, not eavesdropping, but making sure that he could lend his experience if need be. "You can walk to the lighthouse from the other side of the bay."

"You want us to walk from Diego to the tip of northern Madagascar? It's over twenty miles to Cape Bobaomby. There's nothing at Cape Bobaomby," protested Lonny.

"Exactly," agreed Alexis.

"There are fishing dhows at Cape Bobaomby," said Ali. "Maybe one will take you to the Comoros."

"It's not safe," insisted Lonny. He spent every day haunting the sapphire camps. He knew a thing or two about life in the bush.

"It's a good plan." Alexis unlocked a cabinet under the bar and came up with a banana-shaped fanny pack bulging with rolls of money. He also pulled out a sawed-off shotgun with a folding stock and a pistol grip. He draped a bandoleer full of shells across his chest, looking for all the world like a South African mercenary in the Congo. He had prepared for this day long ago, knowing it would come.

"It's a bad plan," said Lonny.

"You either come with me or give me the stone," said Alexis. He clamped his hand over the sapphire and tried to jerk it out of Ali's grasp.

"It's mine!" shouted Lonny, latching onto the chaos of hands.

Ali placed his strong second hand on top of theirs, immobilizing the sapphire on the bar top. "I'll take you to the other side of the bay," he offered.

"Do I have a choice?" asked Lonny.

"Not if you want to keep that stone," stated Alexis.

"Come," said Ali.

The warmth of Ali's callused fingers on the back of Lonny's hand caused him to shudder. The Comorian had poured him coffee when he was hungover, recited the tale of the hippo and the fable of the whale when he was mired in loneliness. They had nothing in common, yet somehow their friendship defied natural logic. Lonny felt ashamed of his city-bred hesitation to venture deep into the Malagasy bush in the face of the old man's persistent optimism.

"Move it or lose it," said Alexis.

Lonny nodded and they let him have the stone.

On their way out the back door Alexis took a backward glance at the nightclub he'd built from scratch. He thought of Bastille Day. His bartenders handed out free beer. The disco was crammed with expats and girls, forty-year-old bureaucrats and their lovelies, the sons and daughters of every Indian merchant and military officer. The DJ was sandwiched in between two women doing a vertical imitation of a horizontal sport. Smiles of pleasure mixed with the odor of sweat and liberated happiness. The music was so loud it hurt and the crowd kept pumping into one another as if the beat would never end. Even then he knew Diego was just another port of call.

11

THE DOCKS

Ali guided the two men away from the Vo Vo, through a maze of footpaths, onto an empty lot that looked like a casualty of war. Thin concrete walls stood castellated against the bright moon, flat corrugated roof panels lay in corkscrewed twists, a trapdoor covered the opening of what looked like a bomb shelter. With the aid of a kerosene lantern Ali led them down into a tunnel where he had once labored. The colossal storm drain was designed by a colonial architect to collect flood waters and channel them to the port. Only the rue Colbert never flooded. The arch was constructed with brick, the sides massive limestone blocks. It cut under the town as mysteriously as the Parisian catacombs.

The milky orange lamp illuminated soldiers' graffiti and attested to common lives lost to a remote corner of the expired empire. Celeste, Ani, Marie-Claire, Sophie, Cecile, Maryam, Betina, Laetitia, Marina, Odile, Beatrice, Yolande, Pascale; the names of different women, some loved, etched into the blocks.

Furry green mold covered the floor like a shag carpet. Large white rats scuttled out of the way. It was like walking through a forgotten corridor of time, as if the men were archaeologists rediscovering a well-known but little documented history of regret.

A full thirty minutes after they entered, they exited the storm drain on a slope behind the tuna fish factory. They continued down the hill past the processing plant, stumbling their way in between immense custom-house sheds and the lighted container park. The tide was beginning to ebb. The night was calm, the air still. They could hear the low thump of the Vo Vo, the rising volume of gunshots and the tinkle of breaking glass.

There was a tramp freighter with a Liberian registration tied to the pier. Below its hulking mass, on the loading dock, a large crowd of men were gathered around an industrial dock light. At first Lonny thought they were holding a rally, but there was a rope hanging from the arm of the light post and it led to the neck of a man with wispy hair.

The mob turned as the three men approached. Lonny was used to walking into huge masses of miners. The sight of so many men gathered together didn't particularly unnerve him. He dealt with unmanageable crowds of curious and sometimes hostile people every day. It was the noose that gave him jitters.

As the mob stepped back Lonny recognized the purple shirt and embroidered gold cross of Bishop McKenzie. Around his neck hung a heavy sandwich board made out of wood. On the front, it read PRÊTRE = TRAÎTRE. On the back, SORCIER—a witch. The priest looked up at the newcomers in wordless misery.

The murmuring mob faced the three strangers angrily. There were four gendarmes leading a mix of dockworkers and custom-house clerks. Most of the men were stripped to the waist in the humid, tropical night. They had batons, sticks and concrete chips from the disintegrating pier in their hands.

The two groups of men were separated by twenty yards. Too far to throw a rock to good effect, but close enough to distinguish each other's features and intentions.

"We have to help the bishop," Lonny whispered to Alexis.

"A little humility might do him good."

"You can't teach a dead man to be humble."

"I have no respect for the man," said Alexis. He

had heard what the bishop thought of both him and the Vo Vo Club. "But I will respect the collar."

The agnostic New York gem dealer, the Muslim Comorian fisherman and the French Catholic naval officer continued advancing until they had were only a dozen feet from the Anglican bishop from Scotland. Not a word was spoken but there was a palpable hate in the air, as if the everyday culture of tolerance and civility that was Diego-Suarez had been peeled back to expose a raw nerve of native Malagasy resentment, jealousy and rage.

Alexis's shotgun was held hip level, pointed straight at the lynch mob. The gendarmes were armed with service pistols. They aimed them at the strangers.

"Let the bishop go," demanded Lonny in French, his voice cracking with the strain.

"Here's the murderer himself," replied the sergeant. Lonny recognized him from the roadblock that morning, a lifetime ago. He was a professional gendarme, not likely to lose his nerve or back down.

"I'm not a murderer," said Lonny.

"I can help you if give yourself up," said the sergeant. The gendarme was impeccably dressed in spite of the late hour and the turmoil of the moment. The round kepi perched on his shaved skull gave him the unmistakable air of authority.

"Let the bishop go," Lonny continued. "He had nothing to do with it."

"A murderer who vouches for a witch," replied the sergeant.

"You have the wrong man," said Lonny. "He never bewitched anybody."

"He did," said the sergeant. "He bewitched the French consul's cook and set a trap for our king."

"Do you know who I am?" Alexis cut in. He slowly extended the barrel of the shotgun so that it pointed directly at the lead gendarme's chest.

"We all know you, Baba," replied the sergeant.

"Tell your men to let the bishop go or you will sleep with the ancestors tonight."

The gendarme raised his hand in a gesture of restraint. The other men were taking their cues from him. If he panicked a number of people were probably going to die right there, right then. The barrel of Alexis's shotgun remained steady. The gendarmes' pistols trembled.

"You have nowhere to run," said the gendarme, aware that his own actions controlled the balance between calm and chaos.

"Back away," commanded Alexis. He swung the ugly shotgun at the mob and they fell back in ripples. The younger gendarmes continued to aim their service weapons at the intruders, but none of them seemed anxious to start a gunfight with the owner of the Vo Vo. He was said to be protected by the spirits. A retired naval officer who had killed many men in the line of duty. A man with a reputation as a champion *morenge* fighter. It was one thing to detain a civilian, quite another to confront an armed man on speaking terms with death.

Ali Mohamed crossed the space between the two sets of men and removed the hemp rope from the bishop's neck. He lifted the grotesque sandwich board off the churchman's shoulders.

The Malagasy hissed at the four strangers.

"Come on," said Alexis. He edged the foursome back out of the circle of light and over to the edge of the pier. As usual there were a number of small dugouts tied to the pilings. Lonny climbed down first, helped the mute bishop, Ali and finally Alexis.

They dug their paddles into the water and escaped around the stern of the Liberian freighter.

"Lord save us," mumbled the bishop, as the workers hurled chunks of concrete at them and the gendarmes aimed their pistols.

"You better pray," shouted the sergeant to the escapees, "that we catch you before Colonel Ratsimanga."

12

THE OCEAN LIKE A RIVER

The Bay of Diego-Suarez was shaped like a ragged three-leafed clover. One leaf created the broad protected cove that stretched from the Pass around Ramena beach to the backside of town underneath Lonny's villa. Another leaf, in its wild and forlorn splendor, blossomed from the opposite side of the Pass and followed the uninhabited contours of the bay until it met Cape Diego. Cape Diego was a spit of land that stuck out into the bay from its western arc and nearly touched the loading docks of Diego-Suarez. Between the port and Cape Diego lay a narrow ships' channel and a protected anchorage. Up past the port there was a third, shallow clover leaf that flooded or flushed swiftly on every tide.

The four men crossed the bay at its narrowest point, the anchorage between the loading docks and Cape Diego. The bracketed channel seemed like a river, the sweep of tide more like a river current than the tug of gravity. Behind them were lights and sound, ahead it was dark and silent.

Ali pointed the bow of the pirogue toward the deserted colonial barracks that lingered over the beach while the younger men bent their antagonistic energy to a new purpose. Ali felt his sinews stretch and creak. The ball of pus in his side rubbed against his arm. He hummed to himself and felt capable and tested for the first time in many years. Ahead of him he could see the prow of a shipwreck and beyond that Cape Diego, dark against the rim of stars.

Lonny's mind wandered while his muscles worked repetitively. He had sensed the presence of the stone at the consulate before he had seen it. He had foreseen the king's murder in the inky depths of his mind before it happened. And he was aware now, as they glided across the vast, tranquil bay, that death paddled with them.

Unlike Alexis, Lonny dealt with bush-bred Malagasy miners every day. He knew how superstitious and unreasonable the peasants could be. The mere sight of a stranger on their land could elicit terror, happiness or greed. Sometimes the contrary emotions erupted simultaneously. He had no illusions. It was one thing to approach a half-dressed, shoeless villager offering up wads of paper money and good feelings. It was something else to approach that same destitute man in want of food, water or shelter. Lonny had witnessed scores of peasants punishing each other without mercy. Denying babies food, burning newcomers out of their huts, cheating the weak out of their possessions. Walking twenty miles across the tip of northern Madagascar was going to be quite a trick.

Alexis had been promoted for thirty consecutive years in the French navy by acting decisively in moments of crisis. He had received the Legion of Honor for pulling a pilot out of a burning helicopter. He had survived two plane crashes, several direct actions against the enemy in North Africa, the South Pacific and the Persian Gulf, and any number of personal conflicts. He was a forceful man by nature and elated that at the age of sixty-four he projected enough energy to unbalance an angry mob.

He had been salting away his profits for years. Between his fat bank account in Paris and his navy pension, he could afford to buy himself a café in Marseilles or Nice. He knew the Vo Vo would never last and he had never expected it to. A foreign businessman in a poor country was in a losing race against the natural elements of corruption, theft and violence. He was lucky it had lasted as long as it did. Slipping away in the night was a hell of a way to go but it beat swinging from a lamppost.

The bishop knelt on the bottom of the pirogue, slowly coming out of shock. The gendarmes had descended on his compound without warning, beating the servants and burning the rectory. Some *côtiers* considered themselves Catholic, some Lutheran, others were professed Muslims, but a true *côtier* was never, ever an Anglican. Before the invasion of the French in 1894, Welshmen from the London Missionary Society had converted the highland royalty while French Jesuits worked over the more pedestrian *côtiers*. When the French government withdrew in 1960, and the highland tribes (now Protestant) dominated and suppressed the *côtiers* (now Catholic) once again, the notoriously democratic Church of England became associated with high-handed bureaucrats and the repressive power of the state.

Bishop McKenzie had been paraded down the rue Colbert twice before. Once after the death of the first president in 1972 and again when the Admiral temporarily lost the presidency in 1995. The first time he had been identified with the black magic of the opposition. The second time with the torturers who kept the Admiral in power. Both times he had been beaten, left in the murderous sun and denied sustenance. Both times he had been considered dead, only to recover and walk among his flock like Lazarus. For these well-known feats he was called a sorcerer. The idol-worshiping and pantheistic *côtiers* denied the Gospel of Christ as the one True Word. They followed no birth to death religion in its entirety, borrowing piecemeal from Christianity, Hinduism, Muhammadanism and Buddhism. Because of their lack of conviction, Bishop McKenzie believed the *côtiers* were easily manipulated in times of crisis, crediting the most far-fetched conspiracies and ludicrous accusations. His ministry had been fruitless. The scattering of seeds on rocky ground. Forty years of wasted energy.

The bishop was surprised at the efficiency of the hatred directed toward him this time around. A noose? For Christmas sake. His pension wasn't much, the Anglican Church of Madagascar was extremely poor, but his mother had left behind a small inheritance in Edinburgh. Maybe his third trip down the rue Colbert tethered like a pet lemur was a sign. Maybe it was time for him to retire and leave the evangelism to less disappointed men.

As soon as the bow touched Cape Diego, Alexis popped over the side of the craft. The moon was so full his exposed figure cast a shadow against the white sand. No lights shone anywhere. Lonny and the bishop followed the navy man onto dry land.

The bishop stood next to Lonny staring back at

the town. He washed his face with salt water and felt reinvigorated.

"I should go back," said the bishop.

"You'll be killed if you return to Diego," said Lonny.

"My flock will need guidance in this time of trial."

"What flock?" asked Alexis.

The bishop chewed that thought for a moment.

"Come with us," pressed Alexis. "We need a guide to Cape Bobaomby."

"Why the cape?" hesitated the bishop. He had visited it several times during his 40-year residence in Diego-Suarez. There was nothing at the cape and only one village on the way.

"We're hoping to find a dhow that will take us to the Comores," explained Alexis.

"The Comores are two hundred and sixty miles away."

"I know it," said Alexis. "But the ocean doesn't scare me and fishermen make the voyage every season."

"We could use your help," said Lonny. Ali was not strong enough to make the trip to Cape Bobaomby and it was rare to find a peasant who spoke French. The bishop knew the way. He spoke the local dialect fluently. He would be a good man to have on their side.

"Who killed the First Rooster?" questioned the bishop.

"Colonel Ratsimanga," said Lonny.

"What if you had given the king the stone like I asked you?"

"The colonel would have killed him anyway."

"I don't believe you," said the bishop.

Lonny refused to accept responsibility for the First Rooster's death. It was like blaming the want of a nail for the ruin of a kingdom. If the king had chosen another horse at the start of the day, or delegated authority to one of his noblemen, or stayed in bed, everything might have turned out differently. If Lonny hadn't awoken that very morning open to the wonder of the world, if other traders had been down the road before him, if he hadn't seen a glint in the corner of his eye, if he hadn't had an accident, hadn't absorbed French on his mother's knee or learned Malagasy from the bishop, hadn't drunk Jaoravo's rum or played cards at the consul's house. There was no end to the circumstances, no beginning to the capricious and interrelated nature of the universe. He traded for the sapphire because of his family background, his training and an emotional failure that pushed him farther from home than he had ever been. His whole life pointed to its discovery. Perhaps the First Rooster's whole life had led him on the opposite course. Without ever knowing it both of them had been heading toward a collision their entire lives, two pilots flying around opposite sides of a mountain the size of the world. Attempting to discover the original cause of the interlaced and overlapping events was as useless as trying to seine salt from the open sea.

"I'm not asking you to believe me," said Lonny. "I'm just asking for your help."

"God will find some use for that golden tongue of yours yet."

"Then you'll lead us?" asked Alexis.

"Why are you here?" the bishop turned on him.

"I lost everything I owned."

"Thank you for saving my life."

"You can repay me," said Alexis, "by showing us the way to Cape Bobaomby." He wasn't enamored with the Anglican bishop, but he realized that an experienced guide would be to their advantage. There were lots of people in Diego—Malagasy, French and Indian—who owed him substantial sums of money. Now that the opportunity presented itself, none of them would object to seeing their largest creditor swing from a lamppost outside the Glace Gourmand or the Vo Vo Club. The faster they made it to Cape Bobaomby the better.

The bishop rolled his head in a circle. These men needed guidance. He could provide it. Whenever two or three are gathered together in His name the presence of the Holy Spirit will make itself known. A priest must minister to those who seek him out.

"It's about twenty miles to Cape Bobaomby," said the bishop. "You need to get off Cape Diego then walk north northeast. I'll take you to the last village. From there you'll be able to see the lighthouse at the tip of Madagascar."

"Are you coming?" Lonny turned to Ali Mohamed, who was still sitting in the dugout.

"No."

"Is there anything I can do for you?"

"Give me money for a glorious funeral."

"Ehh," grunted Lonny. He knew that in the Comoros young men celebrated big weddings, in Diego they celebrated big funerals. Ali wanted to help his family. He wanted his grandchildren to eat meat and gain strength from his passing.

"I don't have any money," said Lonny.

"Give me your ring."

"My ring!" It was so much a part of his hand that he had forgotten about it. His father had given it to him when he graduated from high school. It was fashioned out of 22-carat gold and set with a bloodstone. The soft green chalcedony was inscribed with the family crest and the motto "Truth." Lonny had never understood what that meant, and as he stood there wrenching the solid gold off his finger he understood the family motto less than ever. As if there were only one truth.

"Do not accept less than one million francs."

Ali latched onto Lonny's hand when the younger man slipped the ring into his palm.

"Do you believe," Ali asked finally, "that Muhammad and Jesus are both in heaven?"

"I don't know about Muhammad."

"Eh-ehh!"

Lonny hugged the big man. He loved the old fisherman and could never repay him for what he had done. Ali's children would celebrate his passing more than they respected his life. Once he was an ancestor, a concept Ali neither completely understood nor sanctioned, they would honor him with libations and pray to him for advice. He would die a stranger among the ones he loved, speaking a language and practicing a religion none of them chose to understand.

Lonny pushed the pirogue into knee-deep water then gave it a shove to help Ali on his way home.

"Bon voyage," wished Lonny.

"We will see each other again," said Ali in Swahili.

The old man paddled rhythmically using strength that must have come from his bone marrow. His stroke rose and fell, rose and fell, and before long he had drifted beyond Lonny's vision. The ebb drew him toward Ramena with the blood-warm tide.

"Let's go," said the bishop. He had walked thousands of miles during his ministry. Another twenty wouldn't harm him. Together the three men marched away from the ocean and up onto the shore.

Lonny hefted the sapphire in his hand. The fine white sand squeaked under his sandals like new-fallen snow. He felt free from the constraints of time. The past no longer had any relevance to the near future that awaited him. He concentrated on the moment and all that it brought. The far future did not seem remotely predictable or even destined. Lonny felt the wonder of life open up to him in a way he had never imagined. Like Jaoravo sitting under the mango tree, Lonny lived the moment and found it ever expanding.

13

THE FURTHER DARK

The three travelers crossed the argentined beach and moved hastily through the deserted barracks. The full moon silvered the edges of the palm trees and cast stark shadows across the steep, crescent beach and the vast, lavender-tinted bay.

Cape Diego was the original site of the town and remained the nerve center of the legionnaires long afterward. From the deck of the Officers' Club there were sight lines to the Pass, Ramena beach, Diego town, the old military camp on Amber mountain and the ancient signal post atop Windsor Castle, which surveyed the Mozambique Channel. The French had maintained the barracks on Cape Diego as a citadel if the natives

ever massed. But when they were attacked, it was
not by the Malagasy over land, but by the British
and by sea. The defenses fell on a single afternoon
as kilted Scots mortared the traitorous Vichy.

Into this fort, a neglected monument to mis-
placed ambition, the three men pushed themselves
along at a fast pace. It wouldn't take long for Colonel Ratsimanga to figure out where they were
headed. Across the bay, house fires were starting to
compete with the feeble lights of the town. The
sounds of sustained gunfire and grenade explosions
were clearly audible. Lonny knew the Indian merchants were hunkering down behind their metal
storefront curtains and reinforced concrete walls.
He wondered how the expatriates were faring.
Caught between the gendarmes and the army, they
would lose everything. Their economic power
meant nothing on a night dedicated to settling old
scores. A night of fire, pleading innocents and broken promises.

There was a single white light ahead of the men
and they were drawn to it unavoidably like moths to
a flame. It burned steadily in the black firmament
and they did not know if it was an illusion or a rising planet. As they approached, they suddenly
heard groans, short screams.

A motorcycle lay on its side, its headlight beam illuminating a sheet metal hut set on a concrete foundation. The sounds emanating from the schoolhouse

were fertile with pain. Goose bumps blossomed over their bodies and a shiver of fear shot up Lonny's spine. Screams of rage and agony were overlayed with grunts, slaps and bellows. It sounded as if an angel were giving birth to a devil while two men fought for paternity. Bile rose in Lonny's throat as the scene's outlines became better defined and he stifled the urge to vomit.

"We've got to do something," whispered Lonny.

"Yes," said Alexis. "Keep moving."

The bishop said nothing.

"We've got to stop them," said Lonny.

"How do you know she doesn't want it?" replied Alexis.

"How can you say that?"

"It's none of our business," said Alexis.

"It's none of our business?"

"Our business is survival. Getting to the Co-moros and living to see the light of another day is the only reason we're here."

"But they're raping her," stated Lonny. He wanted to run away too, but couldn't imagine leaving his own daughter in the hands of such brutes.

"We don't know who she is, we don't know who he is. We don't know anything about the situation."

"It's rape," said Lonny.

"What are you prepared to do?"

"Stop them."

"You mean kill," said Alexis.

"What?"

"You'll compromise our escape route." Alexis's first taste of rape had been in Algeria. That delightful, repulsive country. The colonels knew how to win a war and they went about doing it under de Gaulle. The men and women of the Casbah were systematically raped, tortured or maimed. Alexis came to believe that rape was a fundamentally political issue. Rapes would stop when there was social equality between the victim and the perpetrator. Nothing he could do or say was going to change anything over the long term.

"We have to stop it," Lonny said loudly. It was impossible to turn away.

"If you're prepared to kill that man for having sex with that woman," said Alexis, "then do it!"

"But he's raping her," protested Lonny.

"Here's the shotgun." Alexis shoved it distastefully into Lonny's hands. "I'm not going to fix your conscience for you."

The bishop ended their argument by throwing a rock against the tin wall of the shack. It resounded like a mallet hitting a gong. The screams inside the hut temporarily subsided into sobs of grief.

"Well," said the bishop, looking at Lonny. "Are you prepared to defend the weak?"

The metallic weapon sat awkwardly in Lonny's arms. He had never shot a person, certainly never killed anyone. Executing a rapist in America would be unjustifiable, in Madagascar unthinkable. The village would discover this crime and make the criminal recant openly and publicly. The woman would receive a zebu and a village-wide feast by way of reparation. Any children born of this act would be cared for by the man's embarrassed mother. As much as Lonny wanted to turn the rapist into a pink stain, his rational mind would not let him.

In Madagascar murderers were rarely put to death. Neither the judge, the state's prosecutor, the police nor common foot soldiers wanted to bear the weight of another man's destiny. Instead the transgressor was shipped off to a blistering island called Nosy Lava. Forbidden from entering their family tombs, left shackled to logs or handcuffed to their own ankles, they were simply forgotten. The condemned spent the rest of the lives, on earth and in the next celestial one, suffering without respite. Lonny gripped the shotgun ever harder, realizing he had lost his nerve.

"There must be something else I can do," he said, thrusting the weapon back at Alexis.

"Block your ears to the screams."

For the first time in his life Lonny was utterly paralyzed. Disgusted that he knew enough Malagasy culture to let the rape run its course, but not enough to intervene and make a positive difference.

"You're both cowards," said the bishop.

He strode into the school yard and threw more rocks inside the open doorway and against the tin walls of the school until two surprised men emerged. One was the schoolmaster, the other a soldier. The bishop recognized them in the motorcycle headlight and they both recognized him by the sound of his voice. There was only one stranger in northern Madagascar who spoke Antakarana fluently with a Scottish brogue.

"*Shame on you,*" called out the bishop in local dialect.

The men were startled but by no means ashamed.

"*What do you want?*" swore the soldier. "*You damned old sorcerer.*" He buttoned his khaki shorts and swaggered the bishop's direction. He had a general issue nightstick in his hand and was more than ready for a fight.

Ten steps away, beyond the circle of light, Alexis and Lonny held their breath. A confrontation with a soldier was the last thing they needed.

"*Let the girl go,*" said the bishop.

"*She's my niece,*" said the soldier. "*Where should I send her?*"

"*Back to her mother.*"

"*Her mother sent her to me.*"

"*I don't believe it,*" stated the bishop.

"*Are you calling me a liar?*" asked the soldier, edging closer to the bishop with his truncheon raised. The schoolmaster edged farther away, as if he knew something even worse than rape was about to happen.

The bishop stood his ground and it was clear to both Alexis and Lonny the stubborn old Scot was going to be killed for the second time that evening.

"*You wouldn't dare,*" said the bishop. His hands were down at his sides. His feet planted.

The soldier raised the baton and bought it crashing down onto the priest's shoulder. A bone snapped with an ugly hollow sound.

"For the love of Christ!" screamed the injured Scot, sinking to his knees.

Alexis burst from the darkness.

"Enough!"

The soldier turned to face the stranger, uncertain whether to fight or run. The schoolmaster knew. He fled into the night leaving behind both his victim and his brother. The soldier rushed toward Alexis. Alexis raised his shotgun. The soldier paused, evaluating his adversary.

"*Ah zallah!*" said the soldier, wagging his baton at Alexis in the headlight. "*Je vous reconnais, monsieur.*" I know you.

Alexis laid his cheek along the gun stock and the soldier backed away into the darkness.

"You Godforsaken miscreants." The bishop damned them all in the same breath. He knew the amount of energy, time and luck required to receive proper medical attention in Madagascar. If he was able to use his arm again in six months' time he would consider himself fortunate indeed.

Alexis strode into the schoolroom to see if there were more men inside. A naked teenage girl came running out and stumbled off into the bush the same direction as the schoolmaster. She lived on Cape Diego, had never seen a stranger up close and thought the pale-skinned, gray-haired stranger was there to finish the assault.

"Poor girl," said the flustered bishop, unable to soothe her or prevent her escape. He continued on violently, muttering to himself and cursing their situation with words not found in Scripture.

Lonny sat on the edge of the school yard trying to come up with a plan. Two deep cart tracks continued onward beside a line of concrete telegraph poles. Stripped of wire and lacking any purpose, the manufactured poles were an improbable reminder of the development that had washed over the island like a tidal wave before draining into the surrounding sea. They bristled out of the earth like bayonets, sharp and unfriendly. There was no map but in Lonny's recollection of the territory it was another twenty miles to the lighthouse.

"You're not helping matters," Alexis remarked to the bishop.

"A thousand devils on your soul."

"Curse me again," returned Alexis with icy calm, "and I'll break your other arm."

The bishop spat on the ground. It became clear to the man of God that he had landed in this predicament because of mortal fear. In a moment of weakness he had cared more for the preservation of his pitiful life than the Gospel of the Lord. He was not advancing the cause of Christ by running away from Diego. He was not truly helping Lonny or the Frenchman by guiding them off Madagascar. If he had left them alone they would have been forced to rely on the Savior. Through trial and prayer their souls might have been saved.

He had been wrong to accept their help on the docks. His death might have imprinted the lessons of the Bible on the minds of the gendarmes more than another lifetime of preaching. He had not loved his neighbor as himself. He had not offered his whole being to Christ these past few hours. It was a sin of omission. Of deeds left undone. Of sins known and unknown.

"Is there any water around here?" asked Alexis.

"There's water at the village. If you continue north along this road you will be close to it by dawn," said the bishop.

"You're not coming?" asked Lonny.

"I'm going back." The splintered shoulder reminded the bishop of his divine insignificance. It clarified the folly of running from God's purpose. To redeem himself he must confront the unleashed forces of Satan. He must abandon these two sinners and continue with his real mission. He needed to return to Diego-Suarez as soon as possible to mend his bones and gather up what souls as could be saved.

"We can't just leave him here," Lonny appealed to Alexis.

"He's been nothing but trouble since we found him with a noose around his neck," said Alexis.

"He'll be lynched again."

"He gave away our escape route. Now he's cursing our souls to the devil."

"Get rid of the gun," spoke the bishop. His shoulder was beginning to swell. His voice betrayed tremors of pain.

"Why?" asked Alexis.

"He who lives by the sword dies by the sword."

"We'll see about that," replied Alexis. He left the circle of light and began scouting the area.

Lonny gazed after Alexis in dismay. It wasn't his style to leave a man with a broken arm, without food or water, in a hostile situation.

"Don't worry about me," said the bishop, answering Lonny's unasked questions.

"What will you do?"

"The Good Lord will provide."

"I'll carry you as far as I can."

"Tell me, son," said Bishop McKenzie, ignoring Lonny's unrealistic offer. "Do you think it's possible that you are part of something bigger than yourself?"

"Maybe."

"The Arabs call it the will of Allah."

"What does that mean?"

"That we are in the hand of God and no struggle we make can contradict His will."

The high moon was colored like a washed green pear. Its reflection gave Bishop McKenzie the jaundiced look of a man on his way to the grave.

"You believe in Allah?"

"I believe in God Almighty and the voice of His son Jesus Christ."

Lonny had not been in a church since his mother's funeral and avoided the subject of God's existence whenever it arose. What God would let a thirty-nine-year-old woman kill herself? What God would engineer an eight-thousand-mile distance between a man and his daughter? What God allowed women to be raped and men like Colonel Ratsimanga the power of life and death? What God allowed the defenseless to be persecuted generation after generation?

"Good for you," said Lonny.

"The faithless are doomed," responded the bishop.

"All of us?"

"Finished, pulverized, damned to an eternal life in hell."

"Are you telling me that if I don't believe in God I'm condemned to hell?"

"Definitely."

"The word of a man hated by his own congregation," returned Lonny.

"Jesus was so reviled by the people that He was nailed to a cross like a common criminal."

Lonny got off the ground and stared over the low screen of bushes. A murmur rose up across the land like a coming storm. He could make out a vague mob advancing toward the schoolhouse. They were holding lanterns and singing to give themselves courage.

Alexis's shotgun boomed into the air and Lonny saw the lights scatter. There was no time to lose.

"Good-bye, Bishop McKenzie," said Lonny, picking the sapphire off the ground. If the bishop wanted to die in Madagascar that was his choice. Lonny had his daughter to think of. He couldn't afford to let a bout of self-pity color his judgment. He didn't know how close the villagers were, what they intended to do or why. And he didn't want to find out.

"Sapphires belong to God, Lonny. Think about that."

"I gotta go," said Lonny, nervously surveying the moon-shadowed landscape.

Alexis burst into the light.

"Get the motorcycle," he yelled at Lonny.

Lonny righted the motorbike and kick-started it in one smooth motion. The headlight swung away from the schoolhouse and lit up the road. Even with the sapphire in one hand the maneuver presented no problems. Lonny revved the engine and Alexis fired into the air once again.

"May God have mercy on your soul," said the bishop, sinking into shock. He sat in the school yard like a deflated doll, his eyes glassy from the pain.

"Leave him," commanded Alexis. He hadn't shot anyone yet and he wanted to avoid it if possible.

The dirt bike labored to pull the combined weight of the two men away from their pursuers. Lonny steered onto a large concrete field and he realized immediately it must be the old Cold War refueling strip. It was wide and long and utterly smooth. He accelerated, shifted and accelerated until the bike could go no faster. Alexis hung off the back of the bike, one hand on the smoking shotgun, the other wrapped hard around Lonny's waist. Lonny held the sapphire to his chest and bent his knees outward like one of Hell's Angels. Together they hurried west into the further dark.

The smoky yellow fires of Diego-Suarez receded behind them and the stars burned so perfectly bright their distance seemed an illusion. The South-ern Cross pointed boldly to the horizon behind their backs, the seven sisters clustered like a happy family. Orion rotated on the celestial equator, arching over the world from west to east.

Lonny could not see the Big Dipper. The stars of his childhood lay over the horizon and he adjusted his navigation to encompass more recent points of reference. He knew they needed to trace west, onto the larger peninsula, then head due north. They were 14 degrees below the equator. The island lay beneath them to the south and to the north lay freedom. It was a world upside down, where the sky was marked with concrete landmarks and the land was littered with false beacons.

14

INTO THE DESERT

They were over the neck of Cape Diego and well onto the great prow of Madagascar. They were making decent headway, following the well-established cart tracks, putting distance between themselves and the various uniformed men who wanted to kill them, when the back tire of the motorcycle blew out. It was the third time in twenty-four hours Lonny had lost control. This time the bike just slowed and fell over.

Lonny and Alexis lay on top of each other for the moment it took to push off the dead motor-bike. They fell intimately, their limbs entangled like lovers, and separated hastily. They stood clear and looked back to see if there was anyone following.

The sapphire lay on the ground.

"This rock," said Alexis, picking up the gem and tossing it to Lonny, "is the reason I've lost two successful businesses and ten years of work?"

"Give me some credit," said Lonny, catching the stone. "This sapphire is the best thing that ever happened to you."

"What are you saying?"

"You should be thankful I came and got you."

"You self-serving little bastard."

"You'll come out of this richer than you went in."

"That's supposed to make me happy?"

"Why not?" said Lonny.

"You let an entire town go up in smoke for a blue rock."

"Do you think I should have handed it to Colonel Ratsimanga so he could present it to one of the most corrupt dictators in sub-Saharan Africa? What would the Admiral do with the sapphire? Buy another château in France? Use the money to bribe members of the constitutional assembly? Get more land mines to put around his palace? It's not like the man was going to share my discovery with the world."

"And the king?"

"I tried to strike a deal with the king. He tried to rip my head off before the colonel shot him."

"All right," said Alexis. "I don't give a damn about the ethics involved, but I want to know what you're going to get out of this."

"A second chance."

"For what?"

"To see the snow monkeys." Lonny wanted to spend afternoons with Annie watching the funny apes swim in the freezing cold water of the Central Park Zoo, not arguing with Sixth Avenue shysters passing off irradiated gems as European estate jewelry. He wanted to teach his daughter how to pronounce the words on the signs. How to shape those squiggly lines into graphic images, shared memories. The magnificent sapphire could make those wishes come true.

He would never return to the swirl of charity balls. He had no intention of becoming wholesaler to the stars, procurer for high society. Cass's friends and clients couldn't tell an amethyst from a glass bead and they didn't want to either. They purchased things in packs. Grape garnets one year, carnelian the next, spinel earrings with a designer's stamp. Yellow diamonds were the current rage. Blue sapphires were probably out of fashion. Their husbands wrote checks with the enthusiasm of paying the electric bill. Not a one of them had the slightest idea of what it took to bring a gem to market. They treated him worse than a drug dealer or Turkish rug merchant.

"I've never seen a snow monkey," Alexis said.

"Did you ever want a second chance?" asked Lonny.

"There are no second chances," stated Alexis. He was drinking pastis at a café the day his mother, his wife and two sons died in a car crash on the way to the swimming pool. They were all together for the first time in years. He had saved up three months' leave so they could live like civilians. They rented a house in the Pyrenees, went trout fishing, played tennis, hiked the mountains and picnicked whenever they felt like it. It had been a sweet reunion, a second honeymoon with kids and *grandmere*. Georges was ten, Denis twelve, Marguerite forty-nine. They were killed instantly. It had happened eleven years ago but the pain was still fresh.

"If second chances were possible, wouldn't you have asked for one?" said Lonny.

"There is no one to ask."

"I'm asking you." Lonny stared Alexis straight in the eye. A man who hadn't lived in Europe for a decade and carried his disappointments wrapped under a deep layer of forceful living. "I want you to help me get home."

"Why should I help you any more than I already have?"

"We need each other," said Lonny.

"No, we don't. If I leave you for the colonel I'm home free."

"You'll never be able to sell the stone. You don't even know where to begin."

"I'll take a fraction of its real worth."

"You'll never get off this island. You can't speak Antakarana or Swahili. None of the peasants north of Diego speak French."

"Where does your accent come from?" countered Alexis. There was something he had never understood. "I can smell the Pyrenees on your breath."

"It's my mother's tongue."

"She was French?"

Lonny hesitated. They had done business with each other for two years, but they had never been in such a tight spot. They had never faced death together or been forced to confront each other's past. He needed to reaffirm the original reasons for their business relationship. A relationship based on friendship and mutual aid.

Lonny pressed the sapphire against his temple. When examining field specimens he searched for the slightest flaw to give away the internal structure of an unknown mineral. Emeralds encase foreign objects in bubbles; raw corundum derives its hue from alternating bands of color. A conical fracture can indicate onyx, a square break garnet. The Pyrenees was Lonny's best clue to Alexis's thought process.

Lonny did speak French with a slight southern accent, his mother's sole legacy, even though she had claimed to be from Paris after she moved to New York. Because he had grown up in America few French people were able to accurately identify his Niçoise heritage. Alexis's remark that Lonny came from the Pyrenees was more a projection of his imagination than honest intuition. The closest Lonny had ever been to the Pyrenees was the city of Biarritz, where the hills meet the beach.

In Biarritz people took new names after the French Revolution to break the cycle of feudal domination that linked them to a château, a principality or a specific lord. Men created family names like Citoyen, Paysan, Soldat, Fermier. Alexis's last name was Grandmaison.

Biarritz: the jade hills, steel blue ocean, defaced road signs, old farms, schoolchildren wearing black berets. Berets—*Les chapeaux Basques*.

"No, she wasn't French." Lonny drew the sapphire from his forehead and looked his impatient fellow refugee in the eye. "She was Basque. *Euskal Herria*." From the land of Basque speakers.

Alexis rocked back on his heels as the night around them closed in.

"*Euskaldun*," stated Alexis. A Basque speaker.

"*Izena duen guzia omen da*." Lonny pulled out the only other phrase in the Basque language that he had ever learned and always admired—"That which has a name exists."

"*Etxetik*," said Alexis. From home.

"We are cousins," exclaimed Lonny.

Alexis folded Lonny into a bear hug. He did not remember how to speak Basque but the sound of the old language lifted his heart and made him recall the house of his fathers, the tomb of his forebears. His mother spoke to him in Basque before he went to the lycée, where the language and customs of the hills were banned, before his father died, before they moved to the suburbs of Paris and lived in drab apartment complexes. The Basque part of his character was buried inside him like a secret childhood. A place of happiness that existed before the ugliness of the world imposed its will.

Lonny wrapped his arms around the old sailor and hugged him as hard as he was able. Hadn't his years of French history and literature given him the answer like a gift? Hadn't his lifelong, open curiosity for language made him the break he desperately needed in the middle of the Malagasy bush? Can luck be called upon or is it prepared for? His mother wasn't Basque. He had never been to the Basque country. But language is capable of creating its own reality. That which is named exists.

"You're the luckiest man alive," said Alexis. "I always wanted a rich American cousin."

"If I manage to survive Madagascar, you'll have one."

"I'll make sure you dance home with little bells on!"

"Ha!" grunted Lonny. The tension of the exchange and its denouement left him shaking.

"Let's go, partner," said Alexis in a more sober mood. He shouldered the shotgun and checked back the way they had come.

They marched north in silence. The Bay of Diego-Suarez was well behind them, The Mozambique Channel lay to the west, the Indian Ocean stretched endlessly to the east. They could not see the waters that surrounded them over the low barrier of scrub, but they tasted the salt in the air.

It seemed bitter irony to Lonny that he was trekking north. African slaves headed north to freedom from the states of the old Confederacy. They followed the dipping gourd to the pole star, the star which does not waver no matter the spin and tumult of the earth. Lonny shuffled north as well. Except that he was walking north toward the equator, not Chicago. Ahead lay the open ocean, not safe harbor.

The ground was stony and barren. The cart tracks they were tracing, uneven and torturous. If Lonny hiked in the ruts, sharp pebbles pressed against the bottom of his sandals like thumb tacks. If he marched on the hump, prickly tufts jabbed at the sides of his feet. As the tracks wound around contours of the rolling hills, zigzagging across the compass line of demonically straight telegraph poles, the soil changed to sand then clay. His feet blistered. His mouth was parched.

The landscape was barren. A wilderness. A

desert. Not the kind that is natural but something more sinister and depressing. A place where man has come and gone. Hillsides of grass torched to their skeletal roots. The seasonal rains had failed north of Diego. There was nothing but a thin, sooty film covering the soil. The bushes that remained were scraggly and unwelcoming. There were no large trees. A plague of locusts could not have stripped the land cleaner of sustenance.

And yet there was something alive in the small voice of the devastated earth. A boa constrictor lay curled on the track's shoulder. A chameleon swung upside down from a bush, its patchwork color that of the moon-laced shadows. The hoot of a Scops owl drifted in the air like the blast of a foghorn. A Malagasy kestrel flitted from pole to pole hunting the pewter night as if it were day.

As his body fought the land with monotonous repetition, Lonny's imagination grappled with the surrounding sounds. He was a city person and had always been a city person. He had never spent a week in a tent or taken a canoe trip down some frigid Canadian river. His father thought it normal to spend vacations indoors, under fluorescent lights, talking and trading. On business trips to Asia, Africa and South America, the idea of camping in the open had never crossed Lonny's mind.

The night's song teased his mind in new directions. At eye level there were stars that had existed brilliantly for thousands of years and he had never seen them. His first glimpse of the night sky had been a school trip to the Hayden Planetarium. An enclosed space that projected lights and lasers onto a dome above their heads. He left the planetarium marveling at the craft of the show's planners, convinced it was a lie.

How could it be? Lonny asked himself. I have been alive for thirty years and I never accepted the existence of the heavens. Is it possible? How have I come this far knowing only mineral and gem, wholesale and retail, gross sales and net profits, people and paint, books and theories? How is it that I am a father and do not know what to teach my daughter?

He had never intended to get Cass pregnant and once pregnant had argued for an abortion. But now that seven years had passed he understood that Annie's spirit had been meant to walk this earth. She was a divine gift that he had been slow to recognize and too overwhelmed to appreciate. Was God the reason for her conception? Was there really a God?

He wrestled with the presence of the sluggish reptiles, the preying birds and the great bowl of stars. The Milky Way cut across the interstellar void like a band of yellow quartz in a block of speckled granite. The perfection of the night sky and his tiny, painful place in the vast universe dizzied him. As he trudged like a foot soldier into the charbroiled devastation, he was quietly filled with a sense of awe. Overwhelmed by the limpid sky and the tepid air. He felt as if he were staring into the heart of an obsidian diamond so perfectly faceted that it absorbed and refracted the light of his own vision. There was no logical way to comprehend the heavens. Reason and its companions were the wrong tools for the job.

He juggled the sapphire from one palm to the other. It fit solidly into his palm like a piece of sculpted gravity. He was aware of it every breath that he took, cognizant of its heat, its claim upon his energy. Its unfulfilled promise of something better in a world vastly different from the one around him. Instead of a blessing, the magnificent blue stone now seemed like Kipling's golden ankus, a talisman of intrigue. His body fought with the leaden power of the physical world while his mind struggled to grasp the meaning of the stars.

How long had he been walking? When was the last time he ate? His body was in such benumbed condition that it offered no references. As a child his internal clock spun with excruciating languor, drawing out days on the New Jersey shore into endlessly repetitive summers of sand castles, blue fishing and body surfing. The invisible clock beat a tock faster during adolescence but not quite fast enough. He was born with a pressing adult tempo, a 24/7 beat. The sudden lack of a consistent rhythm caught him off balance. He wondered if he had crossed into the purgatory of limbo where the only recognizable unit of time is infinity. The state of being where a person's life is not compared to solar, lunar or geologic movement. It is measured against itself and becomes meaningless.

Alexis had no such problems. He counted off the distance to Cape Bobaomby step by step. He had accomplished so many missions that his mind easily slipped into the gear reserved for emergencies. His senses were alert. His mind active.

They had left Diego at the beginning of the riots. They were hiking down the only road that led to Cape Bobaomby. Therefore, no one ahead of them knew about the death of the king or the riots. It was imperative to stay ahead of the information curve. Once the information overtook them, escape from Madagascar would become impossibly complicated.

There was a sound that Alexis had been tracking subconsciously for some time. It rose then faded away. Like a squad of soldiers running. Or a Jeep climbing and descending the rolling hills. There was another gust of breeze; Alexis relaxed himself for the cooling effect then suddenly stiffened.

"Psssst!" Alexis signaled Lonny.

"What?" said Lonny.

"Chut! Someone's coming."

Lonny looked back down the cart track. He didn't notice anything unusual.

"It's a car."

"Are you sure?"

"I think so."

"Should we hide?"

"No," said Alexis. "We can't let anybody get ahead of us with news of the First Rooster's death."

"Then what?"

"Ambush," said Alexis.

"Who could it be?"

"Either Colonel Ratsimanga or the gendarmes."

"Damn," said Lonny. He had never believed that hiking into the bush was going to solve their problems. There was no place to hide. Nowhere to go. It was easy to find a stranger because the peasants were mortally suspicious of anyone outside their village.

They found a vale where the cart tracks crossed a dry creek bed. The car would have to stop to negotiate the rocks. Lonny lay next to Alexis behind a bush and they waited. Soon a lawn mower–sized engine grew more distinct. A car was making halting progress over the rough track in the dark. Lonny watched the headlight beams fight against the omnipresent night. They jounced and jingled their way forward, swishing from side to side, up and down. It was more like tracking the progress of a zebu with a flashlight taped to its horns than a motorized vehicle.

Alexis held his breath as a Renault 4L drove into their ambush.

Lonny recognized the car from his escapade with Malika that morning.

"It's the colonel," he whispered.

Alexis nodded. He guessed that the colonel had braved deep into *côtier* territory, at night, without scouts or reserves, out of weakness. Alexis had a hunch that the battle for Diego-Suarez might not be going the way the colonel had predicted.

"He's here to make a deal," said Alexis. He shoved the short-barreled, twenty-inch weapon into Lonny's hands.

"How do you know?" Lonny's voice rose on a note of panic. "What are you doing?"

"Cover me," replied Alexis, leaping out in front of the little Renault and standing in the headlights.

The creaking car slowed to a hesitant rest. The soldiers in the backseat peered out at the night like wary tourists. Colonel Ratsimanga opened the passenger-side door and eased himself out. His uniform was crumpled and messy. His shiny boots splattered with blood. His eyes skittish from the reality of battle.

"Where have you been?" the colonel asked Alexis, as if it were normal to find the Frenchman standing on a deserted track, past midnight, miles from the rue Colbert. "You missed the amusements of the evening."

"I don't find anything very amusing about this evening," replied Alexis.

"I heard about your adventure down on the docks," continued the colonel. He stepped in front of the car and waved reassuringly at the soldiers inside. He did not bid them to get out and they did not seem anxious to do so.

"How's the Vo Vo?" asked Alexis.

"*Tsy, tsy*," hissed the colonel. "Burned to the ground."

"Truly?"

"Truly," replied the colonel with a laugh. The Vo Vo had been the scene of a short fight between his men and the gendarmes. After battling them from the *base navale* to the *université*, he managed to corral a dozen of them inside the disco. It helped that they were armed with batons and pistols while he deployed rifle squads, grenades and a heavy machine gun. He offered the gendarmes a choice: surrender or be burned to death. They surrendered. He lined them up on the rue Colbert and torched the Vo Vo as a lesson. "It could have been you," he told the cheerless *côtiers*.

"What are you doing here?" asked Alexis.

"Tying up loose ends," replied the colonel with a satisfied grin.

"How did you find me?"

"Between the gendarmes and the bishop you weren't too hard to track."

"How is the bishop?"

"Does it matter?"

"I suppose not. What do you want?"

"The American."

"I don't know where he is."

"Then you are under arrest for the murder of the First Rooster."

"Me?"

"One stranger is as good as the next."

"Will I get a fair trial?"

"You have your sense of humor," the colonel remarked.

"I don't have the sapphire," replied Alexis.

"I don't care."

"I'm sure we can come to some kind of arrangement," said Alexis.

"You are under arrest."

"There is no logic behind it."

"You will do as I say." Soldiers poured out of the midget car on the colonel's signal.

"There is still time to work this out," cautioned Alexis. "Before someone gets hurt."

"Who will get hurt?" replied the colonel.

"You might."

The colonel drew himself to his full height as he addressed the disco owner. "Come with me peacefully or I will have you tied to the bumper of the car."

"I'm not going with you." Alexis had spent the last several hours congratulating himself for escaping Diego with life and limb. He knew that if he got in the car Colonel Ratsimanga was going to break his bones with a rusty hammer before tossing him down a flight of concrete stairs.

"Do it now!" commanded the colonel. It was the logic of power. The Frenchman would rot in the jail until he signed over his property, emptied his bank accounts and had more money wired from his reserves in France. The soldiers milled in readiness.

"No," said Alexis, confronting him eyeball to eyeball. He had been a real officer in a real military force. Not some kind of third world mafioso directing thugs and terrorizing civilians.

Lonny sprang from the bushes unarmed. "I'll make you a deal."

"Not now!" yelled Alexis.

The colonel swiftly rotated on one heel, stepped forward and kicked Lonny in the balls.

Lonny crumpled, breathless with pain. An electric shock coursed through his arteries and palpitated his heart. The colonel lined up a second kick, to break Lonny's nose and loosen up a few teeth, when Alexis shoved him off balance. The colonel whirled and they faced each other in the weak oblong ring of the headlights.

"*Morenge*," challenged Alexis.

"*Yaa*," said the colonel furiously. He gestured Alexis to come toward him while the soldiers laughed sadistically.

The colonel was ready. A *morenge* match against the disco owner would be a pleasure. The man had a reputation as a champion. He resolved to beat the Frenchman to a pulp, rope both his prisoners to the car and drag them to Diego like trussed boars.

Alexis was unimpressed by Colonel Ratsimanga. It was easy to terrify innocent villagers, to round up unarmed policemen and maul untrained civilians. It was easy to be a killer when you had a gun in your hand and your victims had no recourse. It was cowardly. The colonel was a coward and Alexis had known his type since the housing projects of his youth.

"You're going to regret this," said the colonel, forming a fist with the knuckle out, the traditional Malagasy sign of anger and revenge. The soldiers' attention was riveted on the *morenge* match.

Lonny sat up from his fetal position. His scrotum throbbed, his chest heaved. You're from New York, he told himself. You learned the trade on West 47th. You're not supposed to die in Madagascar. You're not supposed to give up. You're a New Yorker.

The soldiers ignored Lonny as he crawled over to the bush where the shotgun remained hidden. Colonel Ratsimanga had already outmaneuvered him several times in the past twenty-four hours and he wanted to make sure Alexis won the match.

Alexis let the first swing whistle by his face before he stepped in quick as a snake and struck the colonel's kidneys. He had been a black belt in judo before taking up boxing to help pass away the many thousands of hours at sea. The colonel swung again and Alexis whacked him in the face with an elbow. The colonel tried a tackle. Alexis kneed him adroitly, stepped back, stamped on his kidneys. The colonel was wild with rage, the soldiers silent with astonishment.

Colonel Ratsimanga dragged himself off the ground.

"This is your fault." He walked up to Alexis drunkenly. "You are losing. I demand your surrender," as if saying the opposite of the truth could make it true.

Alexis stepped back, in preparation for a final kick, tripped over a rock and fell flat on his back.

"The ancestors are with me," said the colonel. He unholstered a Soviet-era revolver and yanked the trigger.

The first round grazed the Alexis's earlobe at point-blank range. He twisted away, rolling sideways to escape his antagonist. The colonel stumbled crazily behind the spinning Frenchman, firing shots into the pale rocks while the soldiers howled with blood thirst.

Lonny ripped the shotgun out of the bush, centered the metal bead sight on the back of Colonel Ratsimanga's head and pulled the trigger.

The South Bronx street sweeper was loaded with rifled slugs not bird shot. Each slug resembled a Revolutionary War musket ball, except that the modern version was tightly packed into a plastic shell and exploded out of the barrel at three hundred miles an hour. The lead slug blew apart Colonel Ratsimanga's skull like a sledgehammer shattering a pumpkin.

Lonny stared at the space where Colonel Ratsimanga's head used to be. The torso remained erect for an instant, like a chicken with its head cut off, before collapsing on the ground. Lonny instantly realized that he had crossed an invisible line from which their was no retreat. Even if he could give back the sapphire, the soldiers would kill him. Even if he could explain the situation to a Malagasy judge, he would spend the rest of his life on Nosy Lava. There was no longer room for negotiations of any kind.

"Drop the guns!" Lonny shouted at the surprised soldiers.

One cocked the bolt on his assault rifle and Lonny shot him in the chest. It was obscene. Clots of liquid, the crack of bone, the weight of a man falling to ground.

The other soldiers threw away their rifles in a clatter.

Lonny got to his feet to check on Alexis. There was dark blood pooling in his eye sockets where he had been nicked on the forehead. Colonel Ratsimanga's carcass was inert and motionless. The soldiers were staring in a fright.

"It's OK." Lonny bent over Alexis, feeling not in the least OK.

"Thanks," said Alexis. "A couple more shots and I think the son-of-a-bitch would have had me."

"Give up," said a voice from behind Lonny.

Lonny raised himself from a squat and turned toward the voice.

"Drop the gun." It was a soldier with a discarded AK-47 back in his hands.

Lonny swiftly pointed the shotgun at the soldier's chest. "I'm not going to drop the gun. I'm not going to let you hang me. I'm not going to be tortured. I'm not going to Nosy Lava. I won't surrender. Not after what I've been through. No, sir."

The soldier lowered his weapon and sagged toward the Renault.

"*Tsy, tsy,*" hissed Lonny, waving him away from the car with the gun barrel.

The terrified man turned and ran back toward Diego. The remaining soldiers faded fast in the same direction.

Alexis sat cross-legged, with his head in his hands, as if he had a headache that would never go away. Lonny groped in the dark for the sapphire and pulled the stone to his lips. The two men were stuck together now. They shared the bond of life and death. There was no way either of them could ever return to Diego. They needed to keep moving into the unforgiving night.

15

DONIA

The dogs found them first, barking frantically at the bloodied strangers. The two men had walked the warm night through. They were beyond tired and desperate for water. Their dusty legs were tinted red and their feet a mass of blisters. The farthest hill in Madagascar, and the village at its base, were only two hundred yards away when the sun fired the horizon once again and put a torch to the defenseless earth.

The women came upon them next. They dragged the two men away from the circling pack of piebald mutts and pushed them up against the meeting tree in the center of their community. The villagers did not know if the strangers were sorcerers, conjurers or healers. They were careful not to gaze directly at the sapphire lest they bring some curse down upon their heads. The last thing any one of them would have done was touch the mysterious blue talisman.

One woman wiped the dust off Lonny's brow with a sea sponge. Another massaged a fistful of wet leaves across his shoulders. He felt soft and babyish to women used to men with cabled muscles, scarred fingers and rough palms. They giggled over the size of his shriveled penis and swollen testicles visible through a rent in his shorts.

When will it end? Lonny asked himself. Square village huts ringed the tree. They were perched on the requisite seven poles, their roofs thatched with sun-curled banana leaves, the arid soil pounded into a glaze by the tread of bare feet. Loose dogs, goats and chickens mixed with wandering children. What he really needed was a gallon of cold water, a bottle of extra-strength Tylenol and a soft mattress. He didn't suppose there was relief to be found in this far village. It didn't seem like that type of place.

The villagers cherished their squashed mango as much as the first settlers of Connecticut revered the Charter Oak. The difference was that instead of puritanical outcasts worshiping a remote divinity, the inbred, immobile villagers worshiped the tree itself, believing the spirits of their ancestors manifested themselves in the green leaves, the sticky sap and the nourishing fruit. The village existed so far out of the stream of globalization that it could not be considered the third world or even the fourth world so much as another world. A world where the last contact with the civilian government had taken place before the teenagers in the village were born. A world where aspirin was as unknown as the teachings of Jesus Christ, the transfiguration of Shiva, the enlightenment of Buddha or the prophecies of Muhammad.

Alexis slumped beside Lonny in the shade. Rather than growing tall and full like a balanced chestnut, the thick-limbed mango branched horizontally like an espaliered apple. The brooding tree's long, heavy arms were supported by the stems of wild figs growing straight down into the earth as strong as iron lolly columns. The leaves blocked the sun more efficiently than an awning.

"I could use a drink of water," said Alexis, resting the shotgun across his knees. Dried streaks of blood ran down the side of his face. New drops of black blood blossomed at the edges of his makeshift bandage.

"*Is there a well?*" asked Lonny in Antakarana. He knew that village water was usually drawn from the rice paddies, infected with zebu dung and human feces, and he didn't want to add hepatitis, chistosymaisis or some other unrecognizable disease to his list of problems.

"*Tsy, tsy,*" hissed the women. The nearest well

was an hour's walk toward the lighthouse at Cape Bobaomby. As it was a difficult walk when balancing a clay pot on the head and it was taboo to take the path alone or at night, the community siphoned water out of an irrigation channel instead. Children with infected bladders mocked their friends who did not pee bright red streams of blood. The villagers could not conceive of piercing the sacred earth for a new well any more than cloistered monks would deface a sainted cross. The soil belonged to the ancestors and it was as inviolable as the sanctum of a cathedral.

"There's no well water," Lonny told Alexis in French.

"Coca-Cola? Three Horse Beer?" asked the former disco owner.

"*Tsy, tsy,*" the women replied. They had tasted Coca-Cola many seasons ago, when the rice harvest was excellent and the headman had taken it to Diego to be hulled. He came back with several liters of sweet liquid. But they didn't have any soda in the village and they had never tasted bottled beer.

"God help us," said Alexis. "I'll not drink paddy water." He closed his eyes and let the gathered flies settle on his head. His earlobe was torn ragged from the bullet. It hung off his ear like a loose flap of skin.

It wasn't long before the entire village surrounded the two strangers sitting under their tree. Visits to Diego were extremely rare and visitors from Diego were unheard of. Even though the village was only a full day's walk from the provincial capital, there were no cars, bicycles or machines. Nobody owned a gun.

"Why have you come to our village?" demanded the headman in French. He carried a swagger stick, waving it this way and that. Two strangers arriving out of the blue was a malediction equivalent to a drought or a cyclone. Would government soldiers come after them? Soldiers were known for stealing children, draining paddies, raping women.

"We want a fishing boat to the Comores," replied Alexis.

"Then you have not come to our village. You are passing through."

"We are headed to Cape Bobaomby."

The headman translated the reply to the village. He had donned a faded red sash embossed with a hammer and sickle as a symbol of his authority. There was some commotion before the headman spoke again.

"There is a dhow at Cape Bobaomby," he said. "It is ready to leave."

"Excellent!" replied Alexis. "We will go there as soon as we are rested."

"*Tsy, tsy.* There is nothing for you here. Keep walking."

"We need a rest and clean water," said Alexis angrily. It countered the rule of hospitality to deny a traveler a place to stop.

"You have put the village in danger," stated the headman. He didn't know who the men had been fighting or why, but clearly they brought the threat of death with them. It was in their blood, like a virus.

"We ask," said Lonny, "to be your guests for the day." He had not eaten solid food in thirty-six hours, he had been kicked in a tender place and he had marched for close to twelve hours without water. Alexis had been shot twice in the head. He didn't see how they could continue.

The headman considered the request. He was the only resident of the village who had ever lived in the greater world. He had been plucked from the village as a young schoolteacher during the years of North Korean–inspired Communist rule, educated briefly in Antananarivo, then sent back to the bush to explain the principles of Marxist-Leninist Agrarian-Socialism to his uninterested neighbors and relations. The state had never sent any of the promised medical supplies and the postmaster in Diego stole his ridiculously small paycheck. He knew how capricious and unreasoning the state could be. If soldiers discovered the strangers under the meeting tree, they would burn the village.

"It is too dangerous," stated the headman. He feared offending the ancestors as much as the soldiers. The village was built on ground chosen by the ancestors and each family was constrained and channeled by a system of taboos too intricate for rival families to understand. In some families it was forbidden for a sister to sit on the bed of her brother, in others for a baby to eat chicken, fish or avocado. The women of the Joamisy clan were forbidden to squat on the floor while cooking; the men of the Joahauna clan were not allowed to slit a zebu's throat for sacrifice. The whole village believed that if a stranger walked through the rice paddies with an open umbrella the harvest would fail. *Donia*, life on earth, was only a temporary state before true, celestial life began. The invisible and all-knowing ancestors punished taboo breakers according to their own methods and at their leisure. It was always better to do nothing than something, to be passive and avoid controversy than offend the ancestors.

"We will stay until we are rested," returned Alexis.

The headman began translating the insult but several young women shouted him down. The young stranger spoke their language. He had asked for well water. *"Let him speak to the village in the language of the ancestors,"* they said.

The headman faced Lonny and asked him to address the village in Antakarana, but Lonny shook his head. Bishop McKenzie had taught him simple phrases in the local dialect. Beyond the universal greeting ceremony and memorized proverbs, he could only count to a million, ask directions (but not always understand the answer), demand quantities (How much? How many? Where?), request food (Does this village have enough chickens that I might buy one?) and clean water (Is there a well in your village?). Complex negotiations would have to be in French. Lonny knew just enough Antakarana to get himself into trouble, not enough to get out.

"*A hundred tales, a thousand speeches; only one is true,*" prodded the headman. "*I urge you to speak the truth.*"

"*A hundred rivers, a thousand canals; every one ends in the ocean,*" responded Lonny in Antakarana. Formal Antakarana demands an intriguing proverb up front followed by a lengthy explanation. Because of its similarity to Latin and Swahili, where the stress falls on the penultimate syllable, good orations mimicked the cadence of a sermon. He wanted to say that if he could tell them everything they would understand, but he could never explain, the way the bishop could, why the tangle of a hundred lies and a thousand omissions will always lead to the truth. So Lonny simply quoted the one proverb that seemed to fit the situation and closed his mouth.

The headman was baffled.

"*It is better,*" the headman lectured the villagers in the local dialect, "*to meet a sorcerer than a liar. A liar can make a fool out of the most virtuous*

*woman and a weakling out of the strongest man.
How can we tell if these men are sorcerers or liars?*

"Are you a sorcerer?" the headman asked Alexis in French, as he was tired of being made a fool of by the younger man.

"You never know," replied Alexis evasively. The old sailor didn't mind taking advantage of the villagers' ignorance. It might give them currency in place where they obviously had none.

"We cannot force them from our village," declared the headman. *"They will curse us. We must call on the ancestors. They will rise from the earth and confront these strangers. We will ask the ancestors to carry away the spirits of the wicked."*

Even with his eyes closed and flies buzzing around the moisture of his eyelids, Lonny sensed the excitement of the villagers. The rising mood, the way the headman's words drew everyone in the circle closer to him and the tree.

"You are like sick zebu," lectured the headman. *"The poor cannot afford to buy you. The rich want nothing to do with you. You have no place on this earth."* The headman spit angrily at the two strangers and shook his stick as if it were a magic wand that could make them disappear.

"Even the French," said Alexis acidly, "treat Americans better than this."

Lonny wanted to reply but could not. He hugged the sapphire tight to his chest. The rising heat of the morning sun sapped his last reserves of energy and he passed out from sheer exhaustion.

Alexis patted Lonny's arm, huffed the headman a glance of contempt, then closed his eyes. He would have to cut off the remains of his earlobe when he felt stronger.

The villagers atomized into clans. A night with the ancestors required clay pots of rice and rum from the stills. Nourishment would be needed for an entire night of dancing.

The two strangers spent the morning slumped under the meeting tree. At noon they were awoken by old Mama Rosy. She led them to a hut where they ate an enormous quantity of rice topped off with a stew made from spiders, crickets and ants. To help Lonny recover his energy she made him a clay pot of burnt rice water and insisted he drink it. She assured Lonny that rice water was divine, from the ancestors, and would restore his potency. Lonny nodded at whatever she said. The blisters on his feet were so painful that he unlatched his sandals and threw them away.

Alexis took a machete and flicked off the infected portion of his torn earlobe. Mama Rosy wrapped his wounds with healing leaves. She did not believe they were sorcerers. She believed they were normal men. Strangers, full of hidden secrets, but men.

Both Lonny and Alexis ate in a stupor. As soon as

they finished their meal they collapsed under the meeting tree until dark.

Lonny's face was swollen with mosquito bites by the time the evening chill replaced the sun's lingering touch. Drumbeats tapped on his skull like fingers: one two three, *un deux trois, araiky arohe telo*. The sound was dry and sharp. Each smack of a digit against a goatskin hide seemed to have a brief life of its own before disappearing into the stream of rhythm.

The drums reminded him of a celebration in the highlands where the bones of an entire clan had been excavated, rewrapped and honored. He knew the *côtiers* did not dig up their ancestors' bones but appealed to their spirits. In spite of his slightly disorientated state, or maybe because of it, he followed his first inclination. He picked up the sapphire and ambled slowly toward the fluid sound.

Small boys and girls rolled on pathways, drunk off tastes of pure rum. Men were sitting in a place where there was more room between the huts than in other places. Women were spitting drinks into men's mouth's and making lewd gestures with their hips.

Lonny wasn't sure if he was repulsed or fascinated.

"If it isn't the first son of liberty!" bellowed Alexis. He was in his glory, complimenting the ladies in French, making crude gestures with his hands.

His head was bandaged with strips of Lonny's shirt and green leaves. He resembled an escaped lunatic more than a retired naval officer.

"What's going on?" Lonny replied weakly.

"We're waking the dead."

"Is that what they told you?"

"A drop of rum and half these bastards can recite Rousseau. Have a mouthful."

"We need to get out of here before the soldiers catch up to us."

"Bullshit. Without Colonel Ratsimanga the soldiers are useless."

"Lieutenant Rakoto will come after me."

"No he won't. Lieutenant Rakoto can't do a damn thing without orders. And who's going to give him orders? Colonel Ratsimanga is dead. There are twenty midlevel captains and majors. I bet 8 to 1 they're fighting each other like cats and dogs. Not to mention the fact that they're taking on the gendarmes."

"The soldiers will be back to Diego by now. We should leave the village before it gets dark."

"Nonsense. The villagers are putting on a dance for us. Relax, have a drink."

"They're calling up the ancestors."

"Who cares?"

"I don't want to be here when the ancestors wake up."

"Don't believe that boogie-woogie crap. We'll call up our own ancestors."

"It's not funny. I killed the colonel."

"For God's sake, take a load off," returned Alexis. "We're safe."

"I'm not sure about that."

"I guarantee it. Now have a drink."

"I don't want to."

"You'll offend our hosts."

"Nobody will notice."

"I'll notice." Alexis waved to an unmarried villager named Zaina. She was wearing a pair of polka-dotted panties visible underneath a skirt of shredded raffia fibers. Like many *côtiers* with mixed ancestry, she resembled no particular race. She had the wide, full lips of an African. The sharp nose of an Arab. The slim hips of an Indonesian and the round, firm breasts of a European. Her skin was the color of tropical hard wood, smooth and dark, coppery gold in the firelight. From her belly button to her neck she was as naked as Eve.

"We'll raise the dead together, my little deer. What do you say?" said Alexis.

"*Your chicken neck is as soft as a worm*," she replied in Antakarana.

"What did you say?" asked Alexis.

"*Get him some green mango*," the girl yelled to the other women. "*He will need a hand up!*"

"What did she say?" Alexis asked Lonny in response to the laughing villagers.

"*I'll take rum,*" Lonny told Zaina. Alexis guaranteed him they were in no danger and the smooth-faced, bare-breasted woman enthralled his imagination. A drink from her seemed like a reasonable thing to accept.

"*You will feel quite divine!*" yelled Zaina as loud as she could. The other unmarried women, spitting out cane rum on their knees, laughed appreciatively. Lonny recalled it was the custom among wary and superstitious villagers never to accept a drink that was not tasted by the host. But when he felt a warm stream of liquid hit his nose and teeth, he thought, I will die of AIDS. These people will kill me with their diseases.

The spray of pure alcohol made Lonny's eyes stream with tears and his stomach heave. The cane rum was so potent it could have fueled a Peugot. He tried to vomit but his stomach had already absorbed the noonday rice.

The setting sun lit a pale purple fire over the horizon. Another spit of rum and his nerves settled, his fingers tingled. A mauve tint hugged the curve of the earth and seemed to define the limit of human understanding. At the third sip the sky blinked green and shifted across the color spectrum until only the absence of light was visible. Lonny felt like he had been sucked into an alternate dimension of time.

One wall of a hut had been dismantled, opened to the scene. Inside six drummers whacked drums of varying sizes with their palms. The drums were the exact inverse shape of the sapphire. The sapphire bulged in the middle where the twinned crystals joined, the drums were tapered in the middle then bulged out on either end like trumpets. The drummers held the instruments between their knees, or straddled the largest ones, letting the sound shoot out the bottom and resound off the top. With only percussion and rhythm the six men created a whole range of emotion captured inside a nine-beat rhythm: 123, 123, 123.

The headman had arranged a makeshift table of poles near the dancers. He wanted to make sure the strangers' spirits would pass easily into the realm of the ancestors and not linger. They could not afford to sacrifice a zebu, but they had gathered up as much rum and rice as could be spared for a three-day funeral celebration. The space on the table was just big enough for two bodies.

The ancestors called to the living and the new dark aroused dormant passion. Men and women linked their arms around each other's waists in horizontal lines. What clothes the villagers possessed were minimal in the best of times. As the dancers began to move back and forth, ratty pieces of cloth and palm-fiber shirts fell to the earth.

"Would you look at that?" said Alexis. "That's a better crowd than I could draw at the Vo Vo any night of the week."

Zaina took Lonny by the hand and tugged him into the melee.

"Hold this for me," said Lonny. He tossed the sapphire onto Alexis's lap.

"Sure thing, cousin," replied Alexis.

The immediate grip of naked flesh startled Lonny as he joined a zebu line. Hands danced over his hips, back and belly. His left hand wrapped around Zaina's midriff, his right lay across the shoulders of a male peasant his own age. As the drums tapped out an overlapping rhythm the entire line walked forward three steps then retreated the same number. Another zebu line faced theirs and one danced just behind. When they came in contact with either line hands groped in the darkness and quick hip thrusts were thrown in every direction. There was nothing much to it, thought Lonny. Up and back, one two three, *un deux trois*, *araiky arohe telo*. The lines marched in unison like three-stepping Texans.

Old Mama Rosy moved between the lines spitting rum into open mouths. Lonny tried to break out but the hands would not let go. An arm draped over his left holding it down. To his right Zaina interlocked her fingers with his making it impractical to withdraw. There was nothing for it but to keep moving. Struggle as he might Lonny was in for a dance. Nothing short of a fistfight or cardiac arrest was likely to release him from his place.

He struggled to keep his head clear. He took a good look around. Faces were barely hints of the rising moon off bloodshot orbs. Torches flickered at the edge of the confined space. Dark huts and crimson earth absorbed the available light.

Lonny had hidden himself from his sexuality for so long that the music, the impact of flesh and the repetitive hip thrusts overwhelmed his defenses like storm waves breaching a seawall. His adventure with Malika loosened the blocks shoring his defenses and the uninhibited dancing carried them away. He found himself unable to stop his fast descent into the nether regions of physical release. He moved up and back, up and back, no longer fighting the urge to cross cultural barriers and press contact with the villagers. The buttons tore off his shirt. Sweat issued from his pores. His fingers slathered across the bodies of adjoining dancers. Mama Rosy spit more rum into his mouth.

An accordion cut across the bank of drums like a buzz saw ripping through a stand of bamboo. The squealing, pumping rhythm invigorated the villagers like a pealing clap of thunder. Lonny's hips started moving in new directions. His oiled joints felt unhinged. He thrust, rotated, bumped and rubbed his partners in variations he did not know possible. For a brief instant he looked down at himself in amazement, as if he were a spectator and not a participant, then his rational powers fled and his body refolded into the nine beat tempo. One, two, three.

Zaina felt the ancestors rise up through her. They seized her heart and shivered her chest. Everyday worries of water and rice, of demanding parents and hungry cousins, of a womb bursting with fertility and no man capable of planting a tenacious seed fell away. Her breasts hardened, her clitoris swelled. Thoughts of her grandmother, and her grandmother's grandmother, coursed through her in quivers. The ancestors brought her into their line with blessings. They promised to protect her against the jealousy of her sisters and the ravages of bad husbands. Zaina felt herself reincarnated in the body of her own granddaughter, dancing with her descendants, living forever through them. She felt full with the promise of life and the ecstasy of eternity. She did not know if she were alive or in a dream, if she moved of her own accord or the ancestors manipulated her limbs. *Araiky, arohe, telo*.

It was all quite amusing to Alexis. He had danced with Polynesians, Coptic Christians, pygmies, the Jackson Five. He swallowed the rum, moved in step with the dancers and never lost his head. He loved all the zizanie-hula-hula. When the dancing reached a high pitch with the introduction of an accordion, he disengaged himself from the line and went back to baby-sitting the sapphire. He found it mildly jarring that the accordion, so out of fashion in Europe, had become an indispensable part of Malagasy culture. He leaned up against a rickety hut and tapped his foot to the beat. *Un deux trois*, cha cha cha. He had always been a dancer, always liked to dance. It was too bad a well-made accordion lasted several generations.

Hands began to coddle Lonny's aroused cock. Fingers dug into his slick buttocks. He did not try to escape. He moved into the press of flesh. Zaina slid in front of him and he bumped and ground his hips behind her. A pair of hands grabbed his hips and slammed them backward into a muscled pair of thighs. He did not know if he was entering or being entered. He did not know if he was standing or kneeling, falling or swaying. He became one with the eternally isolated villagers. He felt the power of flesh and the elation of creation. He jerked to the pump of the accordion as if he were inside the beat itself, not an individual lost to all who once knew him.

A girl approached Alexis with an odd grin on her face. She carried a charcoal ember in a wire carrier that added a glow to the darkness of the night.

"What can I do for you, little girl?" asked Alexis. She giggled.

"I suppose a bald cat is as good as one with fur."

She handed him a coconut shell filled with palm wine, just as her father, the headman, had commanded her.

"Come onto my lap, little miss." Alexis loosened his belt.

She gestured with the cup and out of annoyance Alexis drank it in one gulp.

"Now come to Papa," he said.

The girl laughed and before he could bend her to his will she escaped back into the lines of dancers.

Instantly Alexis felt a strange paralysis invade his muscles. He attempted to vomit but it was too late. His gag reflex had been suppressed. In a few minutes he would be as rigid as a newly caught fish laid on a wood deck. Death stole upon him without notice. He thought briefly of his comrades who had died in one country or another and he wished there was some way he could warn Lonny. His eyelids were frozen open. He could just make out the shapes of Malagasy peasants dancing under a low moon. He prayed that he would be allowed to join his mother, his sweet Marguerite and the two boys in heaven. The kingdom of glory or the reign of madness awaited. The time for penance had come and gone.

The dancing continued endlessly. A moment out of time and apart from human invention. Dancers collapsing and being hoisted back into line. Whole ropes of peasants hanging on the strength of the creator. Mama Rosy feeding their spirits with squirts of rum.

Zaina pushed Lonny into an empty hut behind the accordionist and the drums. The first ancestor in her family tomb, her grandmother's grandmother, had borne Jao's son. She had seen the pitiful state of her people, led into internal exile by their own weak king, and she felt the need for new blood in her line the way her own grandmother had coupled with a Swahili sailor and the grandmother before with an Arabic slaver. Zaina's maternal grandmother offered herself as a concubine to a French officer until she was full with life and capable of returning to the village with proof of her fertility. Her entire line of ancestors emboldened Zaina to lay the stranger down, straddle him like a washboard and grind him into the floor slats.

Lonny felt as stiff as a maypole as Zaina milled her torso around his convulsive thrusts. He lost whole patches of skin from his buttocks and shoulder blades. He clenched her haunches with the limit of his endurance and she worked him. His body resisted beyond his will. He could not control it any more than he could guide the path of his ranging memories. His mind floated through generations of family history to land upon the age-ravaged face of his paternal grandmother. A debutante. A passionate, careless woman who wore out her youth too fast. He could see her in the Arizona desert riding with the boys of the UCLA polo team. Riding a horse with more vigor than a man, never understanding why her alcoholic brother would inherit the reins of the family business. Tempted by lovers, wed to a jeweler, mother to his father. What are you waiting for? she called to him through the spray of lust.

Zaina had ridden her share of lovers. Some tall, some short. Three different boys from the village and several of the married men. The men appreciated her femininity more than the boys, giving her outright gifts of cash. The boys brought baskets of cassava and letchi but she could gather such things herself. In spite of her past experience never had she felt so aligned to the wishes of her ancestors. It was as if this wooden stranger, summoned by the celestial forces to practice their will, reached a new place inside her. A place where the spirits lived. His bloodless appearance confirmed her beliefs that he was only a reflection of their will, not a real person at all. A materialization of the divine.

Lonny found his head banging against one of the hut's support poles. From the collection clay bowls and burnt vanilla beans that fell over his face he realized with horror he had been pushed into the ancestor's corner. Between debilitating effects of the rum and the physical reality of his battered, naked body he felt he was in a desperate soul struggle with a memory from his past.

"Help!" he called out to Cass, a vision of Cass. She was dressed in a gold lamé halter top and a pair of spotless white pantaloons. She was leaning over her birthday cake, flashing those perfect teeth and that winning smile, showing off her engagement ring. A leafy green Zambian emerald flanked by colorless Namibian diamonds. She looked happy. Happy to be pregnant before she turned twenty-eight. She looked over at Lonny and laughed. As if she were laughing at a good joke. At a cosmic joke. At Lonny.

Encouraged by the stranger's incoherent yell Zaina redoubled her efforts. She opened herself to his vertical axis as if she were dancing on her knees, rapidly shivering to the echo of the drums and the vibrating pitch of the accordion.

Lonny's mother whispered in his ear as he slammed into the corner post on a three-beat rhythm. Her mouth was full of birthday cake. The last birthday cake they would ever share together. It was a mistake, she mumbled drunkenly. If I could do it over again I would take you with me. I didn't realize how much I would miss you. I can't wait to see you again. The pungent scent of vanilla filled

Lonny's nostrils and Lonny realized his mother was eating the same birthday cake as Cass. Vanilla with vanilla frosting. Identical cakes, identical mouths.

"I don't want to die!" protested Lonny as his head banged into the corner pole again and again. He traveled in and out of delirium—the difference between physical reality and the unreality of his strange visions. He reached his hand out to Annie, to wipe vanilla ice cream off her chin. She stood by herself in the middle of a party with no one to take care of her. His feeling for Annie, the vision of Cass and the words of his mother became blurred. He reached his hands up into the dark and toppled his dance partner onto her back.

"I'm alive!" he cried to memories of a dead woman who wanted to embrace her son, to a wife who did not love him and a daughter who did. He drove his shoulders and hips into the hard pack of flesh below him like it was a door that would lead to redemption.

Zaina wrapped her strong thighs around the awakened spirit. Her body began to shake uncontrollably. She squeezed her legs together to heighten spasms that reverberated from her loins in ripples. She gave herself over to the ancestors as cascading waves of heat carried her beyond herself. Pregnant drops of sweat splashed across her face. The stranger burst inside her and she felt his life force pump into her womb like a gift. Everyone was clapping in rhythm. Her maternal ancestors, her paternal ancestors. He would be a king. His name would be Jaojao. The bull, son of a bull. She felt she carried the hope of the world inside her and she was its mother.

Lonny crawled from the hut and lay against its sharp sides. Every muscle in his body was unknotted and elastic. The faces of the dancers remained a wavy blur. The accordion sawed out the unvarying rhythm without a note of fatigue. The moving air reminded him that he was not of the wind but of the earth. Exhausted moans of spirit possession rang in his ears.

A little girl approached him with a coconut shell full of palm wine.

"*M'boulets tsara*," he greeted her.

She held the cup giggling.

Their fingers touched and he stared at her in disbelief and astonishment; he knew better than to drink cat piss on a night made for rum. A cool chill shot down his arm as he took the cup into his hand and lifted it toward his lips. The girl stood against him in the night. He put the shell to his chin and let the liquid dribble down onto his chest while making noisy gulping sounds.

"*Misocha*," he said, and the girl went running back to the headman.

Lonny picked himself off the ground and rejoined a line of dancers stepping to the pattering drums.

There was a commotion when the headman broke the communal trance by holding a flaming palm branch up to Lonny's face.

"What do you want?" said Lonny in English.

The headman lowered the branch and slowly backed away from the dancers. He had prepared the potion in secret, without telling a soul. If the villagers found out that his clan's magic was useless against the stranger they would second-guess his authority. He suspected that the great blue talisman had nullified the effect of his poison, but he didn't dare touch it while the man was still alive to summon its powers. He quickly retired from the celebration to prepare another batch of poison. In the morning there would be other possibilities. The ancestors were watching.

16

BEYOND
THE LIGHTHOUSE

Lonny awoke with the awful feeling that he had forgotten to do something. The fête had lasted all night, or close to it, and spent dancers lined the dirt paths where they had fallen. He was lying next to Alexis in the morbid gray light. Alexis's skin was rubbery and hard to the touch, his mouth gave off the foul odor of palm wine. The sight of Alexis's blank fish eyes hit Lonny like a stun gun.

He could not think properly but knew what had to be done. He reached into Alexis's lap and pried the sapphire from his dead hands in slow motion. His clumsy fingers unclipped the travel pouch from Alexis's waist. He forced his shaking body to unzip the fanny pack and paw through the contents. He found a beet-red French passport, several thick sheaves of 500 FF (*francs français*) notes and ten $5,000 rolls of U.S. bills. He reshaped the cash into pancake-like wedges and divided the money out of habit. He got to his knees and awkwardly shoved three bulging folds in the back pockets of his torn pants. He put another two folds into his left front pocket. He stuffed the sapphire into the nearly empty fanny pack with the remainder of the money and strapped it around his waist. He completed each of the actions as if he were underwater.

A naked toddler pitched unsteadily down the path toward him. Chickens and livestock were beginning to stir in the half-light. A dose of fear quickly cleared the remaining cobwebs from Lonny's dream-like state. He glanced around the village to see if anybody else was awake.

Each hut was aligned with the cardinal points of the earth. The back to the East, the cooking area to the South, the door to the West, and the sleeping area to the North. He had the sapphire and money. The shotgun was leaning against the meeting tree in the center of the village.

The girl saw Lonny moving and opened her mouth, unsure whether to call her mama or scream.

"Shh," Lonny tried to quiet her. He oriented himself to the nearest hut. He needed to go north, to the left. Out the village and along whatever path headed in the direction of Cape Bobaomby.

The girl screamed, "Mama! Mama! Mama!"

Lonny kicked a hen squalling into the air as he ran for his life. There was no time to grab the shotgun. Voices shouted from the interior of different huts. A man lay insensate along the path. Lonny jumped over him and continued the obstacle course. A woman came running toward him. He straightarmed her as she shrieked. In a hundred steps he was beyond the village and into the bush. There was a single wide track that continued the right direction. He flew down it as voices called out.

His bones felt like they had aged years as he put one foot in front of the other. It reminded him of running his first marathon, when every cell in his body was begging him to stop, when his legs cramped, his muscles burned, his gut stabbed knives into his liver.

He pushed himself relentlessly, stubbing his toes on sharp rocks whose tips protruded out of the dry earth like buried icebergs. He was barefoot and bare-chested. Each time he thought he had touched bottom, he managed to go farther, to find a new low he had never imagined.

Lonny jogged unsteadily for more than an hour before the well-traveled path led to a stone trough collecting trickles of water off a high ledge of landlocked coral. He plunged his whole head under the elixir and felt the grit and sand dust loosen. The sweet, limestone water reminded him of what it was like to be somewhere other than in Madagascar, a stranger to the living.

Would they come after him? How long would it take?

When he lifted his head from the water trough, he saw the dramatic 120-foot lighthouse marking Cape Bobaomby aglow with the first orange rays of sunlight. Its brown limestone walls so blasted by buffeting winds they might have been caressed smooth by a million hands. Lonny gazed up the slope leading to the tower with the same wonder prairie town adolescents feel when they stroll the canyons of Manhattan. He was filled with awe that such a tremendous feat of labor and architecture dared to exist. Only an artist, he thought, could have built such a monument in such a forlorn place.

Lonny hiked the slanted tip of northern Madagascar to the foot of the octagonal tower. The entrance to the lighthouse was open, the old steel door guarding the threshold lay on its back. Piles of zebu skulls buried the floor. It had been abandoned as a navigational aid and achieved totemic significance in a culture centered around death and fertility. A pagan temple for landlocked peasants unconcerned with the sea. As a death pole to the moribund French empire, it dwarfed the most lurid fantasy.

Lonny entered the lighthouse and climbed up the interior stairs. The spiral staircase was made of wrought iron, beautifully turned and sculpted. Up he climbed, oblivious to the gaps made by rusted-out steps. Viewed from the sea, Europeans saw the amber headlands as hazards to be marked and avoided. The Malagasy gazed out from that same spot and saw infinity extending to every horizon. They called this numbingly distant end of the earth *bobaomby*, "the place where cows are born." Lonny wanted to see what he could see. To see beyond Madagascar.

He felt the first twinges of vertigo when he stood inside the eight-foot-tall Fresnel lens. Its round sides were made of solid glass clapboards, chipped and cracked by a half century of weather. What remained of the balcony were fragments of steel decking held by cast-iron struts and rock buttresses. Lonny stepped onto the gaping deck and clung to the iron rail.

He could distinguish the hill, the meeting tree and the village several miles to the south. To the north, where the swift currents of the Mozambique Channel collided with the inert mass of the Indian Ocean, a ridge of water curled into a backward C. The constantly collapsing ripple stretched to the end of time. Below, to the west, lay a cove to the Mozambique side of the tide rip. The sun was beginning its ascent, the rays reflecting off the water and hammering into the red island. But clearly, no more than a few hundred yards away, were four Swahili dhows lined up on the sand like fat seals. A fifth stood at anchor in the shallow cove.

With the prospect of salvation close at hand, Lonny closed his eyes and let the breeze blow on his face. When he opened his eyes a thousand startling hues and variations of blue confronted him. Clouds sped by below him as their shadows crossed his face. The sky was below the ocean, the ocean part of the sky. All the blues, the hues, the shades, the intensities, the color values and nuances of a lifetime tried to knock him off his foolish perch. Each patch of blue was an entire color in and of itself. The world seemed like a giant sapphire rainbow and he frozen inside its cornflower blue resin.

He took refuge inside the gigantic lens but was just as disoriented. The wavy silica trapped him like a specimen in a jar. A paramecium or a blood platelet suspended in antifreeze. The red soil of Madagascar swung up beneath him and the blue ocean pressed down from above. Instead of a beacon of safety, the lighthouse was a trap: a familiar-looking object that was as different from the lighthouses of his youth as he was from the boy who had once held his mother's hand on the way to church.

He had traveled the length and breadth of Madagascar, stayed in dank concrete bungalows and crammed inside kidney-knocking bush taxis. He had seen mass starvation, men neck-deep in the sewers of Antananarivo groping for minnows, the festering limbs of the condemned. For two years he had traveled to the thorny deserts of the south, down the silt-laden rivers of the west and into the psychedelic forests of the east, purchasing kilos of colored stones without so much as a hangnail. He had supposed that the gift of languages, the knack for making new friends and a healthy dose of independence had been the keys to his self-preservation. But his sense of cosmic entitlement was profoundly shaken by the sight of Alexis's corpse. It created a void where there had been self-assurance, and emptiness tilted him off balance.

When the nausea and the seasickness subsided Lonny crawled down the stairs as warily as an aye-aye. Back on the trembling earth he peered into the sapphire. He held it in front of him so that it would capture the light the way it had that moment, two mornings ago, when he'd bought it from Jaoravo. It is all because of this? Lonny asked himself. He held the stone, his Planck length of wonder, in the palm of his hand and stumbled onward like the survivor of an airplane crash. For all its glory the largest, most precious sapphire he had ever seen was but a timid reflection of the heavens.

17

THE SWAHILI

Lonny stumbled down the slanted headland to the bluff overlooking the sandy beach and the protected cove. His toes resembled mashed sausages. His head pounded from the dehydrating effects of the rum. He pushed himself onward as if that last five hundred yards were the final mile of the New York Marathon.

Swahili crews were scraping trails of algae and moss off the wooden hulls with sharp shells, pounding rags soaked with shark oil into the seams of their lateen vessels, preparing for their voyage back to the Comoros. There was a fifth dhow anchored in waist-deep water. Its open hold was stowed with dried fish. The sail was freshly patched with rice sacks, two plastic water jugs were fastened to the aft rail and there were cooking pots stashed in the triangle before the mast. The front quarter boards were carved with elaborate swirls and painted white. Eyes in the shape of crescent moons were affixed near the bows.

Acres of fish wallpapered the rocks near the beach. They were split down the middle and left to cure in the sun. Occasional douses of salt spray preserved them for the voyage. Lonny took a deep breath of foul stink and worked his way across sharp boulders, odd-shaped ledges and over the fish themselves to get down to the beach. His soles left bloody marks on the sand.

"*Salam alekem*," Lonny cheerfully greeted the first Swahili sailor he met.

"*Alekam salam*," responded Abdallah.

"I wash your feet," Lonny continued in Swahili.

"I let you wash them."

"Good trip?"

"Very good."

Abdallah stared at Lonny. The Swahili are a practical people and they speak a practical language. The sailor regarded Lonny as an *mzungu*. A white. A skin color. No more, no less. There were rich whites and poor whites, dumb whites and clever whites, helpful whites and cheating whites. It had been a long time since he'd heard a white man speak his language. Abdallah waited for the white to reveal his intentions.

"Where is the captain?" Lonny gestured toward the readied dhow.

"Why do you need him?"

"I am a traveler. I want to travel to the Comoros."

"Which island?"

"Mayotte."

"He is not traveling to Mayotte."

"I will change his mind."

"No, you won't," said Abdallah, looking over the lean traveler. He had met dozens such men, hitchhiking their way across the oceans, thinking trips in wooden dhows across treacherous expanses of ocean were an adventure. These backpackers rarely had much sense or money.

"Where is the captain?" repeated Lonny. There were twenty or thirty men working on the other boats just down the beach. They were shifting their eyes his direction.

"I am the captain," replied Abdallah. He was a short, powerful man who used his head as well as his back. He had three wives, fifteen children, a house in concrete and a farm on the island of Anjouan. He liked to take reasonable chances but not tempt the hand of Allah. He fished hard and he fished well. His dhow was always the first to leave the fishing grounds off Cape Bobaomby each season.

"*Parlez français?*" tried Lonny. He wanted to express himself more fully in French.

"*Non français*," retorted the captain. The four islands of the Comores, as the French called them, had been a French colony until three of the islands had voted for independence in 1975. He had gone to lessons, he had learned about "*nos ancêtres les gaulois*." He could converse better than most American college students in *la belle langue*, but he remembered the Moroccan teacher who beat him when he mistook a *le* for a *la*. Swahili is a gender-neutral language. How is a small boy ever supposed to know that a house is feminine and a boat masculine? It made no sense. He refused to speak French to the *mzungu* because the language brought back ugly memories.

Lonny debated switching to English but held back. He didn't want to reveal more about himself than was absolutely necessary.

"OK. *Sawa*," replied Lonny. Ali Mohamed had spoken with him at length in Swahili. They had traded proverbs, spoken of each other's families, joked, punned. If he opened his soul to the language, memory would carry him.

"*Kahawa?*" demanded Abdallah, mocking his pronunciation.

"*Sa-wa ka-ha-wa*," rhymed Lonny, letting his humor overcome his fear. He laughed as he made his phonetic pun and Abdallah grinned. The men working on the dhows didn't seem particularly in-

terested. It was the end of their short season in
Madagascar. The wind kept changing direction and
they had work to do before their voyage home.

"The dhow is ready to travel," continued Lonny
in Swahili.

"With the tide," replied the captain.

"I want to travel to the French island called Mayotte," said Lonny.

"I'm a fisherman," said the captain. "Not a
ferry."

Lonny waded a few yards through the tepid water
to the dhow. The salt water pierced his jagged
wounds like needles but he gave no sign of the pain.
The boat had a spindly mast slanted forward, a lateen sail unfurled to shade the fish from the first sun
of the day. On the stern there was a weather-beaten
twenty-five-horsepower engine.

"I'll pay for a new engine," proposed Lonny,
bouncing from foot to foot. "A forty horsepower."

"You don't have enough," said Abdallah. The
captain was not impressed by the *mzungu*'s claims
of wealth. What did he have besides a supple
tongue and calm, direct eyes? He was skinny and
exhausted.

Lonny pulled a fan of paper money out of his
front pocket. He waved it at Abdallah like toreador
taunts a 2,000 pound bull with a red cape. He knew
it was a dangerous thing to do, a good way to get

thrown over the side of the dhow when they were on the open ocean.

Abdallah strode into the ocean, snatched the money and counted it very slowly. Lonny looked over at the sailors. The men looked across the cove at him.

"Why do you want to travel to Mayotte?" said the captain.

Lonny took out Alexis's passport and showed the red cover without letting Abdallah touch it.

"I'm French," said Lonny. "Mayotte is French. I am a Frenchman who wants to go to French territory."

"It is not enough money," said the captain.

Lonny unzipped the fanny belt, withdrew more packets of French francs and handed them over.

The captain counted the bills again, very slowly and deliberately.

"This," said Abdallah, holding up the money, "is adequate."

"Let us go," said Lonny. He climbed over the stern of the wooden dhow and sat inside the vessel. There was a small afterdeck, just big enough for the helmsman and two or three others. Between the afterdeck and the mast, there was an open cargo hold stuffed with dried fish. The wooden planks were joined together by dowels. The ropes were made of twisted sisal and hemp. Except for the pintels joining the rudder to the stern post, there wasn't a scrap of metal on the whole vessel. It felt good to Lonny, the way a boat should feel. He didn't dare wait until the villagers, Lieutenant Rakoto or the gendarmes from Diego caught up with him. He wanted to be out on the ocean, sailing into the wild blue yonder before any of them discovered he was gone.

"Hurry has no blessing," quoted Abdallah.

"There are bandits following me," said Lonny.

"Who can attack us?" Abdallah made a sweeping gesture that took in the forty sailors and the four other dhows.

Lonny lunged for the cash and managed to get good grip on some of it. "We leave right now or no deal," said Lonny, hanging precariously over the stern of the vessel.

Abdallah tried to tear the paper money out of Lonny's hand, but the American held tight. A five-hundred-franc note ripped in half.

Abdallah frowned at the fistful of cash they were fighting over. Somehow he knew it was not going to be as easy as it seemed. They would be sailing against the tide. He wanted the high water to float them over the reefs and sweep them away from Cape Bobaomby. If they left now he would have to use the engine and there was precious little fuel left after a month of fishing 250 nautical miles from the Comoros.

"It's no good," said Abdallah.

"Are you a cheat or a captain?" demanded Lonny.

"I am the captain," replied Abdallah, defending his honor. "You hired me."

"We go?" asked Lonny.

"*Sawa*," said Abdallah.

Lonny released the money. He sat on the after-deck restlessly, waiting to see what would happen. He couldn't stop the spasms wracking his legs. If the captain called for his crew, they could be sailing in a few minutes. If the captain decided to steal his money then leave him behind he wasn't sure what he would do next. It depended on how closely he was being followed and by whom. He had no way of knowing.

Abdallah yelled for the crew. Six lean fishermen disengaged themselves from the others. They were hard from a diet of fish, their curly black hair bleached a tint of red due to the blinding rays. The men gathered around their captain and he discussed Lonny's haste openly.

"What is your word?" the captain asked the crew.

"We go!" replied the crew. They were men used to reacting quickly to new situations. The *mzungu* was a good catch. They were fishermen. They should take their bounty and run for home. The captain was a frugal man, but what was a liter of gasoline compared to a new forty-horsepower engine? They could motor through the reef then hoist the sail.

"*Sawa!*" said the captain. They had been on Madagascar for nearly a month. Living in the shadow of the boats. Gutting fish and telling stories. At home were wives and children, girlfriends and cousins.

The crew shouted to their fellows and the other sailors came up the beach. The captain explained the situation to the gathered men. They waded into the ocean to rock the dhow off the sand and push her into deeper water. Once the keel broke free, the crew climbed aboard the laden vessel and began poling across the cove toward the coral reef. The helmsman started the engine and bucked the incoming tide. The crew leapt to the lines and hoisted a long boom to the top of the short mast. A triangular sail hung down off it. The dhow was sluggish, wallowing against the swirling currents of the cape. Between the poles, engine and sail they barely made it through the gap in the boundary reef.

"Fantastic!" exclaimed Lonny. The sail was patched in so many places, with so many different kinds of material, that it looked like an Appalachian quilt. As it filled with wind he felt free of Madagascar. He had the sapphire strapped to his waist inside Alexis's fanny pack. Nothing lay between him and Mayotte except the open sea.

"They are killing us!" shouted a sailor.

Lonny spun around as tiny waterspouts erupted between the dhow and the land. A squad of gendarmes lined the bluff, firing their pistols indiscriminately. The dhow was about three hundred yards out and gaining momentum. The gendarmes must have left Diego the night before. The sight of the colonel's body, followed by the discovery of Alexis's corpse, probably delayed them a few hours.

"They're too far," said the captain.

The contrail of a rocket-propelled grenade arced out from the beach and headed directly for the wooden dhow. It sounded like one of the model rockets Lonny had built as a child. The white contrail grew longer as the rocket zeroed in on the vessel. SSSSWWOOOSSSSHHH!

The RPG punched a small hole the size of a shark bite through the thin sail and continued another five hundred yards. It exploded with a geyser the height of Old Faithful.

"God is great!" shouted Abdallah. He made an obscene gesture toward the gendarmes.

"Amen!" said Lonny, too stunned to say anything else. He touched the place on his forehead where the bishop had made the sign of the cross. The wind continued to push them farther out of harm's way and the helmsmen increased their speed. A flap of loose material snapped against the otherwise taut sail. The vessel slipped the lee of the Grand Island and rolled heavily through the swells.

18

OFF MADAGASCAR

Abdallah tried to avoid eye contact with Lonny but found it hard to stay angry at the *mzungu* with a fresh wind at his back, a hold full of fish and a following sea. The dhow scudded along on a permanent broad reach. The wind came over their aft quarter at a forty-five-degree angle and the men slept in the shade of the single great sail. The dimpled brow of Madagascar slipped over the horizon like an indolent crocodile.

A truck full of gendarmes and a rocket-propelled grenade added up to more than a band of thieves. Abdallah blamed the traveler for endangering the dhow, yet he knew he should have refused the sugar-tongued *mzungu* the moment he walked down the beach. He had risked his vessel and crew by coveting an engine he did not need.

That evening the lookout spotted a sea turtle and hooked it with a large gaff. They cut the bloody flesh into hunks and feasted on the red meat. Lonny felt like he was witnessing the dissection of the last mastodon at an Explorers Club supper, but he was well past moralizing his fellow man. He ate quietly and slept beautifully on the wide stern boards near the tiller.

Lonny awoke the next morning to the blast of an air horn. The crew was alert and agitated. A black inflatable boat, filled with armed white men, was three hundred yards away and approaching at full speed.

"*Légionnaires français*," said Abdallah.

In his panic to get off Madagascar Lonny had not given much thought to what lay beyond. French naval ships stopping in Diego supplied a penal company of legionnaires on a group of forlorn atolls named *Les Iles Glorieuses*. Lonny had just discovered their location. One hundred nautical miles west of Cape Bobaomby, a hundred and sixty miles east of Mayotte. A brigade of disposable, antisocial delinquents serving out their enlistments as far from the general population of France as geographically possible.

If it was a routine patrol, the legionnaires would

want to question Lonny about Alexis's French passport. If he threw Alexis's passport overboard, he wouldn't have any papers whatsoever. The Comorian fishermen were neutral, but a white man traveling without proper documents toward the politically volatile, coup-prone islands would trigger an immediate reaction. And if the French were actively searching for him at the behest of their consul in Diego, he was in real trouble.

"Hide me," said Lonny.

"You motherless crab," swore Abdallah.

The Swahili captain grabbed Lonny by the arm and forced him over the far side of the dhow into the ocean. Lonny grasped for a trailing line as the fanny pack dragged him under. The crew ignored him. They were on the other side of the hull gesturing wildly at the no-nonsense legionnaires. The dhow slowed noticeably as Abdallah spilled wind from the sail and the motorboat latched on.

"Where is the American?" Lonny heard a voice demand in French.

"Is that a fish?" responded Abdallah.

The boat dipped as a boarding party searched the vessel. Lonny let himself trail behind the stern until he was hidden beneath the tiny outhouse. He let go of the rope and grasped the inside of the wooden toilet seat.

"Where did you come from?" demanded a legionnaire.

"Mahajunga." Madagascar.

"Where are you going?"

"Anjouan." The Comoros.

"Why are you so far off course?"

"Bad wind," replied the captain. The French lacked legal jurisdiction in either place.

The dhow was only drifting at one or two knots but Lonny didn't know how long he could hold.

"We're looking for an American," the legionnaire said one more time.

"Good luck!" laughed Abdallah, gesturing at the forlorn sapphire sea, the complete absence of other vessels or islands.

"Dirty bitch." The legionnaire slapped Abdallah across the face.

The wooden dhow rose as the legionnaires transferred their weight to the inflatable. Lonny knew they weren't going to give up that easily. He worked his way over to the rudder. He exhaled three times, took a deep breath, then used the rudder post to pull himself underwater. Water-survival techniques were a requirement at boarding school. He swam around the rudder until he was under the dhow itself, wedged against the bottom of the hull like a barnacle. He would drown if he stayed there longer than thirty seconds.

The bottom of the speedboat dropped behind the dhow, lingered, circled the stern slowly, then swept around the bow and accelerated. Lonny blew bubbles out of his lungs until there was nothing left. He tracked the prop whine as it disappeared into the wide ocean.

He let go of the rudder post and floated out behind the dhow.

"Here," croaked Lonny. The helmsman tossed him a line and the Swahili fishermen hauled him aboard like a kingfish.

"Why didn't you say you were American?" demanded Abdallah, in French, the moment they laid Lonny out on the small afterdeck.

"You going to throw me back?" returned Lonny, gasping for breath.

"What did you do?" asked Abdallah.

"I killed a soldier."

"A plain soldier?" demanded Abdallah.

"A colonel."

"Ahh," said Abdallah. He translated the conversation to the crew. The fishermen nodded and clucked their tongues. It was murder to kill a soldier doing his duty; it was political to kill a colonel. Any group of Comorian men who had survived forty governments in twenty-six years understood the implications.

"Will the French be looking for you in Mayotte?" asked Abdallah.

"I don't know," said Lonny.

Abdallah shook his head in disgust.

"I agreed to take you to Mayotte," said Abdallah.

"I know."

"Do you have more money?"

"No."

"What's in the waist pack?"

"A stone," said Lonny. It was an all or nothing gamble. He no longer harbored any doubts that Abdallah would push him overboard. "You want to see it?"

"You are more trouble than you are worth," replied Abdallah angrily.

"I feel that way myself sometimes."

"A deal is a deal."

"Yes, it is," said Lonny.

Abdallah refused to speak with Lonny for the rest of the journey and Lonny was careful not to rile the captain any further. He confined his gaze to the ocean vista and caught sight of humpback whales standing on their heads. Their horizontal tails stuck out of the seascape like billboards lining the West Side Highway. Two nights and three days later, on Friday, five days after he had purchased the sapphire, the dhow entered the grand lagoon encircling the low rounded hills of Mayotte. They came in through the *Passe en S* and headed directly toward the gap between the main island and that known as Petite-Terre.

Mayotte was administered by France but claimed by the three sister islands of the archipelago that made up the Federal and Islamic Republic of the Comoros. On Mayotte the population consisted of native Mahorias ruled by white French bureaucrats posted from Europe. French legionnaires provided the muscle to keep everyone in line. The complicated political situation was the result of repeated colonial mistakes and history's profound disinterest.

Petite-Terre was a small island off the island of Mayotte. The French kept their administrative and military offices isolated from the general population. A ferry plied the sea between the administrative center and Mayotte, much as a ferry used to ply the bay between Cape Diego and Diego.

As they neared the yacht anchorage on the main island Abdallah told Lonny to jump.

"Closer," protested Lonny.

Abdallah bore down on the tangle of luxury yachts bobbing in the lagoon. When he was in the thick of them, he shouted to his sailors and they heaved Lonny overboard with roguish good cheer.

"Bon voyage! *Safari njema!*" Lonny called out sarcastically from the safety of the salt water.

Abdallah made his second obscene gesture of the trip and turned his back. The fishing dhow continued on, nearly spearing a half-million-dollar megayacht with its long mangrove bowsprit.

Lonny swam to the ferry landing. His pants stuck to his legs, his fanny pack dribbled sea water. There was a young Mahorias woman soaking her ankles who followed Lonny's progress with some amusement.

"Friends!" said Lonny cheerfully in French by way of explanation.

"They must not like you," said the woman. Her face was painted with a yellow daub that Mahorias women use to keep their skin healthy.

"They don't," said Lonny. He fished a wet 500 franc note from his pocket and begged the young lady to buy him some shorts, shirt and sandals. To his surprise, she not only agreed but actually returned with the clothing and a receipt. Mahorias maidens were used to the pranks of young men and took their antics in stride. She obviously enjoyed Lonny's distress. Lonny offered to buy her a coffee but she just laughed and sauntered away.

Lonny decided it would be best to hover below the radar screen, not risking a phone call or E-mail. He had six thick folds of dollars and one sheaf of French francs. He was back in the developed world, or the pre-independence colonial world, and he wasn't sure what that meant in the year 2000. The roads were reasonably well paved, electric wires hung overhead, a few brightly colored, recent model cars cruised some of the streets. He ordered a cup of tea at a waterfront café and noticed several of the French patrons drinking alcohol. The Mahorias served them grudgingly; the French treated them as if they were mentally handicapped. It never occurred to the bons vivants that serving alcohol on the Muslim holy day was the equivalent of masturbating in a church pew.

Lonny strolled down the oceanfront boulevard overlooking the yacht harbor. He had $30,000 to make his next move but it needed to be a quiet one. Three hours after Abdallah and the crew dumped him inside the grand lagoon, Lonny found just what he was looking for. A small American flag snapping from the port stay of a forty-two-foot yawl. He borrowed a dinghy from the landing and rowed out to the moored vessel.

"Ahoy there," shouted Lonny.

No response.

"Anyone aboard?" he shouted again.

"Who wants to know?" came the reply in English.

"The IRS," said Lonny.

A head immediately popped out of the companionway.

"Listen, my man," said a middle-aged yachtsman, sizing up Lonny. "You about gave me a heart attack."

"I've been looking for a guy like you," replied Lonny. The man was suntanned and weathered. The boat seemed well kept and well used.

"Why's that?"

"I'd like to make you a proposal."

"Where you from?" asked the sailor.

"The Big Apple."

"You're a long way from home."

"Don't I know it."

"Come aboard," said the other American. "I'm always open to interesting proposals."

Lonny grabbed a stainless steel stanchion and climbed onto the gleaming white deck. His toes were healed after three days of sea air and didn't leave any marks. The cabin top was trimmed in teak, the wood oiled and rubbed to a soft glow. A tarp was stretched across the cockpit for shade. It reminded Lonny of a liqueur advertisement in a society magazine.

"My name's Rob Hunnywell. People call me Fishy."

"That's perfect."

"Would you like a cold Coke?"

"You don't know how much that would mean to me, Fishy," replied Lonny. He followed the other man belowdecks and found himself seated at a varnished dining table. The interior resembled a well-appointed apartment on Central Park West. Understated and assured with a million-dollar view.

"A boat like this must rent for a tidy sum," said Lonny. He felt socially awkward after five days on the run.

"Six thousand dollars a week on Martha's Vineyard," returned Fishy. He wore his auburn hair in a ratty ponytail. His shorts were bleached from the sun, his eyes red from smoking too much marijuana. Nobody in Oak Bluffs would recognize him now. A middle-aged bond broker gone hippie.

"I like that," said Lonny. "A man who knows the worth of his labor."

"I maintain the boat. Why shouldn't I know?"

"Hard to make that kind of cash around here though."

"Impossible."

"I suppose French tourists might want to charter with an American," Lonny got up a head of steam. "But the French won't have it. They keep the jobs for themselves. Make you fill out all kinds of paper-work."

"In triplicate," agreed Fishy.

"You working your way around the world?"

"Trying to."

"How would you like to make Vineyard rates for a few weeks?"

"Come again?" Fishy was caught off-guard. He had woken up to a nice breezy day. He was thinking about rolling himself a joint, playing the guitar, maybe inviting one of the French boys over for a cocktail.

"I'll offer you five thousand dollars a week to take me to my next destination."

"You smuggling something?"

"Me, myself and I."

"Are you for real?" asked Fishy.

"I'll have that Coke now," returned Lonny.

Fishy handed him an ice-cold can of Coca-Cola.

"Tastes good in a can," said Lonny, studying the navigation aids. The single-side band radio, the Global Positioning System, the weather fax, stacks of charts piled on a bunk. The black elixir bubbled down his throat deliciously.

"Different than in a bottle."

"You said it."

Fishy reached into the yacht fridge and grabbed himself a beer.

"What's this all about?" he asked. His fellow American didn't look or act like a tourist. He was a man in trouble who might bring more trouble. But then again Fishy had been sitting inside the lagoon for weeks, racking up mooring fees, contemplating a liquor run to Grand Comore. He could fit a hundred bottles of whiskey in the bilge. Each bottle would bring a $50 profit on the Islamic black market. The truth of the matter was that after fourteen months at sea he was flat broke. He didn't want to return to life with a tie around his neck. He hadn't found a solution either. If he didn't do something soon he was going to lose the yawl.

"Fishy," said Lonny. "How did you make the money to buy this yacht?"

"I had an opportunity to participate in a stock offering and I took it. I didn't do anything illegal."

"If you had passed up that opportunity, would you be here?"

"I might be. Who knows?"

"Think about what I've offered you," said Lonny.

"Why's that?"

"Two reasons. First, it's an opportunity that won't come twice. Second, it's a chance to do a good deed."

"What's my good deed?" asked Fishy.

"Helping a fellow American."

"You get somebody pregnant?" asked Fishy. His fellow American was definitely easy on the eyes. Girls would go crazy for a man with his physique and attitude. Boys too.

"Yes, I did," said Lonny. "I handled it very badly but I'm going to make it right. Now, do you want to make five thousand dollars a week? Or you want sit here staring at this stupid lagoon for the rest of your natural life?"

Fishy guzzled the beer.

"How many weeks would we be sailing for?"

"How long does it take to get to South Africa?" countered Lonny.

Fishy pulled a tube of English Admiralty and French Marine charts off a bunk. He spread them across the center table.

"We could gunk hole down the western side of Madagascar. It's totally unspoiled."

"I'd rather not go there," grimaced Lonny.

"How about Mozambique? The folks are supposed to be dynamite."

"Can't we go somewhere without people for a while?" said Lonny. "Just sail on the ocean?"

"I know where you're coming from," said Fishy. "A little too much civilization can crowd you if you're feeling fragile."

"That's it," said Lonny.

"How about a nice long jaunt up to the Aldabra Group?" Fishy pointed to some uninhabited atolls due north of the Comoros. "Then we stock up on supplies at a neat place in the lower Seychelles." He pointed to an island several hundred miles from the first destination. "Finally we make a long sea leg around Mauritius, La Réunion and southern Madagascar. If we batten down, we'll make it in three weeks. If we take it slow, six weeks."

"Let's take it slow," said Lonny. In six weeks things would cool off considerably. Anyone tracking him would assume that he had died, been murdered or was back in New York. Nobody would suspect that he was reading books and eating grilled fish on a yacht in the middle of the Indian Ocean. "I've got plenty of time."

"Sounds like fun," said Fishy, extending his hand. "What's your name?"

They left Mayotte that evening. Lonny lay inside a sail locker when a customs officer completed a routine check. He spent the next few weeks aboard the glistening, well-stocked yacht cooking, sleeping and dwelling on his escape from Madagascar.

He could not renegotiate with the First Rooster, reason with Colonel Ratsimanga or bring Alexis back from the dead. At each juncture it seemed to Lonny as if things might have gone some other way. If only he had been a different person, Madagascar were Montana, the moon were made of American cheese. His head got wrapped in such a tight knot of contradictions that he decided to let the whole thing go. Nobody, not even himself, knew the truth of the matter. Some days, when Fishy was snorkeling or sleeping, Lonny took out the magnificent sapphire and polished it for good luck.

The thought of seeing Annie again made the monotony tolerable. He spent whole days thinking up plans for summer vacation, like taking her to Mexico so she could improve her school yard Spanish. He even allowed himself to dream of Annie as a confident young woman on her way to college. When she was older he looked forward to showing her the world. The museums of Europe, the gem mines of Australia, small cities and towns away from centers of power.

Six weeks and thousands of miles of blue water cruising after they left Mayotte, they cleared the Cape of Good Hope. They left behind the warm waters of the Indian Ocean for the cold Atlantic. They arrived in Cape Town after dark and tied up on the waterfront below the spectacular, American-style mall that dominated the harbor.

After their voyage together in isolation they didn't have much left to say. Fishy had gamely argued theories of modern art and French literature ad nauseam. Lonny had read every book on the yawl and learned to plot their position using a sextant, a noon sight and Greenwich Mean Time. They needed each other and got along well enough to complete the voyage without incident.

"I'm going to take a walk around the city," Lonny told Fishy. He wanted to get away from the harbor before any customs or immigration agents made their appearance.

"Good luck," said Fishy.

Lonny snuck away from the sturdy vessel and wandered unmolested into the glowing city.

19

ROUNDING
THE CAPE

Cape Town is the last great colonial city in all Africa. The elegant whitewashed villas of Mogadishu have been reduced to rubble; the fine seaside promenade in Luanda broke under waves of terror; Nairobi sprawls as mundanely as it ever did. Yet the former Cape colony, gone native for more than a decade, retains its original air. Real highways are awash with miles upon miles of flowering agapanthus; the yacht club is lined with varnished sailboats; the cable car running to the peak of Table Mountain departs on schedule. The botanical garden showcases a thousand brilliant varieties of native African flowers that surpass description. Nelson Mandela, imprisoned for a life span within sight of the city lights, made it his home. And like all renowned colonial-era cities it hosts a grand hotel named after a venerated hero of the empire. A place where hardened voyagers met up in Victorian splendor before rounding the Cape of Good Hope to confront the desolate reaches of Antarctica, the grasping masses of India, the parched Australian outback.

Saturday evenings were slow at the Admiral Nelson Hotel. The change of government, rising crime rate and sinking fortunes of the South African Rand led to an empty lobby. But there were standards to uphold and the general manager would have summoned the police at once if it weren't for something so steady and calm in the visitor's eyes. The man's hair was stiff with dried salt, his face deeply bronzed, his gaze so piercing it frightened the desk clerk. Former guerrillas become cabinet ministers had that same look. They had been tested, proven. They had seen their own lives come and go. They were no longer afraid of living.

"I'd like a room," repeated Lonny.

"But you don't have any identification. Not even a credit card." The manager glanced distastefully at the lumpy, grimy fanny pack in Lonny's hand.

"I've been robbed," said Lonny. "This isn't my country. I'm from New York."

The Swiss-trained Sikh instantly lit up. He reached into a desk drawer and withdrew a photo of Lonny in his Columbia days.

"Are you Mr. Cushman from New York?" asked the turbaned manager, studying the picture.

"Yes," responded Lonny, caught out, unsure what the identification meant.

"Your father has been searching for you." The manager delivered the news as a matter of public knowledge.

"My father?"

"Yes, sir, from New York, sir. I believe he is in Johannesburg or Durban at the moment."

"I need a room."

"I'll ring your father," replied the manager. "There's a cell phone number here. I'm sure I can get him on the line." The manager turned over the photo and began dialing without further discussion.

"It's ringing, sir!" said the manager. He indicated a private phone booth across the lobby where he expected Lonny to pick up the telephone.

Lonny whistled irritably as he walked across the plush lobby to the mahogany-paneled phone booth. The other guests, an elderly South African woman wearing a string of black South Sea pearls and a pair of tourists waiting for a horse-drawn buggy, hustled out of his way. After seven weeks on the run Lonny had not expected to bump against his father's tentacles within five minutes of making himself known.

Lonny picked up the trilling phone and shut the glass door of the booth behind him.

"Hello?" said Lonny.

"Lonny, is that you?" said Cal Cushman.

"With whom am I speaking?" asked Lonny.

"Your father!"

"What do you want?"

"The embassy in Madagascar told me you were a missing person."

"Do I sound missing?" asked Lonny.

"Do you have the sapphire?"

"I'm holding it in my hand."

"Prize ribbon blue? Starry night? Twinned crystals?"

"Right to the bottom line, eh, Cal?"

"Don't do a thing. I'm in Johannesburg. I'll handle the South Africans and broker the sale."

"This is my stone," said Lonny. For the first time in his entire life he felt equal to his father. He had made the journey off Madagascar alone and back in the world he felt free from the old constraints. It was just like that.

"Are you out of your mind?" said Cal.

"I'll sell it on my own terms."

"I've got a client."

"How's Cass?" countered Lonny.

"Look, I'm sorry," backtracked Cal. "She filed for divorce. I hired a lawyer to represent us."

"What do you have to do with it?"

"My granddaughter's involved."

"I want you to stay out of it," said Lonny. He felt

completely out of place in the plush surroundings of the five-star lobby.

"You can't expect to go away for two years and come back to the same place," said Cal.

"I was only out of communication seven weeks."

"A lot can happen in seven weeks."

"Yes, it can."

"Will you meet my client?"

"Will you let me handle the negotiation?"

"I'm not sure you're up to it," said Cal, back to his old self. "This guy's very shrewd."

"It's my stone."

There was an unusual silence on the other end of the phone and Lonny knew his father was wrestling with his temper.

"Nobody changes my blood pressure like you do."

"I am going to sell the stone my way," said Lonny flatly. "Either you can have a piece of the transaction or you can stay out of it. Your choice, Cal."

"It's your stone, Lonny."

"Then how much should I ask?" continued Lonny.

"He's good for ten million dollars. He claims the sapphire used to belong to his great-grandfather."

"Is he Malagasy?"

"He's an Arab."

"Are you sure about this guy?" asked Lonny. "I'm here without a passport, a South African visa or hard cash. What if he tries to have me arrested?"

"I'll contact the American embassy to get you a

passport. I'll send over someone from the South African government to clear your immigration status. You sit tight and meet the client. If everything works out you'll have a passport and a visa by tomorrow morning."

"I need money," said Lonny. He knew that if Cal gave in on this point their father-son relationship had moved into unexplored territory.

"A jeweler in Cape Town will drop off a hundred grand."

"You mean it?"

"This is your show," said Cal Cushman.

"Great," said Lonny. He hung up the phone and slid open the door of the telephone cabinet in a daze.

"May I escort you to your private cottage, Mr. Cushman?" asked the bed-rumpled assistant manager. A front-desk clerk was busy typing in his reservation. The general manager had left to deal with other problems.

Lonny nodded wordlessly. In one phone call he had been transformed from desperate fugitive to expected guest. He didn't know that his father had spent the last seven weeks searching the continent for him, contacting every jeweler, gem trader and hotel manager within five thousand miles of Diego-Suarez.

Inside the plush, private cottage Lonny stripped off his clothes and let thick streams of steaming water blast layers of salt grime from his body. He had learned that fresh water was a precious commodity on a forty-two-foot sailboat. He put the sapphire on the bottom of the shower stall and gazed down at it. A tree branch rustled outside his window and a brooding sense of vulnerability overtook his calm. He called the head of security and demanded three armed guards posted outside his room. He couldn't afford to slip up this late in the game.

By sunup he was dressed in a conservative gray suit, his hair washed and styled, his ragged beard shaved clean, his skin and fingernails manicured to a glow. Lonny knew full well what was expected of a salesman. As a boy he had sold T-shirts and magazine subscriptions, traded stamps, coins and baseball cards. In college he cut his teeth on textbooks, CDs, vintage cars, paintings and diamond engagement rings. Anybody can buy a gemstone, only a professional can sell one for a profit.

As the sun rose brilliantly he sat alone at the private pool, sipping iced tea under the shade of a parasol, thumbing through a stack of European celebrity magazines. The first person to arrive at a quarter to eight in the morning was the jeweler. His son had attended NYU and he was happy to do Lonny a service. His terms were a 2 percent delivery charge and 5 percent daily interest. He left the money at Lonny's feet in a calfskin briefcase.

About 10 A.M. as Lonny enjoyed recent copies of his favorite New York tabloids, the bellboy announced the arrival of Peter Mbeki, Minister of

Home Affairs for the Republic of South Africa. Lonny stood up to greet the short, muscular African. He had no idea his father had enough clout to summon up a person of the minister's stature.

"Pleased to meet you," the minister greeted Lonny expansively, as if he were a distinguished invitee on a state visit.

"It is an honor to meet you," replied Lonny. He ordered a bottle of Johnnie Walker Black Label whiskey from the bellboy. He was no longer an outsider peering into Africa. He understood the terrifying power of a high-level cabinet minister. The man could confiscate the sapphire from him as easily as expelling a breath.

"You know Africa well, eh?" asked the minister.

"I try to conform to local custom."

"It's best for all concerned."

"Yes," said Lonny.

"You have some sort of problem?" asked the minister, moving directly to the point. He lived in Cape Town and stopped over at the request of a prominent member of the diamond cartel. Even on Saturday morning he was impeccably dressed in a three-piece suit with a yellow silk tie and Italian leather shoes.

"A very small annoyance," returned Lonny. "Hardly something a man in your position would be concerned with."

"Anybody may come to me," replied the minister. "From the poorest squatter to the richest American tourist."

"Yes," said Lonny.

"This is a democracy. I am here to help every people, black, white or colored, overcome the inherited bureaucracy of my country."

"Yes," said Lonny.

"Some things require a quiet word with the right person. Other issues can be quite time consuming and costly."

"Yes," said Lonny. He lifted the briefcase off the ground and showed the minister the contents.

"We are still finding our feet." The minister gestured toward the money contemptuously. "We don't want to be like the other African countries paralyzed by corruption and backwardness."

"South Africa is a great country," returned Lonny, closing the case and putting it next to the minister's chair.

"Tell your friends South Africa is a good place to do business."

"I will, Minister. But at the moment I seem to have lost my passport and visa. I cannot prove I entered your country legally and I don't want any problems with the police."

"A visa? It's just paperwork," replied the minister dismissively. "A polite businessman such as yourself would not stay at the finest hotel in our country if he were a criminal."

"Thank you for understanding," said Lonny.

The minister grunted but he did not seem in a hurry to go anywhere. He did not inquire any further into the circumstances that found Lonny in South Africa without proper entry documents.

"Have you seen our leopards?" inquired the minister.

"On a previous voyage."

"You have been to my country before?"

"Colored diamonds are my father's specialty. I used to accompany him on purchasing trips."

"I have been to your country as well."

"Did you have a chance to visit New York?"

"Obviously. Seattle, San Diego, New Haven. All the important cities. My daughter earned a doctorate at Yale."

"Congratulations, Minister!"

"And to you, Mr. Cushman, for living in such a splendid place."

The minister sipped his whiskey with pride and they both regarded the obscenely clear water in the swimming pool. It could have slaked the thirst of an entire village. A striking woman in colorful South African wraps strode across the grass and accosted the silent, self-satisfied pair.

"Leonard Cushman?"

"That's me," said Lonny, rising, staring into a face he had been sure he would never see again.

"I can't believe you're alive," said Malika. In the

wake of the riots she had spent nearly four weeks in Antananarivo trying to cobble together an official version of the events. It was frustrating, thankless work and she had threatened to resign from the Agency if they didn't take her off the mission.

"Malika!" Lonny said warmly. "May I introduce you to my guest?"

"I was spending the weekend at Stellenbosch"—she ignored his overture—"when the American ambassador in Johannesburg contacted me. He wants to know how a troublemaker and a thief like you got into his country."

"His country! We're all your niggers, ehh?" asked the minister.

"This is the Minister of Home Affairs for the Republic of South Africa," said Lonny neutrally, surprised by her rancor. "We were just having a drink."

"Oh!" Malika regarded the minister with a mixture of surprise and suspicion. "Mr. Minister, I didn't expect to see you here."

"What is this ridiculous costume you're wearing?" The minister turned in his seat to glare at her. "You're not South African. You're not even African."

"I don't see how my clothing has any bearing on the situation," replied Malika.

"Did you bring my passport?" asked Lonny.

"No!" stammered the unsettled CIA officer. She was supposed to identify Lonny and report back to the embassy. She had not planned on running into a minister. "We have a notarized deposition from your father, a copy of your birth certificate and a photocopy of your previous passport. The embassy will confirm you are a U.S citizen."

"Wonderful. It's my preferred status."

"But"—the budding diplomat recovered her poise and remained true to her purpose—"the embassy wants to know how you entered South Africa. The ambassador must ascertain whether any host country laws were violated."

"I am an American citizen in need of an American passport," replied Lonny. He ignored the seductive body encased head to toe in native South African garb. It was clear to him that she wasn't there to help. "My past problems should have no bearing on the present situation. However, if you need to know, my presence in this country is entirely legal. Will you confirm that, Minister?"

"Certainly. The government of the Republic of South Africa confirms that Mr. Cushman is a visitor in good standing."

"There," smiled Lonny. "You have the word of the minister himself. All I need is my passport."

"The ambassador in Antananarivo had a report that you were being pursued by the Malagasy military authorities. Was that a false report?"

"If I knew who took the report maybe I could straighten out the situation," replied Lonny.

"I did."

"Then this must be the consular visit you promised me in Diego."

Malika's caramel cheeks turned a shade of ebony at the memory of abandoning Lonny to Colonel Ratsimanga. In her shame and confusion she turned on the Minister of Home Affairs. "Is the minister willing to send me a letter confirming his statement?"

"If you are saying my word is not good enough I will protest your inebriated and offensive remarks to the Secretary of State!"

"Sir, I don't drink alcohol."

The minister, who had begun life as a diamond miner, swallowing rough stones and protecting his belly from knife thrusts as he ran to the latrine, did not tolerate contradiction very well. He threw a full tumbler of whiskey into the diplomat's face.

"You positively stink of alcohol!"

Malika unraveled her orange torso wrap and used it to wipe her face. She balled the thin cotton wrapper into a soggy mass and threw it at the minister's feet.

"I will accept the minister at his word," she said.

"I'm sorry it has come to this," said Lonny

"I'm surprised you made it as far as you did," she retorted, as if his early death in Madagascar would have saved everyone a great deal of hassle. The opposition coalition had crumbled with the assassination of the First Rooster. The constitutional assembly had been dissolved. The American ambassador was in the process of being transferred from Antananarivo to Bujumbura, Burundi. The Admiral was back in charge and he hadn't bothered to send aid to Diego-Suarez following the riots. Any hope of truth or reconciliation was gone until the next round of donor negotiations.

"Your passport might take a few weeks," she added.

"You owe me one," said Lonny.

"I don't owe you a damn thing."

Lonny hardened his eyes. Then speaking slowly so she could feel the intent behind every word, he said, "If I don't have that passport by noon tomorrow, my lawyers are going to sue you and your employer in federal court for official misconduct."

"Screw you," said Malika. The man was threatening to blow her cover while caught in the act of bribing a foreign official.

"And screw this corrupt, pathetic excuse for a democracy." She leveled a blast at the minister. She walked backward a few steps, then turned and stumbled across the grass. She hated herself for seducing Lonny, she hated her job and most of all she hated Africa and everyone in it. If she had joined a law firm in Chicago none of this would ever have happened. A group of waiters jumped sideways as she swore at them and strode unsteadily toward the exit like a wounded lioness.

"Bureaucrats!" declared the minister. He rose and shook hands with Lonny.

"I apologize for the unpleasantness, Minister."

"You're a lucky man, Mr. Cushman," said the minister, picking up the case of worn hundred-dollar bills. "As a courtesy between old families I'll give you forty-eight hours to leave my country before I have you imprisoned."

Lonny ordered a hamburger, french fries and a Coke as an early lunch. The taste of red meat and fried grease was a pleasant reminder of American fast food. Yet it felt strange to eat alone. He picked up the phone and called Cass. It was seven hours earlier, 4 A.M. New York time, when he got through to her cell phone. She was in a yellow cab returning home after a night on the town.

"This is Cass."

"Hi, it's Lonny."

"I thought you were dead," said Cass.

"You're the second person who's said that today."

"What are you doing?"

"I'm on my way back to New York."

"Why are you calling me?"

"I thought I'd give you some warning before I showed up."

"Why would you show up? You ruined me."

"The role of the tragic young bride hardly suits you." Lonny voiced the words and regretted them at the same time. He closed his eyes and forced himself to slow down, to stop himself from saying something irreversible.

"You cheated on me."

"Yes, I did," said Lonny.

"You wanted me to have an abortion."

"That was my mistake."

"You're a son-of-a-bitch."

"We are legally separated," Lonny said. "I hope you can forgive me for the past."

"I filed for divorce."

"It's not about us. I'm coming to New York to see Annie."

"I'll get a restraining order."

"I have a right to see Annie," Lonny continued calmly.

"What's wrong with you?" asked Cass. "You sound different."

"I want to be a father to our little girl. I'm sorry for everything else."

"You should be," said Cass.

"I want joint custody. I'm willing to work with you or fight you."

"See you in court," said Cass.

"I'll be there," returned Lonny. "You can count on it."

He was startled by the emotionless bleep as Cass cut the conversation short. He hadn't expected things to be better simply because he had returned from the great unknown. He gazed at a neon blue kingfisher poised over the wind-ruffled pool. Gone was the drama of survival for its own sake, the *morenge*, the *salegy*, the midnight sailing. He still had to fight for Annie. Still.

Evening descended like a familiar friend while Lonny completed his travel arrangements. Whether or not his father's client chose to honor their appointment, he intended to leave South Africa before the minister's deadline. He strolled over to a trellis of cascading morning glories tinted with the night's first dew. They were hanging in ropes from the roof of a neighboring cottage.

"They are splendid in the morning," remarked a voice in the half-light.

Lonny breathed deeply before turning. He sensed a connection to the stranger like a magnetic current.

"Seyyid bin Seyyid, at your service." The man held both his palms together and inclined his head. He wore a plain white kanzu and a red-and-white-checkered head scarf that looked like a tablecloth swiped from a cheap Italian restaurant. Two black cords embroidered with gold and silver encircled the piece. The whole thing sat low and tight on his head as if it were a helmet.

"Leonard Cushman, at your service." Lonny returned the bow. "Have you come for the sapphire?"

"Yes."

Lonny ushered the man into his secure cottage. He asked the hotel guards to wait outside and the men did what they were bid with stolid reluctance. The sheik wore a ceremonial dagger prominently displayed at his waist. The sheaf was encrusted with rubies, emeralds and diamonds. It had a priceless rhino horn handle, like a museum piece, but a real blade. The guards left the door open so they could monitor the situation. The beefy Afrikaners' paranoia appeared to be their sole redeeming quality.

Lonny unlocked a steel closet with a key hanging around his neck. Next he punched in an electronic code and opened a miniature hotel safe normally used to keep traveler's checks away from the maid. He unwrapped the sapphire from its chamois cloth and placed it under a xenon desk lamp atop a white felt pad.

"God is great!" exclaimed Seyyid in spite of himself. He held the stone under the light and let the dazzling color bathe his fingers. Like the sapphire miners who sold him rough, Lonny studied the man's face, not the stone. The sheik obviously knew what he was looking for.

"It is just how they said," continued Seyyid, almost unaware of Lonny.

"How is that?" asked Lonny. He too had been overwhelmed at first sight. It was a costly error.

"It is the true stone. The Vision."

"Whose vision?"

"Let us talk," replied Seyyid.

Lonny locked the sapphire back into the safe, installed the armed guards, then led the sheik back into the evening shadows and around the lighted swimming pool where they both sat on bar stools. Together they examined the halo of light creating a dome over the glassine water.

"It is said that contact with the Vision produces second sight. The ability to foretell the future."

"Perhaps 'feel' the near future is a better description," responded Lonny, his emotions finally put into words. How had he known that Jaoravo would sell him the stone? The First Rooster was going to die? That Alexis was Basque? That Fishy was the right man to get him off Mayotte? Was it coincidence? Luck? Destiny? Or had the stone helped him discern the near future through a fog of possibilities? Nothing could be proved, nothing repeated.

"Yes," replied the sheik, pleased with the correction. The sheik spoke with an American accent perfected at the Harvard Business School. The knowledge of similar vocal sounds, a common grammar and identical vocabulary words made their communication easy. Although their conception of honor, legality and justice were diametrically opposed, the American language provided them with common ground.

The Vision was the prize of Zanzibar in the days

when the sultanate of Oman stretched from the harbors of Muscat to the rivers of Mozambique. It was stolen from the royal palace in 1856, days before the death of Seyyid bin Seyyid, the greatest sultan ever to reign. A man who sent slave caravans across the continent to the Congo. With the stone missing and the heirs divided, the British ripped the sultanate in two. Eventually the English outlawed the slave trade, assumed control of the island and colonized the mainland. The throne had never recovered from the theft of the Vision.

The scrolls described the sapphire in exact detail and Seyyid bin Seyyid had no doubt whatsoever as to its legitimacy. There had been rumors that the stone had been smuggled to the Comoros. The sheik did not know how the Vision had been transferred to Madagascar, nor how it had been lost beneath a mango tree for most of that time. Yet now, only a century and a half later, it had resurfaced on the open market. In time to change the destiny of Oman once again.

Lonny knew better than to ask the sheik how much he would pay for the sapphire. He must set the price, but like Jaoravo he wanted more. He wanted to chaperone Annie's first-grade class on field trips. Buy her stuffed animals and compliment her on self-portraits made out of macaroni. He wanted to be the father his father never was. He wanted to be present when she needed him, a warm hand to push the button at crosswalks and hail yellow cabs in the rain.

Seyyid bin Seyyid laughed grimly to himself at the downfall of his uncle the sultan, known throughout the kingdom as "the Fist." His cunning, severe uncle who had conceived heirs through invitro fertilization. A man who could not bear the touch of a woman and claimed to rule a people. Once Seyyid bin Seyyid owned the sapphire the royal family would rally to him. Paratroopers would toss his uncle out the door of a helicopter. Nothing would be remembered of his reign in a few short years.

The Vision had been known inside the sultanate since antiquity. It had left its specially constructed palace to voyage to Zanzibar on the trade winds, in the robes of Seyyid son of Seyyid. The sultan had taken the stone with him to impress the importance of Zanzibar on the minds of his subjects. More wealth flowed into the sultanate during those times than any other in their entire history. With the death of the great Seyyid bin Seyyid and loss of the Vision, Oman had dissolved into tribal warfare and the sultanate had contracted to its original boundaries. Only in the last thirty years had military victory, duty-free shops and free trade zones invigorated the Islamic kingdom. But now something else was needed. E-commerce threatened the viability of airport malls. The next sultan needed to invest in the people, in grammar schools and universities. An educated populace would be the salvation of the realm. Once the new Seyyid bin Seyyid kicked his uncle into the sea the floodgates to knowledge would open. He would be an enlightened sovereign who instilled confidence and loyalty in his people.

"How much do you want?" asked the sheik, far too anxiously.

Lonny sipped iced tea while his guest drank fruit juice. The neatly trimmed cottages and perfectly mowed grass seemed surreal. Something to be encountered in the opulence of Palm Springs not surrounded by the great thrash and tug of Africa. Above him the chiseled face of Table Mountain rose like a displaced version of Mount Rushmore. Beyond his sight the ocean swirled around the tip of the continent. A verdant, lovely spot contested by all who ever laid eyes on it. Because of Madagascar he was aware. Because of Madagascar he was awake.

"I want 100 million dollars," said Lonny.

Tears of disbelief welled in the sheik's eyes. "Think of the poor who will suffer to meet your demands. The mothers and fathers who will be stripped of their livestock. Allah the merciful have compassion on my people!" The sheik appealed directly to heaven.

Lonny gazed at the sheik. The Arab's soul seemed at peace, his tears real. A man who did not mind crying in front of a commercial adversary if it would bring him a commercial advantage. If Cal had been present he would have said, "Another buyer, another liar."

"I am sorry for your people," remarked Lonny.

"Your father will sell me the stone for a tenth of that price." The sheik dabbed at the corners of his black eyes with the hem of his robe.

"My father is only acting as an agent in regards to this sale. The sapphire belongs to me. I'd rather throw it in the ocean than haggle."

The sheik regarded Lonny intensely. The American's inflexibility reminded him of the mujahideen. Warriors who took an oath to die for a holy cause. "This sapphire must have cost you a lot, Mr. Cushman."

"You'll never know."

"I have a brownstone on the Upper East Side," said the sheik. "It was renovated last year. There is a new roof and the best security system money can buy. It's a stone's throw to the United Nations."

"It sounds nice."

"Think nothing of it. It belongs to you."

"I welcome your generous gift, but it does not change the price." Lonny had overwhelmed Malagasy miners with similar presents: a used Renault 4L, a moped, washbasins for the extended family. The exchanges created a sense of obligation in an otherwise straightforward transaction.

"The sapphire," said Lonny, "has no equal. It is a

gemologically perfect crystal weighing 2327.39 carats in the rough. It has unmatched clarity and a delicate, sublime color. It could be cut into a cube, a pillar or a sphere. There is no kingdom in the world with a finer stone. All I ask for risking life and limb is 100 million dollars in cash. It's worth every penny."

"The price will make you world-famous."

"I don't want publicity," said Lonny. "Take it or leave it."

"I accept your price," said the sheik, realizing there was nothing to be gained from further posturing. He would draw from the family positions in European equity markets. Once he became sultan he could sell his uncle's Air Force jets to recoup the loss.

Lonny extended his hand to the sheik. "It's a deal."

The sheik grabbed Lonny and kissed him on the lips in a raw Oriental display of affection. Lonny hugged him back, not knowing what else to do, unsure of what the future held. The sapphire known in Madagascar as *vatomanga,* and in Oman, Zanzibar and beyond as the Vision, continued its reign of good luck. In the next millennium the sapphire would change hands thousands of times following economic revolution, bloody war, royal marriage and constantly shifting national boundaries. In all of its reincarnations, whether hidden in dark vaults or on public display, it radiated promise. Lonny's interaction with the solid blue light amounted to a nanosecond in human history, less in geologic time.

Between wisps of E-transfers and legal faxes as thick and intricate as honeycomb, the sapphire left the Republic of South Africa on Sheik Seyyid bin Seyyid's private plane that night. Lonny paid his father a 10-million-dollar broker's fee and put 90 million dollars in an offshore account. He settled his debts, paid the hotel bill and chartered a jet to take him to New York the next afternoon. He felt like a professional in every sense of the term.

There were several Dutch blondes sitting evenly spaced apart at the hotel bar and Lonny asked one to accompany him for the evening. Her professional name was Jolie. She studied computer science and was looking for a way out of Africa.

"Do you have AIDS?" she asked.

"I don't think so."

"When were you tested?"

"Never."

"Have you slept with the blacks?"

"Who are you calling black?"

"The Africans, dummkopf!"

"Aren't you an African?"

"I'm South African."

"Well, I've slept with all kinds of Africans. What makes you any different?"

"You probably have AIDS," remarked the girl.

"I hope not," said Lonny, and he began to laugh very softly to himself.

"What's so funny?"

"Isn't this the Cape of Good Hope?"

She would not caress him or kiss him. He paid her an exorbitant sum to stay for the night and she agreed as long as he kept his boxer shorts on. He lay in the cool, starched linen sheets but could not sleep. He drew Jolie close to him and the mere warmth of her curved spine staved off despair.

He raised his groggy lids the next morning as empty and hollow as he had ever felt. He was disgusted with himself for trying to buy intimacy. The richly decorated five-star hotel room felt as sterile and corrupted as a private medical clinic. The humdrum of everyday life pitiful.

Jolie awoke and showered. She slipped back into a sequined cocktail dress that fit her as perfectly as an ostrich-skin glove. In the distance muted church bells vaulted fences and security guards to ring dully through the windowpanes.

"Are you coming?" she asked.

"To breakfast?"

"To church. Today is the Pentecost."

"Are you going to church?"

"Who needs the Lord if not the sinners?" she asked.

"What?" said Lonny. The phrase vibrated an

emotion in the back of his head like an organ note that reached beyond conscious memory. He opened the windows onto the tiny lawn with its private pool and the bells tolled louder. The sun disoriented him and his forehead throbbed with a migraine.

He stepped through the low-set window, crossed the ground-level veranda and dove into the pool. The water was cold and forceful and took the breath right out of him. He felt the temperature shock slap him in the forehead and descend in quivers throughout his whole body. The dive renewed his desire to see Annie again with such jolting electricity that it felt like a baptism. When his head breached the surface the world took on a new power. The primary colors stood out like lightning bolts against a backdrop of 18 percent gray.

"Dance me to those bells," said Lonny, as he wrapped himself in a thick, terry-cloth bathrobe.

The prostitute smiled. She kissed him on the cheek then extended her arms as willingly as a debutante. They spun past the uniformed guards and down the long, immaculate driveway. The very asphalt was swept of dust. Palms planted by vanished English aristocrats hovered.

"Do you know what a prodigal is?" asked Lonny, turning counterclockwise.

"No," said Jolie, keeping the beat. "What is it?"

"I'd like to find out."

The air was limpid and the possibilities limitless.

His life was a third of the way passed by. The bright Atlantic glittered with promise. Lonny was among strangers thousands of miles from home, but he was going home and he had faith that a life of neglected parts could be redeemed and made whole. Lonny and the prostitute waltzed into the city with the spring of a long-forgotten Easter in their step.

Acknowledgments

Thanks to the members, trustees and director of the Institute of Current World Affairs, 4 West Wheelock Street, Hanover, NH, 03755. Their generous financial support allowed the author to live and travel throughout Madagascar, the Indian Ocean region and Africa.